THE GODDESS OF PROMISED LAND

LAMENTATIONS

BOOK TWO

Rachael Roberts Bliss

Jan-Carol Publishing, Inc
"every story needs a book"

The Goddess of Promised Land: Lamentations
Book Two
Rachael Roberts Bliss
Published August 2023
Broken Crow Ridge
Imprint of Jan-Carol Publishing, Inc.

This is a work of fiction. Any resemblance to actual persons, either living or dead is entirely coincidental. All names, characters, and events are the product of the author's imagination.

ISBN: 978-1-954978-95-9
Library of Congress Control Number: 2023942808

You may contact the publisher:
Jan-Carol Publishing, Inc.
PO Box 701
Johnson City, TN 37605
publisher@jancarolpublishing.com
www.jancarolpublishing.com

To my children: Robert, Miranda, Joshua, Renee, and Matilda.

They made my real life exciting and fulfilling

so later I could dream of the Goddess herself.

Author's Note

Remember baby Sophia-Emma, the newborn baby of color found in a pasture at the Promised Land plantation? Now she's a teenager with her own story to tell. I call this second story *The Goddess of Promised Land: Lamentations*, and Sophia-Emma has plenty.

Join me as we find our young protagonist feeling the pull of the Almighty to seize who she is meant to be. Only now, she has family problems to deal with. Her mother, Loving Foster-Jones (formerly Amanda), is one of them. At times Sophia-Emma wonders who is the real mother, she or Loving.

Lamentations takes you to Sophia-Emma's confusing and traumatic world in historic Africatown, Alabama, settled by freed slaves at the end of the Civil War. But there's a world around her that needs transformation. Will she play a part in that? For now, she has to deal with her dysfunctional family and a puppy who's adopted her. Torn between desires for a normal life spiced with love, and understanding the miracles randomly emanating from her spirit, Sophia-Emma is looking for answers, even if the search takes her to a place where racism puts her life at risk.

This book explores mature themes including racism, generational trauma, and references to sexual assault, and may not be suitable for young readers.

Introduction

How often have you as a spiritual person wished you had been taught about a woman who came down to earth to show us how to make our world better with a feminine power not dependent on violence or punishment? If you believe in the Trinity as many Christians do, can you imagine the Holy Spirit, often considered feminine among early believers, taking its turn being incarnated on Earth as a woman instead of a man?

This is what my fictional series *The Goddess of Promised Land* attempts to do. In *Genesis*, we witnessed baby Sophia-Emma's courageous mother who knew no limits in protecting her daughter, whom she found in a pasture on her family's old plantation while an eagle circled above her. Years have now passed as we now offer the second book in this series, In *Lamentations*, we find our hero Sophia-Emma taking on leadership in her family and community. But with that come dangers that even a Spirit-Goddess will find challenging and life-threatening. Can she survive to go on with her mission?

Chapter 1

How doth the city set solitary that was full of people?
(Lamentations 1:1)

Was she afraid?

Damn right, but there was no one around to tell.

Sophia-Emma, teen and nerd, a few minutes ago had sneaked out of her family's back door ahead of Hurricane Abram. She wanted to once more savor—maybe for the last time—this small world of Africatown, Alabama, USA, where she'd lived, played, and worked most of her life.

Abram was picking up speed, making the lone explorer hurry around to her favorite places before the monster storm came in to rearrange the struggling town's furniture. It was only late June, and already the Gulf was getting out-of-its-mind rowdy. Some folks 'round there kept blasting recent ancestors for ignoring the early signs of climate change back in the nineties. Yet all those huge tanks at Magazine Point said that everyone was guilty, even present day folk. A tangle of pipelines were still flowing into this tank farm through some pipes as long as sixty years. Sophia-Emma was now fearful whenever she heard a hurricane was forecast to hit her town. Could the pipes endure one more onslaught? Would this be their version of Katrina?

She shifted her gaze to the now empty two-mile long Cochran-Africatown Bridge above her head. The trucks that carried industrial cargo across it were now parked somewhere in safe places that would protect them from approaching Abram. How Sophia-Emma had wished her community hadn't approved its construction long ago before she was brought here as a baby. The marshes, fishing wharves, small homes, and grocery stores were now all gone. In their place, only sprawling tank farms, barges, and coal terminals. The once pristine Mobile River had been ruined with chemical spills and outright dumping.

Not too long ago, one of the Africatown residents painted a mural of the Clotilda at the base of the bridge. Sophia-Emma passed by it many times before today. The painting told the story of a buried ship that in 1860 illegally brought over the Atlantic the last captured slaves, more than 100 of them, from Africa. Many of these slaves' descendants still lived here in this tiny town they had built after they regained their freedom following the Civil War. She wondered how the incoming storm would mess with all of their descendants and the things they cherished.

Sophia-Emma knew she needed to get back home, but there were so many last looks to file in her melancholy mind. She looked over at the old cemetery where all the dead residents were buried facing east toward their African ancestral home of Benin. Old-timers talked about being part of the Yoruba tribe that had existed from times immemorable.

Giant raindrops were now plopping on Sophia-Emma's head. The wind was picking up, but for the most part, other storms off the Gulf started like this, too. She walked on, wanting to visit Hog Bayou and Shell Bayou. Then there was Third Creek where it met the Mobile River, flowing near Kimberly Clark and the Asphalt plant.

"Stop it," she shouted to the wind as she zipped up her waterproof jacket. Sophia-Emma felt her bushy dark hair blowing across her face, along with needle-like sand caught up in the wind. But she couldn't stop yet.

Before long she was walking against the wind. In other storms during her short life, the wind would come and go. But now the wind's velocity was building and building with each second. The small girl fell flat on her face, but even that didn't stop her. She was up and moving so she could get to some last looks at the factories and refineries.

Finally Sophia-Emma could barely stand up against the wind and the sand-ladened rain. The skin on her face felt as though it was being sliced to shreds. She turned around, thinking she had been defeated and let the wind blow her home the long way, flowing with the blasts rather than against them.

Other noises now bombarded her. She was too afraid to look behind herself, but the storm seemed to be throwing tree branches at her back. Meanwhile, the rain was drenching her, so much that she couldn't even see where she was headed. For the first time, the wandering teen wondered if she'd be the first victim of this hurricane. Would she die out there in the streets?

"Dammit, Wind," she screamed at the top of her voice while being drowned out by Abram's slams and punches carrying her along his cruel gales. Boards put up over windows were being violently pounded. A couple palm trees were being plucked out of the ground like weeds. Street lights were dimming as electrical wires, now broken by falling branches and debris, sparkled like dying embers of a campfire.

"I must find some type of shelter or I'll die," Sophia-Emma told herself as the power of darkness was overcoming her. All she could hear back was howling, pounding, chaos, the end of the world.

Once again, she screamed until her voice took on the sound of fingernails on a chalkboard, simultaneous with wheels squealing around a sharp corner.

"I say to you, Wind. I say to you, Rain, no more. Stop this ruckus right now!"

Silence. Her world was now quiet. She heard a pine needle drop. Then she cried out in relief, gratitude, and fear.

Chapter 2

Sophia-Emma noticed neighbors in the hood slowly and cautiously starting to emerge from their homes. They didn't pay her much attention, for which she was relieved. She knew they were probably as confused as she about what the hell Abram was up to. This lull couldn't mean the eye of the storm was over them, signaling that half the storm was over. No, he seemed to have gone to sleep or simply called it quits. Yes, people were avoiding the live electrical wires scattered everywhere, but why did the wind become tame so suddenly, as though a gentle giant had walked through their little town and swept away hurricane winds and rain with his broom?

Now Sophia-Emma saw some familiar faces. Mama, Daddy, and little bro Christopher were heading her way. Even her best friend, Harriet, tagged along with them at first, then ran ahead of the old folks, and Christopher took off behind her. She kicked her friend's shin. Sophia-Emma immediately leapt backwards, almost losing her balance.

"Girl, what you doing out here in this mess?" Harriet asked, not seeming to notice how hard her kick had been.

"Just looking and capturing photos to remember the hood, getting some *before* hurricane sights right here on my phone and filed in my heart. Planned to go back later for the *afters*."

Her mama, now caught up with the other two, interrupted the conversation.

"Girl, you crazy? Out here in the middle of a Category Four hurricane?" Sophia-Emma's mama stood nearly on top of her with her index finger close enough to pick her daughter's nose.

Before she could come up with a plausible answer, her daddy had caught up with his wife, growling at her like a rabid dog. "You're grounded forever," he commanded.

Sophia-Emma tried to bring some common sense into the conversation, "Yo, I wore my sensible jacket zipped up, rubber boots. And I just about back home. Gaw! I had work to do out here."

Her mama knew what she meant. Harriet? Not so much. Her dad, as usual, insisted his daughter was going through a teen-age phase, as he thought a few years ago she was in an adolescence phase.

While so many neighbors were looking around and raising their arms in gratitude for the Almighty's second miracle of the year, Sophia-Emma's mama and daddy were out for the jugular.

"What in the world are you doing out here in the middle of a hurricane?" Her mama wouldn't let it go.

"Dammit, girl, you have no idea how you scared us. Our most dangerous hurricane of the year, and you're out for a little summer walk while your family going crazy inside our home, down on our knees begging that you'll be meandering in the front door any minute. I swear, Pulsar, she's damaged, insane."

Her mama pulled at the very top dread on the top of her head, the one she always twisted and pulled. She bit her thin lips. Poor thing, Sophia-Emma thought. Too bad she had to be born with similar genetics to the George W. Bush lineage. But that was another story.

"OK, I made another mistake. Will you forgive me one more time?" Her daughter was trying to boost both of her parents' sense of forgiveness.

"But guess what? Dah! It's. Not. Raining." Sophia-Emma joined the rest of the neighbors in raising her arms up to the heavens in praise of what was probably a miracle from heaven.

The next thing she knew, her mama was herding her two children home, while her husband stayed behind talking to folks about the effects of climate change and his so-weird daughter's escape from home during the storm.

Harriet caught up with the threesome and started giving Sophia-Emma the same flack as she'd received from her parents minutes ago. Poured into her short shorts and revealing tank top, she scolded away.

"Why in the world did you get out in this storm and risk your life, Soph?" she asked as her friend was trying to stay ahead of her mama's butt-slaps behind them. "Just being indoors, I was shivering with fear like a hairless Egyptian cat lost at the North Pole."

That's when Sophia-Emma blew up. She'd thought that if anyone would understand why she seemed so quirky, her best friend would. Not quite.

"Go to hell, Harriet," she shouted and tried to out-walk the bickering.

The nerdy teen had told her countless times that she knew bits and pieces of what was happening to her, but couldn't clarify it yet. Like everyone else, she still didn't quite know who or what she was or would be. This hurricane thing was just another example of a strange power she wished she didn't have.

"I was going to write a book about you, girl," Harriet teased. "But you so way out there, I can't understand you at all."

"Then forget it," Sophia-Emma snapped. "You're no help at all. I need your opinion, and all you want to do is make money off me and my quirkiness. I gotta get home."

She hung her head the rest of the way home, wondering about this journey she seemed to be on. Maybe it was a project, not a mission, or vice-versa. Sophia-Emma was completely confused and tired of being a mess, designated as the hood's weird kid.

At one time, she'd thought her mama would at least understand. But all she did these days was give her advice on how not to end up like Granny Foster, the mother she loved to hate.

And her daddy's advice? "Not the right time. Maybe later," was his usual response.

Little bro Chris? She laughed at the thought. No, he needed to enjoy his childhood, so she left him alone, except when they built Lego stuff together and she walked him to the pool.

The mosquitoes and their buggy cohorts by now were venturing out into the misty twilight. They momentarily distracted Sophia-Emma's habitual thinking about her predicament. She'd been thinking of splitting from here for a while, getting away from the chemical smells, the bugs, the stagnating heat, this hood, where she'd lived way too long.

She knew what Harriet would say if she ran this thought by her. "You ain't gonna do no such thing. You ain't old enough. Why, you not even graduated yet."

Then Sophia-Emma knew how she'd respond: "Don't give me a guilt trip. The work pulling at me is daunting. If my gut's telling me right, I need to get away and figure out these signs and crazy powers I seem to have.

Harriet gave her a peeved look.

All of this weird stuff started when Sophia-Emma was placed on Earth. Unlike most children who didn't remember much before the age of three, she remembered everything as if she'd inhaled her first breath yesterday.

She had been placed by soft loving dark hands up the river from here on Granny Foster's old plantation, not far from where many long-oppressed humans were buried. A creature with flapping wings circled above. Nameless at the time, she didn't know when it would swoop down and carry her away as dinner. It was then that she as a baby learned to cry in harmony with the spirits all around her.

A pretty woman with a deep tan emerged from the big house—a barefoot woman dressed in brilliant colors. She strutted toward the crying critter, probably with no idea what kind of creature it was. The baby herself wondered what kind of object she was. If she was there to be food for the creature flying in the air above, would this woman protect her from it, or would she consume this choice morsel herself? She remembered being wet and ragged, probably repulsive to this creature wrapping her white arms around her. This big creature was to become her mother, who later said she'd also feared this baby. She'd stopped in her tracks, sickened by the odor of excrement. Then it was like she awoke from a spell. She didn't offer it to the eagle. She also didn't open her mouth like she wanted to take a bite. Instead she carried this little creature back to the big house where it cried even more. There the old creature, smelling like a fire, spoke with a terrifying voice. Even though the newborn creature didn't know her words, she sounded like thunder, crashes, wild critters. The younger creature—the lady who'd picked her up—took the baby from that big place and said she would care for her, at least for a little while. Like a tiny garden in the wild, she was fed and cleaned. From there she and the colorful woman she called Mama had adventures together. She loved this baby so much she even produced milk for her from her own breasts. The baby's fear turned into smiles of comfort. To this day, Sophia-Emma still didn't know how she got in that field. All she knew—or thought she knew—was that she exited before that day from a dark warm place.

Bringing Sophia-Emma out of her nostalgic thoughts, a small puppy yelped behind her, like it understood all the mixed-up memories going through her head. She bent down to stroke its head. "You don't want to hang 'round me, little puppy. Go, find your ol' lady," she urged.

The small ball of fluff seemed to not understand what Sophia-Emma was saying. And to be truthful, she didn't try too hard to persuade it to get lost. She knew this wasn't a good time to adopt a puppy, reminding herself that she needed aloneness and privacy so she could figure out this life through which she was walking in a stupor.

Thinking had recently become so central in her life. She'd enjoyed being an innocent, dependent baby. Everyone should have such an easy childhood as she'd had. But now was the time to move on, said that little voice deep in her heart.

Sophia-Emma, at last in her pre-Hurricane Abram home, walked through the dark boarded-up house. Clean water was still in the bathtub in case water sources became contaminated from the storm. With no air circulation, the entire house stunk like a sweaty towel. Surprisingly, the power was back on. The refrigerator was purring while the air conditioner was struggling to lower the humidity inside.

Mama was back at her easel painting and Christopher to his Lego characters and our two cats, Corker and Clare. The kitties don't seem to care if Sophia-Emma stopped the storm or not. They had tiny square pieces of colorful plastic to push under the couch, chairs, and every other place where they could make them hard to reach at clean-up time.

Chris looked at Sophia-Emma as though she intended to scold him. "Don't get on me, sis," he pleaded. "Sophia-Emma need to scatter these little devils so I can see what it's like to be hit or stepped on—you know."

She shook her head in disbelief of little boys' fantasies and then shifted her attention to her mama's new painting in her studio corner looking over Three Mile Creek. I caught her in the middle of getting a perspective of Daddy's portrait built around a fishing pier along the Bay.

"What's the matter with this? It's missing something, but don't know what. You got any ideas?"

"Well, why don't you put some water behind him?"

Hesitantly she agreed. "Maybe that's it. I'll try. Hmm."

Her question became the perfect lead-in, as Sophia-Emma's anxiety about her life's purpose.

"Mama, it's time for me to go and do what I was put here for."

Her mother gave her a questioning look and leaned a little to her left, ran her hands through her dreads and asked, "What you talking 'bout, girl? Sophia-Emma, your work's right here right now in this house and hood. We all love you."

This was her affirming lead-in. Soon would come her forbidding.

"You add laughter to our days and you're too darn young to even think such a thing. There're people outside of our piece of dirt here who won't be as accepting of you outside the hood. Kids who look like you have been dragged behind trucks with red flags criss-crossed with a big blue X. Why you can't even trust the police to be on your side." She then became insistent. "You're not going anywhere, my girl. Worse yet, you could get shot."

She turned back to her painting, but she knew Sophia-Emma wasn't accepting her stock answer.

"Mama, I don't care whatcha got to say, I'm still leaving. Now, before you begin to wonder what you did wrong, you did nothin' wrong. You're perfect, and I'm not saying this to be flattering. It's true."

Her mama wasn't flattered. "Your daddy should be here in 'little while, as soon as he gets done talking to Ross about all that climate change, diseases, and storms. We can talk more about this then."

Sophia-Emma knew this wasn't easy for her mama, but it wasn't for her daughter either. She needed time to think. But before doing that, she passed by a mirror above the sink in the bathroom. She was clearly no Beyonce, maybe more like Miss Piggy, but a darker one. Her entire image reminded her of one of those healthy smoothies, a little bit of vegetables disguised with the flavors of strawberry or raspberries. In her case, her coarse hair said African; the shape of her eyes, Asian; the deep blue of her eyes, European; ruddy complexion, American indigenous; her nose, Mediterranean; and her full cheeks, Polynesian. She saw herself as a mess. Other times while in a better mood, she told herself she was the best humans had to offer. She turned around to examine her butt, a Jennifer Lopez butt. She shook it a bit and moved it around like Jello in a bowl—a large bowl.

"Yelp, I'm human. But am I something else, too?" she waited for the girl staring back at her from the mirror to tell her what.

Chapter 3

Chris knocked on the bathroom door. "I need to go. And you need to go out," he yelled. "Please?" He took a deep breath and screamed louder. "Right now, or you'll slide in my pee out here."

Sophia-Emma knew she would miss that boy when she left. Even he was a mixture of black and white, prompting her to occasionally call him Peanut Butter. Her mama and daddy, however, were of a dying generation. Her mama, rosy vanilla; and her daddy, rich coffee with no cream.

As Chris slammed the door behind him, his sister heard the outpouring of liquid nature. Meanwhile Sophia-Emma's soul started to yearn for the nature of heights, valleys, greenery, growth, decay, critters, and danger. She told herself that she had to go now to that lonely place where she could wonder and wander. She would force her parents into conversation about this when they gathered at the table tonight to break bread.

Until then, she busied herself by going through her closet and bureau drawers. The stuff landing on her bed were sheep, the chosen; those on the floor, goats, the rejected.

She found the hand-me-down backpack hanging from the back of the door and began stuffing the items on the bed into it—sweaters, boots, heavy socks, underwear—knowing that this was only the beginning of what she'd need. Closing her door, she looked in the mirror again and began to rehearse the plea to her daddy to let her go. It had to be presented tonight with her most assertive voice.

The puppy at the front door diverted attention from her rehearsal. His yipping was a constant reminder of what not to do herself when she made her plea tonight. Why did this little guy have to follow her home today when no one in the house wanted a new puppy? But he seemed to be starving, so Sophia-Emma searched the fridge. Maybe the leftover roast her mama had served last night. No one would miss a small snippet and some gravy.

Little Guy inhaled the snippet and begged for more. Once more, she couldn't ignore his pleading eyes. She opened the fridge and gave it more puppy-food, which the night before had been people-food.

As Little Guy devoured his second helping, Sophia-Emma discovered she was in love with her little black shadow. She would have more pleading to do, asking that this sweet, sleek little creature be admitted into the family. Maybe her parents would let him accompany her on the trail up to Clingmans Dome in the Smoky Mountains, where together they could be closer to the Creator. Was she ready for this job that seemed to be calling her? Little Guy would give her support, even protection without scolding, unlike what humans liked to do.

Chapter 4

Doing what Sophia-Emma always did when she was stressed from indecision, she collapsed amidst the clothes still on her bed. She weaved the strands of her long coarse hair into thick tough braids and then unweaved them again. Sleep overcame her anxiety as Little Guy curled up into a ball at her feet, making her feel electrified with love, peaceful, so-so peace . . .

The next thing she recognized was her daddy at her side, staring down at Little Guy now under her arm.

"What's this? Hadn't we decided no more dogs until we got Tuffy out of our hearts?" he asked her. "I hope you're not thinking this tiny mutt can replace Tuffy. Looks to have some Pomeranian in him, not anywhere near Tuffy's lab lineage."

Nevertheless, even he couldn't resist rubbing Little Guy's tummy. This led Sophia-Emma to conclude that her old man could be flexible on this. She explained why the puppy was there.

"He followed me home, Daddy. He's helping me relax and, well, he brings me peace. I do kinda like him." Already she was strategizing if it would be better to alert her daddy about her plan now rather than wait until she had an audience around the dinner table. She took a stab at it.

"Oh, by the way, I'm leaving for a little while, Daddy. Now don't get your blood pressure up. I gotta go on a hike just for a few weeks."

Her daddy didn't respond as she'd hoped.

"Don't give me that line. I'm not letting you go off on your own till you're an adult. Subject closed, especially after your little escapade today out there in Abram. Plus, white supremacists are on the prowl. Not a good time." Her daddy turned and headed for the door, adding one more command, "And no puppy."

"Daddy, you know I've usually been responsible. But I'm not a kid anymore. I know you ran away yourself once."

"None of that." He seemed surprised that she reminded him of that incident. "Remember, I was much older than you are now, and I had jail time breathing down my neck. You don't. Prison is not a place black folk wanna end up."

"Daddy, I have so much weighing on me. I can't explain it 'cause it's not clear what's going on. I got to get away. If I don't get your blessing, you'll have to literally tie me down. There's a calling in my head and heart that I can't ignore any longer. I'm not asking permission. I'm telling you that as of tomorrow I'll be gone for a short time. But only a short time," she added.

"You ain't going nowhere, sweetheart, while I'm your father. Now get down to supper."

He may have had the last word in this skirmish, but the campaign would go on in the kitchen in a few minutes.

If that conversation wasn't enough, seeing Mama at the table with a stern expression on her face, and hands plastered onto her hips, made Sophia-Emma's day even worse. Christopher gave her a wink of warning as Sophia-Emma approached the dinner table.

"So where did the roast beef go that I was saving for supper tonight?" Mama showed her an empty container with tiny puddles of gravy around its bottom.

"Because of this, we're having macaroni and cheese tonight, emphasis on the mac," her mama complained. "Didn't you know I planned to have hot roast beef sandwiches and mashed potatoes tonight? You know that lots of fatty meat makes your complexion a mess and . . . and what's that little black furry creature at your feet there? Did you feed that mutt all our expensive roast?"

Her daughter responded with a quote from the Bible, "*I was hungry and you gave me to eat.*"

"Don't get smart with me, young lady. Now put that dog outside and sit down."

This was so unlike her mother. But today was no ordinary day.

Her daddy gave his daughter a look of solidarity with her mama, daring her to bring up any intention of leaving any time soon. Sophia-Emma surrendered and decided this wasn't the right time.

While she focussed on her simple meal amidst an atmosphere of God-awful tension ruling out the family's normal camaraderie, Sophia-Emma regretted that this meal now being shared with them would be her last for weeks, maybe forever. What if she never saw this family portrait again? She didn't want to remember them like this. Her eyes filled with tears and she excused herself.

Disappointed that she'd chickened out of talking her way through this, Sophia-Emma knew there was no chance that family members would be giving her their blessings before she headed out the door. All the more reason to leave this little town immediately. She had lots to think about, to meet challenges, overcome evil, maybe even lead the oppressed into true freedom. She knew she couldn't do all that from this place.

Back in her room, she stuffed more necessities into her camping bag, topping it all off with her old piggy bank. Tomorrow she'd take all it held to a bank. She needed so much to eat on and provide other necessities for the hike on the Appalachian Trail to Clingmans Dome.

Finding her hiking boots at the bottom of her bag, she dug them out and put them on with a pair of hardy socks she had put in with the goats earlier. She made her bed, neatly arranged all her rejected stuff back into drawers and the closet. Then she wrote a note to her parents and Chris:

Sorry, but I have to leave for a while. Don't worry about me. You always knew I was put here for a purpose. Mama, you raised me right. Now I must go. I'll come back, God willing, when the fruit is ripe for harvest. Hope you'll greet me back with open arms. Thanks so much for your love since my newborn year and my childhood up to today. No one ever said this parting would be easy, but y'all have prepared me well.

Love,
Sophia

PS: I think I'll just be Sophia from now on. And I'm not taking my cell phone, so you won't be able to track me. If necessary, I'll call you from a pay phone.

For one more time Sophia took a panoramic glance at her newly neat and inviting room. She threw her bag out the open window and then squeezed through it herself, climbing carefully down the old maple tree near the house. No one seemed to notice from inside the house as she rushed to get out of sight, edging her way north toward the bayou. She felt propelled by the sound of someone following her. She was too scared to turn and confront the person she assumed was behind her. Whoever they were, they were gaining on her. Was it her dad? It couldn't be her mama. She ran with a limp since she injured her ankle a few months ago. Christopher? No, it was bath time. She started running, pushing herself faster than she thought possible. Every cell in her body now failing her, she crashed when she came to the Shell Bayou.

Falling into the slippery and sharp river cane, she decided to confront her pursuer. Sophia saw that it wasn't a human after all, more like a black bear or a cub. As it got closer, she saw Little Guy, not quite a bear, but nevertheless, a friend for the journey ahead. She caught up and jumped on her lap, going so far as to apply his tongue to Sophia's lips and sucking little bits of food left over from the disastrous meal. Sophia laughed and cried till she had to catch her breath and rest. She glanced behind her and saw her home off in the distance. Then she realized there was one more person she needed to see before she left.

Chapter 5

Sophia needed to decide where she'd sleep tonight, but she also needed advice. She'd hoped it would have come from her parents. She blew that idea. But there was still Miss Mildred Washington. They'd been like two pairs of eyes and ears in Africatown since Sophia as a baby had moved here with her mama and daddy so long ago. In their early days of friendship, they'd conversed with their eyes. Still could, if communication with voices seemed too harsh or when there were no words yet created that meant what they felt in their guts.

Only the elderly wise women, mostly grandmas, *heard* Sophia's eyes. Miss Mildred was the best. Another was Miss Tillie who worked for her mean grandma, Mrs. Louise Foster of Promised Land, who'd never even given herself a chance to *hear* her only granddaughter with her eyes.

Miss Ina May from a holler in Virginia—who got Sophia's mama and daddy out of trouble when the bad white supremacists were trying to take her away from them—was a fun lady to meet eye-to-eye. And she was good at hearing true spiritual words, too. But she hadn't seen her in years. Still remembered her, though.

So tonight Sophia found herself walking over to see Miss Mildred. She planned to tell the wise mentor about her decision to leave home. It wouldn't be the first time. She'd always shared plans with her. Maybe this time she could recommend ways to get her mama and daddy to not worry about her disappearance. Thank God, she lived just a few blocks away over by the old factories in the Magazine area, where Sophia wouldn't be seen. Little Guy seemed to hear what she was thinking now, too. He followed along like her shadow.

Miss Mildred was in her front yard, repairing her flower garden after the mean winds and rain of the afternoon's hurricane. She looked up and motioned Sophia to visit awhile. She was a tall strong dark brown woman as kind as a breeze and as smart as a preacher.

"My girl, what have you gone and done now?" She gathered her hair back into her normally neat little bun. Sophia stepped back and looked Miss Mildred in her eyes, which were saying that she already knew what Sophia was up to.

Sophia fired back with her big mouth, "I gotta do this, old lady."

"Your daddy just called to ask me about your whereabouts. Of course, I told him I knowed nothin' about your doins'." She paused and clicked her tongue. "So now you tell me, girl. What that bulging bag on your back? And while I'm givin' you a hard time, keep your little mutt out of my damn garden, ya hear?"

Sophia found herself tuning out from the scolding, so her mind could take a picture of her old friend to carry on her journey. Kind eyes that pierced through the teen's marrow. Dirty, rugged, but soothing hands. Coarse, wild silver hair clasped in a flowery scarf. Beads of sweat illuminating a holy glow.

"Now let's git up on the porch and have a little talk about your apparent plan to leave our town."

"And that's what I want to talk to you 'bout." The soon-to-be-fleeing girl, in a purple rocking chair, leaned toward Miss Mildred, who had settled onto the wide porch swing.

Sophia began to bare her soul through her eyes. "You know we been eye-talking about my mission of late. I don't know what I'm s'posed to be doing. And the voices are getting louder and louder. Do you think maybe I'm crazy? Maybe schitzo?" Sophia's eyes showed a frightened expression.

Then she switched to mouth-talking. "All I want to do is go away for a few weeks. I don't know, and see where I s'pose to be or doin'. I got this deep feeling I need to start, but I got too many distractions 'round the hood to hear what this power tellin' me. It's like static on wifi when I'm too far from a router. Gees, I gotta get closer to my teacher who informs my heart. Know what I mean, Miss Mildred? Hell, I can't speak how impatient I feel this minute. Can we let my eyes talk to yours again?"

Miss Mildred gave her one of her pitiful looks like she was making a fool of herself, but she wanted to use her mouth.

"I know what you trying to say, girl, but you just a peepsqueak by human standards, like that little ball of black fur by your feet. You don't know what grown-up is yet. Your mission—which I admit could be heaven-sent—it'll wait." She said. "Remember, when Jesus went on that holy journey, with his mama and papa, how he got too big for his britches, talking to the temple big shots? How did his mama, the Virgin, put him in his place? I guess she whooped his ass and then he shut up and lived under their roof eighteen more years." Is that what you want from your mama and daddy now?"

"If I's a mama, I'd probably do the same thing, but I know my mission is calling now. It's not like I leaving forever—just a little while—so I can know what's up. You get me?"

"And you can't find that in the hood? My girl, we got water here like the Sea of Galilee. We got fish—lots of 'em. And we got the sickly, the oppressors, the harlots. It's all here on this little spot of land."

"Old lady, can't you see? I. Need. To get. Away. I've tried to do it your way. Been down in the Bayou, in the market, even with my bros and sistas. I've talked to our ancestors at the cemetery, those in the shut-down paper plant, the stinking dump. All that makes me want to get far away even more. I gotta go to the unknown—at least to me—where I ain't never set my feet before."

She pounded her hand on her chair's armrest. "I don't want to do what my old man did. No, I need a hallowed spot where my maker meets me. No mama, no daddy, no pesky little bro. Can you keep a secret and just encourage me, please? All you gotta do is reassure Mama and Daddy that I okay. I come back quick as I can, maybe to stay. Tell 'em my heart is urging me I gotta go. I find a way to call if I mightin' get in trouble."

Sophia didn't think Miss Mildred was convinced yet, but at least she was thinking about what she'd tried to explain. It was best to give her a chance to say her piece and pray she'd say what her mentee wanted—needed—to hear.

"Okay, I see I ain't changing your mind, baby," Miss Mildred finally spoke. "So tell me where you goin' so I can send out a rescue team if you in trouble. My lips, other than reassuring your daddy and mama, are sealed." With that, she figuratively zipped her lips.

But Sophia needed more, especially some wise advice and reassurance. Maybe that would come later. Miss Mildred had spoken her piece. She waited now for the details of what she was expected to keep her mouth shut about.

"Now here's my plan," she started. "I'm on my way up to Clingmans Dome in the Smokies, on the Appalachian Trail, which starts up in Georgia. I plan to catch a ride, maybe a bus tomorrow, probably to Gainesville, Georgia. From there, I'll find a group of hikers I can link up with from Springer Mountain, where the trail starts. Clingmans Dome is about two hundred miles from there, about twenty days at maybe ten miles a day."

Miss Mildred shook her head like the girl had no idea what a big chunk of getting away she was about to bite into. But she kept her mouth shut till Sophia was done talking.

"Comin' back, another twenty days. I'll stay up there somewhere 'bout a week, so at best I be back in maybe two months. No big deal, huh?"

"Miss Mildred now had her chance to comment, which she did with no qualms. "It a big deal if you're a young woman of color, my child.

Surely, your mama has had *the talk* with you by now. If not your ma, surely your daddy."

"I know *the talk*, Miss Mildred. But you know and I know that I'm here to fulfill a mission. Nothin's going to happen to me. A power beyond any of us is watchin' over me with a team of angels all around."

"You crazy, girl. Wake up and be real. Even Jesus himself was killed by folks from his own people, chile. Sometimes we expected to use some ol' common sense. Wait here. I got something for you."

As Miss Mildred moseyed away to go into her house, Sophia started worrying about Little Guy sleeping at her feet. Would he be allowed to travel on Greyhound with her? Maybe she'd have to hitchhike instead. Just let folks think she was taking the bus. Little Guy awoke and jumped on her lap, as though he knew she was worried.

Miss Mildred joined Sophia on the porch with a bag of gadgets—pepper spray, pocket knife, small but powerful flashlight, small book on self-defense moves, and even a prayer book for women traveling alone.

"Now my girl, why don't you stay with me tonight so you can get a fresh start tomorrow at the break of day."

Sophia was overjoyed, but didn't want to seem too eager. "I can't do that. Plus you probably tell Mama and Daddy, and they come get me and lock me up in the house for the rest of summer. Can't do. Sorry."

Miss Mildred, bunching her long flowery skirt into a ball on her lap, got a peeved look on her face. "Now you hear me, girl. I do no such thing. We go back a long time, me and you. I promise you, my lips be sealed regarding your where-abouts, 'cepting in matter of life and death. I want you safe tonight. Tomorrow, you on your own, baby."

Sophia glanced through the window behind them at the welcoming soft bed in the extra bedroom. She also knew Miss Mildred would send her off with a huge breakfast of country ham, biscuits, gravy, and grits the next morning. There was no way she would turn this offer down.

"But what about Little Guy here?' Sophia lifted him up to Miss Mildred's eye level.

"No, you don't, young lady. I just had my carpet cleaned, and puppies have a way of messing 'em up their very first night. I don't know what you goin' do about this little fella while you gone on your trip. Buses, you know, don't allow dogs. He probably belongs to some other folks 'round here anyways. He too friendly to not have owners somewheres."

"Well, I might deal with that tomorrow," Sophia said to make Miss Mildred think she agreed. "I'm sure God will help us find the owners if they're still around. But I'm too tired to think about that now. For now, I'm wonderin' about tonight." She scratched Little Guy's neck. "He'll bark all night if we leave him outside by himself. Can I keep him in the bathroom? You don't have carpet there. I really kind of love this ball of fur."

As she'd hoped, Miss Mildred gave in and the three of them settled into the little, but immaculate home, the one her mentor moved into some sixty years ago with her barber husband Martin. She never talked about children of their own. Sophia thought maybe that was why some days she seemed to be deep in sorrowful thought and didn't notice when Sophia walked by her house. But tonight she was on top of things. Sophia could see some of the sparkle she used to radiate when she was happy. Her smile tonight was genuine, not pasted on. A Godly woman, some would say. That was why the two of them had been attracted to each other for as far back as the teen could remember.

After a good-night snack of chocolate-chip ice cream, they called it a night. Sophia tucked Little Guy into a wadded up old blanket on the floor in the bathroom with yesterday's *Press-Register* right next to it just in case.

The young girl wished she could have hopped in bed with Miss Mildred, but knew that her childhood days were now over, and grown-ups didn't sleep with old mentors anymore.

Chapter 6

Sophia woke up ahead of the seagulls as the smell of savory fried sausage and eggs, coffee and grits infiltrated her nostrils. Miss Mildred was in the kitchen creating breakfast for two. In the bathroom, she noticed Little Guy sniffing the aroma, as well.

He was also getting antsy, so Sophia led him out to pee and poop. She wished she had a treat for him. Old Tuffy always had looked forward to his little nugget of something or other that he gulped down as soon as it touched his mouth.

For breakfast Sophia's nose had guessed correctly, except Miss Mildred had done her one better. She's added sliced muskmelon—sweet, juicy, and cold. At that moment she wished her mama had learned to do *Breakfast 101* from Miss Mildred. If she were home about then, besides sleeping, she would soon be pouring out a bowl of cold cereal for her first meal.

On the front porch, watching the sun beginning to poke its fiery self over the bayou, Miss Mildred and Sophia had a moment of quiet. The younger was thinking she might never see this kind of foggy morning—with it's singing and chirping birds and its sultry heavy air—again. For about the first time, she couldn't guess what Miss Mildred was pondering.

Breaking the silence, Sophia talked about memories at her side through childhood. "Remember when we used to play *Paper, Rock, Scissors. Hide and Seek* and *Rummy*? We sure had fun, huh?"

For once, her old friend said nothing, but her eyes, with their tears, said it all. They eye-talked again. By now, this had become almost second nature, Miss Mildred reached over Sophia finally and gave her the longest, tightest hug the teen had ever received from a human being. The old woman touched one of the girl's tears and joined it to one of hers now on her cheek. An outsider would have thought both were performing in a Ken Burns documentary with melancholy music softly playing in the background.

They both laughed. Then they cried. No more words could be spoken. Sophia hurt and already missed her mentor.

But the trip had to begin. The young girl backed up, leaned into her backpack and put her arms into its straps, at last standing up and feeling a tug on her back. A rush of courage crept up her spine. Miss Mildred scooped up Little Guy and the two young critters were on their way out of Africatown.

Miss Mildred knew Sophia had no intention to search for Little Guy's original owners, and consequently, that Sophia wouldn't be catching a bus to Gainesville.

One more stop before leaving town. Sophia decided to connect with Harriet and tell her about her quest. Maybe she would give her a ride to Springer Mountain. They'd been friends since dance lessons as five-year-olds. Sophia knew she was probably still asleep, but no harm hoping.

So she sat on her friend's porch for an hour, wishing for some type of life to awaken inside the sleepy yellow house. This was the first time the teen missed her phone, so much that she was tempted to get a cheap Tracfone like Miss Mildred suggested last night.

Little Guy, at her feet, was taking his first nap of the day. His little tummy was full of sausage gravy and biscuits, transporting him to dog heaven.

Sophia rearranged the stuff in her backpack and discovered she had nothing to keep her dry in case of rain. Also nothing soft to lie on, no blankets. Not even a water bottle. She couldn't go home. Just remembering all she'd forgotten for her trip, she became nervous about this quest. But then, what did Jesus bring with him when he fasted for forty days on some Middle Eastern mountain?

In a worsening mood, she decided she could wait no longer for someone in Harriet's home to wake up. She'd already stayed too long. She had to leave town ASAP. Maybe she'd hitchhike to Atlanta and find a ride there to Gainesville. One of the first places her folks would look would be around here—at her friends' homes or at Miss Mildred's, maybe one of the bayous. They were probably already driving all over Africatown searching for her.

Sophia dashed off Harriet's front porch to a part of town where people probably wouldn't look for her—over by the refineries, across from the cemetery, in the hidden areas of the bayous where the alligators hung out. She saw her family car near the school. No one was in it. She sneaked into Union Missionary Church nearby and waited in the women's restroom. She had no idea how long Little Guy and she held out there in perfect silence, reminding her that another thing she forgot to pack was her watch. She'd always depended on her phone to check the time.

After what seemed forever, Sophia left the restroom and cautiously looked outside a crack in the church door. The car was gone. Next step was to take Little Guy into the woods owned by International Paper. Her day was slowly creeping into midday. She'd accomplished nothing so far. By tonight she'd have to get to an interstate highway and hook up with a kind-looking driver at a truck stop. An entire day was being wasted, and she was still in Africatown. All because of Miss Mildred's kindness and Harriet's late sleep-in. But most of all because she had no guts and was a procrastinator, she told herself.

The girl and her puppy slipped into the old graveyard. Kids were always out that way tripping and tipping over old grave markers and drinking. Jamal (Gator), an old friend from the pool, happened to be there. He smelled like weed soaked in beer. Sophia took up his offer between beers of a ride to Love's Travel Stop, a decision she regretted as the young driver zig-zagged all the way there. Once, as she gazed out the back seat window, she noticed that he was driving south on a northbound lane. She kept an eye out for blue flashing lights behind then, something they definitely didn't need tonight.

"Have you seen our ancestors' graves lately?" he asked as Sophia obsessed about his driving. "There's one there that I'd never seen before," he reported while he swerved side to side.

"Yeh, I know. My daddy added another a few months ago. He dug up an old slave's bones from an old plantation over by Selma. Her name is Cecilia." She didn't explain that the plantation belonged to her grandmother.

"Say, I'm glad to take you wherever you're going," Gator offered as Sophia gathered Little Guy in her arms and thanked Gator for the ride. She'd had enough of Gator's sky-high driving, so she ignored his offer and went on her way.

In no time, she realized that she'd traded one scary situation for another. Now Sophia was in the midst of horny old white guys going in and out of the showers so they could impress some desperate hookers when they later bedded them in the cabins of their sixteen wheelers or nearby cheap hotels. Too bad Little Guy wasn't Big Guy yet.

Nevertheless, Sophia knew there had to be a few nice folks around. She'd seen them before on trips with her family—good, generous, and safe people among overwhelming numbers of others who could only be described as weirdos. She entered the busy center and looked for those good, generous, and safe people. The smell of enticing foods, like steaming hotdogs, fresh doughnuts, and nachos, became distractions as both Sophia and Little Guy started to salivate. It'd been a long day since breakfast with Miss Mildred. Consuming some of those aromatic foods into empty bellies became priority number one. Sophia took Little Guy into a restroom stall. She nearly scared her puppy to death when she crushed her piggy bank by stomping on it. The piggy's insides cashed in at $234.92 in dimes, nickels, quarters, and a few bills. All of it was scooped up and dumped into her backpack, leaving pink and blue ceramic pieces scattered all over the restroom, except for a few chunks that went into her pockets for protection, if needed later. First purchase was a box of dry dog food, and a collar and leash for Little Guy. Then came food for herself.

For a few swift moments, the two of them fell into sublime comfort out on the curb eating their food. Sophia shared with Little Guy her sizzling foot-long hotdog with melted yellow cheese. Realizing that her food tasted better than dry dog food, Little Guy licked Sophia's fingers and even her teeth. As she wadded up the wrapper, both craved for more. But they had to find a ride. The night was upon them.

Inside the center. Sophia searched up and down the aisles where shoppers were looking for snacks, examining bottles of milk or orange juice, soap, products that nice people, preferably women, would use. She struck up a conversation with one.

"Sorry, just got out of that traffic maze in Atlanta. Going the other way," said one small woman, who backed up to keep her distance.

Another responded to her request, "Nope. Never pick up hitchhikers, especially those with dogs. I don't care what they say. It's not over yet."

There was no third. In a way, that's not quite true. There was. And he was a cop. Someone must have squealed on the two who didn't quite blend with the usuals found at night alone at a travel center. Before she knew it, Sophia and puppy were at the Mobile Police Headquarters. Sophia would answer no questions, something like what Jesus did when he was turned over to the Roman officials. But the police went through her backpack and found her ID.

"Dammit. I'm not very good at escaping my hometown," she told Little Guy. Next time I won't make it so easy for the cops. At least, he's not put his knee on my neck yet."

Sophia's mama and daddy came and picked the girl and dog up at police headquarters. Wisely, her parents were silent on the way home as the runaway moped in the back seat. Her only consolation was her little brother's arms wrapped around her like he'd lost his best friend. Once home, each family member simply went to bed.

That was it. Sophia knew tomorrow an entirely different dynamic would take over. She cried herself to sleep, partly because she'd failed and partly because she dreaded the scolding ahead bright and early the next day.

Chapter 7

Next morning Sophia's parents awoke her early—out of spite, she assumed. First, her daddy had his say before heading over to fight his favorite corporate polluters, the ones he often described as stompers on people of African descent. But today he was stomping all over his daughter with his words.

"Do you have any idea the pain you caused your whole family with this running away business? You know this requires a punishment." He waited in silence for a response. Sophia said nothing.

Then in a deep loud voice, her daddy spoke again, "Do you understand?"

She nodded, but still didn't talk. Instead she stared out on the porch where Little Guy was ripping the screen door, begging to be let in so he could rescue his cohort in crime.

Her father, realizing that he was getting nowhere, other than looking wimpish, concluded, "I'm too angry to pronounce your punishment now, young girl. Your mama can think more rationally. But whatever she says you do, you will do, ya' hear?"

He started to leave her room, but turned around and faced her one more time, leading Sophia to realize he wasn't finished yet. "I do hope you realize your punishment will be immediate and it'll make you realize how you put all of us through hell."

Finally Sophia was awake enough to have her say: "But Daddy, surely you understand that my time here with you and Mama is limited. I must be about my mission and . . ."

"Now, stop this craziness right now," her daddy cut her off. "You're our adopted daughter. I know your birth story. Your mama has shared it with me and dozens of others hundreds of times. She might not have birthed you, but you were hers from Day One. She even fed you with milk from her own body. She didn't have to do that. Most babies do fine on bottles, but she was willing to sacrifice her own body for you."

She could see now that he was tearing up. "Your first mission, girl, is to serve and be loyal to your earthly family. Now, once you get your GED and you want to start a mission outside of this family, we can't stop you. But today, you belong here in this house with this family and in this community. Forget the A.T and hitch-hiking to Georgia, that mutt who's ruining our door out there, and yes, even Miss Mildred."

"Daddy, no. I won't do that. Miss Mildred knows me better than anyone on earth. I'll not stay away from her." Sophia got out of bed and walked past him through the narrow doorway, refusing to meet his eyes, but touching his body as she walked past him, essentially daring him to stop her.

Out on the porch, she cradled Little Guy in her arms and cried on his soft slick coat. Her daddy followed. He appeared uncomfortable dealing with the situation, like he wished Loving was up to support his stand.

"I've said what I have to say, Sophia-Emma—and that's your name. Your mom is going to take it from here. But don't you ever walk out when I'm talking to you again."

Sophia-Emma momentarily hoped he would just take her over his knee, spank her, and get it over with. At least he could spit in her face or shake her a little. Instead he kicked the door of his little gray Smart Car, denting it. His daughter felt it was all her fault. But geez, she hadn't been planning to leave them forever. And she'd been kind enough to leave them a note assuring them she'd be back someday. Parents were the pits. Just because her mama rescued her and took risks with her, she didn't own her. Yes, she was a mama's girl, and she let her tell her story over and over something like this:

"After she rescued me from the eagle out in the pasture and after a fight with Grandma Foster, she took me to a campsite where she was living with her boyfriend Peter. Sadly, some white nationalists shot him in the back and killed him the next day. From that day on, she was determined to always be my mama. She called me her lifesaving miracle that day. But those racists weren't done with her yet. We escaped to a place called Sanctuary. That's where we really got to know each other. She even tricked her boobs into thinking she was my birth mama, and she fed me like that for three years. I can remember the day she weaned me. I was devastated.

"Anyway, Daddy came into the picture when they got together to play cribbage one night at Sanctuary. He helped her face a grudge she had against Grandma Foster when she almost died. I remember him saying he loved me from that day on, but my first love was my mama Loving. Her real name was Amanda, but to this day, she still goes by Loving."

(Sophia-Emma hoped she would appreciate her name later this morning when her case would go into its sentencing phase.) But back to her story:

"The three of us had to leave Sanctuary and the state of Virginia when the white nationalists came for us there. But Miss Ina May saved us. The rest of my childhood days were spent in Africatown—some call it Plateau. Mama and Daddy figured the white nationalists wouldn't look for us where people of color lived. So far, so good."

While Sophia-Emma was digging into old memories of Africatown, her mama joined her out on the porch. Both of them seemed to have rehearsed what they'd say. Daughter started by saying, "Mama, I'm sorry I worried you." She hoped while she was speaking that her mama noticed that she was now taller than her, especially apparent while they were sitting side-by-side in the swing.

"I know you are, sweetie. But you've always had a mind of your own, and I'm baffled about how I can deal with that without breaking your spirit. Maybe now I have a small inkling of how your grandma was flustered with me. Of course, I think you know why I couldn't follow her lifestyle, and I have another inkling that there's no way you'll follow mine." Loving grabbed her daughter's hand and squeezed it.

"That said, as your mother, Sophia-Emma can't let you do things that'll put your life in jeopardy. No way will she let you do that. And when you do stupid actions like yesterday, I have to punish you, as I'm sure you expect . . ."

I butt in. "But Mama," I plead, "you know I'm not an average child. I think I was put out in that pasture as a baby by some spiritual forces. Nobody has come forward after all these years claiming they lost or abandoned a baby on that day. You's my only mama. You know where I'm going on this, don't you?"

"Sophia-Emma, you can't know how many times I've tried to put the puzzle together about how and why you got here on this planet. Forget the pasture. I've compared your birth and childhood years with those of Jesus in the Bible. But as your mama, I need to treat you as a normal smart-ass teenager. Yes, I know you have a special mystical power—like communicating with your eyes. No other person in this family can do that. That's why I'm going to let you keep seeing Miss Mildred."

"That's my mama! Smart move," Sophia-Emma squealed. Then she shut up, knowing more edicts would soon be pronounced by her mama. Nevertheless, she planted a big kiss on Loving's cheek, in an effort to persuade her to go light on whatever punishment was coming.

Since Loving seemed to be in a relatively good mood, Sophia-Emma knew that she had to push her on another concession, which was keeping Little Guy.

"I love this sweet puppy here. We've bonded, so I can't bear the thought of losing him. Can I keep . . . ?"

Her mama was silent. She looked across and down the road. Already the steam from last night's heavy dew was beginning to resemble a magical land of ancestral natives observing the wild beyond, listening for calls of animals near the camp, watching the tribe's children gather around a new toy a father made from willow and river cane. Even though Mama was born into an old southern white family, for nearly half of her life she had turned her back on her own people and had gradually assimilated into the cultures of those not white, originally the Muscogee, followed by Africans, brought here against their will.

"Let's put Little Guy on probation," her mama answered while her daughter was daydreaming of ancestral days. "We'll see how well he can behave, how well he can be a part of our family, and if we can be sure that someone around here hasn't lost him."

"I think you're saying he may end up being our next dog?"

"Maybe, but you'll have to pay for his shots and buy his food. No more roast beef or any other meals waiting for us humans in the fridge. Got me?"

Sophia-Emma was reminded of her now broken piggy bank. "Hey, did you notice I already used my own money to get him a collar and leash?"

Her mama smiled and nodded in agreement. "I did. I never said you were irresponsible, just impetuous."

Now that she'd succeeded in securing approvals on her major requests, Sophia-Emma felt she was on a roll and was ready to press for more, but also preparing herself for the gauntlet.

"Sophia-Emma—and that's who I'll call you until your dying day—I've thought about what's an appropriate punishment for you. And here's what I've come up with:

"First, you'll help out more here at home. Take care of your little bro. I'm trying to make a go of my paintings. I need your help."

Not bad so far, Sophia-Emma thought as she nodded affirmatively.

"Two, study for and take your GED test. I won't have you stepping out into this world without some type of academic document. You're smart. Shouldn't be hard, right?"

Aw, damn. No fun there, Sophia noted as her mother moved on.

"And three, I want you to organize this community to do a service for our town—maybe develop an anti-litter campaign, raise money to have a memorial put up for the founders of our town, or set a goal of making these refineries accountable to us."

This demand was the most difficult. Finally, Sophia-Emma found some words. "All that just because I gone one night?" She felt blown away and wondered if she'd ever find time to sleep. "Thanks a lot," she said as she kicked the porch railing, stubbing her big toe, in the process.

"Once you've accomplished what I think are fair and adequate goals, I'll grant you more independence to find your mission," her mama continued. "I'll even help you get the time you need to more clearly see your next steps."

"So that's it, huh?" Sophia-Emma asked. "You're sure not going to make my summer fun, though. Guess I gotta try since you're the boss. Remember, if I get the message from above that I'm needed on a special project, you need to clear the path. This isn't about me or you. It's about being in unity with the one who sent me here," the young girl warned.

"I'm not holding my breath waiting for this to happen," her mama said with a grin, like maybe her daughter needed to get real with the real world and not fantasize that she was some type of angel looking down on this tiny town.

After Loving left to start her painting for the day, Sophia-Emma took Christopher over to the playground. She listened as he described his fear while she was missing. She apologized, but made a promise to herself that someday when he was older—he was only six now—she'd tell him more. She asked him if he ever talked to God, or if God talked to him.

"Not much lately," he answered. But I remember long discussions with some space aliens around him when I was being potty-trained. They let me know that I really could let that poop out and that all my insides wouldn't come out with it."

A marvelous concept, his big sister told herself.

"But now, we don't talk much anymore," he confided as they walked to the playground. Sophia-Emma told him to not give up. He promised that he'd start saying his prayers again every night. Maybe that would help.

Chapter 8

Once back home, Sophia-Emma washed the dishes and loaded the washing machine. To please her daddy, she hung them outside to save electricity and the earth. After sandwiches for lunch, she decided to call the Mobile Community Action Center administrative offices to inquire about local GED classes.

"There are no GED classes in your area because the agency's offices in Plateau were closed long ago," the voice on the phone informed her. "You'll have to take classes downtown."

Sophia-Emma couldn't believe what she'd just heard. Her anger boiled up from her belly to her throat. Lots of friends in Africatown had dropped out of their schools, which were worse now than before Africatown had been taken over by the Mobile City School System decades ago. Plus the big shots insisted on calling her town Plateau even though residents preferred re-establishing their town as Africatown. Being mostly swamp land down by Magazine Point, it certainly wasn't on a plateau.

Spouting off like a kettle on high heat, she phoned Harriet, Gator and some other friends who dropped out of school, and asked them to call other drop-outs, too.

"Some folk might ask how I expect to get a bunch of drop-outs to have the gumption to form a group to benefit our education," she explained to Gator, who was having a sober day. "Haven't we already been failed by the system? They assume that we'd all rather play video games or sell dope. They don't wanna put ten minutes of their time into making GED classes available here in the hood where it belongs."

Her friends hadn't seen her so fired up since her neighbor Tomae had been sent to prison using evidence based on rap lyrics he'd recorded describing gang violence. Then there were Black Lives Matter protests and demonstrations to remove Confederate monuments. This was one more knock-out in a never ending saga around racist actions.

"My gut tells me they be wrong this time, too," she said to Harriet.

Then she called Community Action again and complained. "Let me tell y'all nay-sayers a bit more about why an intelligent girl like me needs a GED. I no drop-out. Mama has home-schooled me because she say I always been too smart for public schools. She still not too happy I don't talk like her, but I know how to talk, just don't do it."

"I'm sorry that we can't help you closer to where you live," the voice from Community Action said.

"I don't need your apologies," she retorted. "Now back to getting my GED. Since I don't have an actual school where I attended, I need to get a GED—General Equivalency Diploma—just as good, but without a big party afterwards."

That was the day Sophia-Emma and her homies set Tuesday, August ninth at five o'clock for their first meeting at her place.

She baked brownies for twenty and bought lots of cokes. Five friends showed, including Harriet and herself. They discovered that organizing was hard work. Or maybe she just didn't do her homework before the meeting.

But it wasn't a big loss. They used this occasion to rebuild relationships and stuff themselves on sugary goodies. Eventually they decided to talk about what they had to do next to get GED classes restarted in Africatown.

Sophia-Emma's mama heard them debating next steps to get more kids like them involved. Being a former organizer herself before becoming a mother and painter, she reminded them that organizing *was* hard work.

"You don't plan a meeting and tell people to come," she explained. With a root beer in one hand and a brownie in her other, she sat down with the five to share a few ideas, such as setting up one-on-one meetings with natural leaders around the hood.

"Who looks up to these kids? Go visit them. Appeal to their self-interest," she stressed. "Ask them what could they do if they were able to get their GED."

She told them to get names of other leaders before leaving their first one-on-one meetings, and then visiting those people, and asking for more names from them, over and over. "Decide on a date for the meeting and get them to commit to bringing at least four other people with them."

Loving was on fire. Her enthusiasm bubbled up as she gave hints on organizing. Sophia-Emma saw an amazing mother whom she'd never seen before in her true element. She smiled at the others, proud to be her mother's daughter.

"Day after day you meet with people. Build up interest. Meanwhile research the closing of the Mobile Community Action Center on our side of town. Why here? Who is your target? Who holds the power to change this situation? Which of the powerful do you get on your side?"

Sophia-Emma glanced over at Harriet and saw her shaking her head like she was at a revival with Loving as the preacher.

"And don't forget to call folks back a day or so before you meet. Remind them of their commitments and tell them how important their involvement is. Finally, promise food, especially when you're dealing with kids your age."

Sophia-Emma that night realized that even though her mama was white and all her friends were people of color, this seemed to make no difference. Of course, her mama dressed the part, sprouting dreads and married to a native son, a local hero, who himself was trying to make the hood a safer place to live.

That night the former runaway found a mission. She wasn't yet leading lost souls to God like she'd figured earlier. She decided that only her Creator knew who she really was, why she had been put at this particular spot on Planet Earth, or how all of this would wrap-up.

Harriet and Sophia-Emma went out on the front porch after the other four had left. They mapped out the next couple of weeks. Then it was on to one-on-one meetings with leaders and officials whom they thought would be on their side. Before the final accountability gathering with live bodies answering questions and approving new GED classes back in Africatown, another planning meeting also had to happen.

In addition, they'd get the media to turn out, besides promoting it on social media. This re-opening of the Community Action Center would be on everyone's tongue. The two friends could see how they could be advocates for their neighbors. Sophia-Emma's head was bursting with a love for power, but she was also afraid that her energy would be used just to satisfy her ego. The power bug had bitten.

"Harriet, please watch me," she urged. "All this stuff about power we talked about tonight scares me. Don't let it go to my head, please. I gotta be humble, not proud. If that means working behind the scenes, great. Will you be the face of this campaign?"

Harriet looked at her in surprise.

"I think you're thinking too far ahead. Let's let leadership rise up on its own," Harriet answered. "In a few weeks we'll all know better what each of us is suited for." She sarcastically added, "Has God spoken to you lately?"

Harriet had always been Sophia-Emma's best friend. She'd descended from the original settlers of Africatown and was proud of it. She quit school as soon as she turned sixteen because at the time she was planning to marry Jordan Baker (Mousetrap). But now he was serving time in federal prison on interstate drug sales. She told her friend she'd wait all the while he was gone, but lately Sophia-Emma had seen her flirting with other guys around town. Aside from getting horny for some male TLC, Harriet shared that she'd decided to search for a job so that when Mousetrap got released, he'd have a home to come to.

Harriet grabbed her purse and prepared to leave. Sophia-Emma noticed how cute she looked when she talked about Mousetrap. Her bright red perfectly sculptured lips spread across a full dark face while her round eyes exploded with excitement and a touch of exhaustion.

"Girl, you need to get yourself a man," Harriet said as she mounted her bike. "A man awakens your whole body, like from a breeze to a hurricane, but with more umph than Abram had."

Chapter 9

No guys for me, Sophia-Emma thought. She was here to complete a mission. First, she needed to understand what kind of mission she was assigned to here before she could even think about the opposite sex. She also had to work herself out of the penalty box into which her parents had caged her.

So for the next couple of weeks she and Harriet would talk to every drop-out with leadership potential that they could find. People who had no drop-out friends might wonder how a drop-out could be a leader, or conversely, why would a leader drop out of school? There were no easy answers, but she knew both happened. Some students dropped out because they were bored, bullied or banished—the smart, the abused, and the ones who fought for their rights. She searched out the banished first. One was Moses Welsh (Bulldog).

She found him one afternoon hanging out around the basketball court not far from her house. He consented to talk for just a few minutes while cooling down after a workout. As he was wiping the sweat dripping from his face with a big torn towel, Sophia-Emma noticed how short, but tough he was. On the court, his lack of height probably made him bolder, a good character trait for a leader.

"What's up, bitch?" he asked.

Sophia-Emma told him upfront this was the last time he'd call her a female dog.

"So why we meetin'? He could see that he'd just blown his chance to make it with her. "Whatcha want, girl?"

"Oh, just wonderin' what you up to these days since they kicked you out of school last winter. Your old lady musta felt like whoopin' your rear end, huh?"

He rose from the bench to his feet and started dribbling his gray basketball. "Com'on girl, I don't want to talk about it. Old news now anyway. You working for that fuckin' school now?"

"You crazy, Bulldog?" I never set foot in that cage. But hell, I gotta get goin' on with my life. Video games have started playing me now." She hoped she could get a smile out of him. It didn't happen. "But let's get serious, despite what I said a couple minutes ago, you pretty cool dud 'round here. And I need your slant on how we can get goin' on GEDs. I'm thinkin' of startin' a church someday, but can't get a loan without proof I finished school."

She noticed a tattoo of Malcolm X on his forearm. "Hey man. Who did your Malcolm X? Now there was a powerful speaker."

Bulldog knew there was a purpose for all her syrupy compliments, but he played along and let the sweet stuff lift his mood. "Good 'semblance, huh? Wanna open my own shop someday. I can't even think 'bout opening a shop till I get my GED."

Bulldog looked like someone had thrown a quart of vinegar in his face. He became quiet and wiped more sweat from his face, gradually moving his towel down to his arms where little droplets of body fluids were turning into salt.

Sophia-Emma took this as a cue that their meeting was about over. She turned to walk away.

"You know what they did to me, don't cha? Over there at LeFlore?"

She didn't say a word. Instead she slowly turned back to face Bulldog and saw a tired angry man.

"I called one of those people who sit behind a desk all day a *Hitler*, and I was gone that minute. Couldn't even get my stuff outta my locker. I'll never set foot in that looney-bin again, so help me God."

"You kiddin' me, man." Sophia-Emma said without thinking ahead again. "Bulldog, someday we're going to win our just due. But for now, do you wanna GED?"

Since she'd already practiced her spiel at home, she felt sure she could convince Bulldog to come on board.

"Let me tell you another travesty that's keeping folks like you and me in the poorhouse. The Community Action Center has been closed down here in Africatown for decades. Why am I mad? That's where GED classes used to be. Now instead they want us to get downtown. Any other hood where they've shut down the Action Center? Don't think so. Why just over here, Bulldog?"

"Ain't no diff'rent than usual, sista."

"That's why this kinda stuff stops here, man." She shouted louder than she'd intended. "Let me ask you—are you with me, man—to join some of us in the hood? We're gonna put those big shots on the hot seat, come September. You do want to get your GED someday, don't you, Bull? You know why they turned you down again this year to work on the dock? How 'bout pumping some life into this old town doin' somethin' you got a passion for, like that tattoo center?"

"Hey girl, now you're talkin'. Let's get this thing on the road. I'm tired of all this aggravation folks give us here."

Sophia-Emma and Bulldog bumped fists and went on talking. "All you have to do for the next couple weeks is to get the word out in the hood. Some of us are planning and organizing meet-up over at the old Union Missionary Baptist Church on Thursday, August twentieth, six o'clock. That's when we'll strategize how we can win on this issue.

A couple weeks later in September, watch us fill that place up with folk like you and me and other homies, even old folk. On that night people'll be peeping in to see what's goin' on. That night we gonna make demands of all those bigwigs who think they can close down what's important here. And just watch. If they don't show, or if they stall or short change us . . ."

By now she had Bulldog's full attention. He'd stopped bouncing the ball and was nodding his head as she spoke.

"One more thing Bulldog: Since you're one of the main bosses in this battle, you need to be at my house August twentieth, six at night for pizza and planning. I'll need to know that night how many you can commit to show up on Thursday, September third for the community meeting. That means bring 'em all in, man, so we can wear those bigwigs down."

"I'll be there, Soph. I know some bros who'll show up with me."

Sophia-Emma walked a little closer to Bulldog and gave him a high-five.

"Remember, at our pizza gathering a week or so earlier, we'll be going through our strategy, who to put on the hot seat, who'll be our main target. What will be our demands? Who'll get us on social media, TV, and in the *Press-Register*? With your help, we're gonna rock. Now what date you comin' to my place?"

"August twentieth, six o'clock. Putting it on my phone now," Bulldog repeated.

Sophia-Emma raised her thumb in agreement. "And Bulldog, it's crucial you work with me on this. Call every drop-out you know, the head homeboys and their followers about the September community meet. We puttin' this town on the map, man."

As she got back on her bike, she remembered one more thing. "Hey man, who else can I talk to about this?"

Bulldog seemed to think a bit before he shouted out Purple Moon's (Nico Watson) name.

"He was being bullied by the football team for coming out as gay. But that was then. Now the guy's built like Ali in his best years. He gave her Purple Moon's contact and she was off to reserve the space at the church for the two gatherings in August and September. She then thought about all those little old church women who were probably just as mad about the closure of the center as her drop-out buddies. Maybe

Miss Mildred or even her own mama could bring some of them into the fold.

At the church, Preacher Anthony Jackson was pumped that Sophia-Emma was taking on the GED project. "Praise the Lord, this is what this neighborhood needs," the pastor said. "I'll be there. I can welcome the people to our historic fellowship center. I'll have our members spruce up the room, putting real flowers on the table . . ."

"Father, uh Preacher–I'm sorry, but I don't know what you want to be called–Your idea is fine for our organizing meeting on August twentieth, but the tables have to go for the September gathering. We're gonna have folks crammed in like threads in a silk blouse. Maybe we should consider the sanctuary instead, since you have pews there.

"Let's look at the sanctuary and then we'll decide," the Rev said.

The two walked over to the church where Sophia-Emma was overcome with the holy presence of the place. Could this sacred spot with flickering candles near the altar, the baptismal font holding calm waters, the plush red carpet with matching pew cushions, a solemn place of worship, all be transformed into a battleground for oppressed people? She needed time to think a while on this.

"I love this spot," she said to Pastor Jackson. "Which do you think would be better for what we need to do in September?"

"My child, this is the house of the Lord. Sometimes my God wants silence. Sometimes he wants noise for what is good and righteous. Let's pray about it now."

This was the first time she'd been asked to pray with a preacher–anyone for that matter–other than before meals with Miss Mildred sometimes. She couldn't tell Pastor Jackson that she didn't know how to pray. She assumed he meant talking to God. She'd been more inclined to do the other kind of prayer, where you went into a closet and said the *Our Father*. But by now, this pastor had gotten into a pretty good rhythm.

". . . by your guiding force, you bring the powerful down and rise up the pitiful. Hear our prayer, we beseech you, Holy Savior, Son of the

Father, let your Holy Spirit come down and anoint our sanctuary this day and every day, through Christ, our Lord, Amen."

Sophia-Emma felt her body wanting to float over the altar, to the holy water in the baptismal font and sprinkle it around the pulpit, on the altar, over the Bible. She literally had to control her hands by tucking them under the pew cushion.

"Pastor, I'm enthralled by the holiness I find in this sanctuary. Can I have some time here alone? I won't be long." The young girl felt like such a grown-up at this moment.

As the pastor walked back to the church entrance, checking the poor box and whatever ministers do while waiting for worshipers to leave their churches, she knelt on the red carpet before the dancing light of a candle. She whispered to the godhead who people worshiped there.

"I kind of think I'm part of your triangle right now. Am I crazy, or could I be a part of you two? Why am I here on this planet? Did I ask you that today? I don't remember any of this deciding stuff. I do know that I long to merge into the essence of both of you. I miss our camaraderie everyday. Forgive me, Father, if I've lost my mind. I can be weird at times. Bless me and let's get together real soon, just to catch up on what's happening in this big world."

She rose from her knees and reverently backed away. Something was missing from her request.

"Oh yeah. Amen."

A deep sense of peace overwhelmed her as she left the sanctuary. She felt the need to go outside and breathe a sweet breeze that didn't happen much in this part of town. Upon opening the church's front door, she saw an eagle resting on a branch of a pecan tree, limbs swaying as a sweet breeze romanced them. It didn't fly away, insisting instead to simply look at her as she looked back.

She finally grabbed Rev. Jackson's arm. "Maybe I'm too superstitious, but I think this is a sign from God that we should meet in the sanctuary here in September. Okay with you, Pastor?"

Riding home, the sun on the western horizon settling into the Gulf almost blinded Sophia-Emma. She got off the bike and walked the rest of the way home, still in a semi-trance following her experience in the church and with the eagle—not as a predator but a protector. If only she could know more about her relationship to God—each of the persons of God, that was—as that church seemed to believe.

But for now, she had to get back to organizing, back to washing dishes from a meal she'd just missed. Then there was folding the laundry and making more calls. Sophia-Emma didn't know if she'd find time to at least rest her eyes before starting all over again tomorrow.

On the steps to her front door, she saw a line of marching fire ants, one part of creation that she'd always thought the world could do without. The regiment seemed endless. Within minutes they were on her clothes and in her hair. A nightmare had begun.

Chapter 10

Attempting to leave the ants outside, Sophia-Emma tip-toed into the house and noticed a horde of them clinging to her sandals. They were tiny but treacherous. She could feel welts growing on her skin, so she changed gears and ran straight toward the bathtub. There she immersed herself into a fresh stream of hot water. The ants rose to the top of the water, actually swimming toward Sophia-Emma's upper body where they continued to chew on her more. Pulling the plug and spreading soapy lather all over her body, she didn't have time to think of what else she could do to be rid of these rabid bugs, She stood up, closed the shower curtain, and turned on the shower's hottest water her body could tolerate, aiming it on spots where they clung in teams. All the while, she was screaming and crying like a frightened baby.

Her mama rushed in and tried to calm her daughter. In turn, many attacked her. She climbed into the tub herself, still clothed, frantically stripping because the ants had attached themselves to skin under her clothes. Her daughter started picking the angry ants off her while her mama did the same for her. Then Pulsar finally walked in to see what all the commotion was.

"Get out," her mama yelled at him. "Call an exterminator. Fire ants are biting us. Don't let them get on you. It's like they're possessed by some evil force. Shit! Dammit! Ouch!"

Echoing her, Sophia-Emma hollered even louder, "Daddy, they're coming in from the front porch. Noticed them when I came up the steps—thousands of 'em heading straight for me. Had to climb into this tub to get them off, but they stick to me like I'm fly-paper. Can't stand this and won't stay in this house any longer. Gotta do something. Please do something, please!"

All the while she was screaming at whoever could possibly help, the hot steamy water continued to spray both mama and daughter. The ants' nibblings worsened. Sophia-Emma peeped outside of the shower curtain onto the bathroom floor and the outer rim of the tub. More were still racing into the tub, replacing those that had washed down the drain. Sophia-Emma wondered if they'd cling to the inner sides of the drain rather than be washed all the way down into the sewer.

For what seemed an eternity, the ants wouldn't let-up. As both women picked off ant after ant, most came right back. Sophia-Emma's entire body was reeking with pain and bubbling up with welts. Both were prisoners of these invaders from hell. At this moment the younger victim saw them as killers, eating her one tiny bite at a time. And they were biting like they hadn't eaten in days, even months.

"Don't these things belong outside?" Sophia-Emma managed to ask her mama. "If I don't get them off me in a few minutes, I'm going to slit my wrists. Can't stand this. Help me, Daddy. Help me, anybody!"

While she was frantic and begging for death, her mama was proclaiming surrender to some divinity she'd never heard of. She was sitting, hands over her face, crying, moaning, surrendering, at the back side of the tub's floor.

Finally, after what seemed a decade, her daddy brought in the exterminator into the bathroom, despite both his wife and daughter being naked. They turned their backs to the stranger while he talked to Pulsar. Christopher stared a hole into both women.

"I'm not quite sure how to go about this, man," the exterminator said. "Probably least dangerous is, uh . . ." He dug into his bag, "Have to make the two ladies put these masks on, ask them to not breathe any more than they have to. I'm going to spray this area with insecticide, which will kill the ants within seconds. After that, I suggest the women wrap themselves in clean towels and go to the other bathroom to rinse off."

"We have just one bathroom," her daddy said.

"Well, then have them rinse off by the kitchen sink while I de-ant the entire place, the porch, and around your home's foundation."

Sophia-Emma yelled, "Give us the damn masks and get started. Christopher, get us some towels from the laundry baskets. Sir, tell us when we can leave the bathroom."

Both women took one last long deep breath and put on their masks that looked like gas masks from World War One. They picked off more ants and prepared for the onslaught of poison, a fog that permeated the entire bathroom.

"Okay, wrap in towels and leave," the exterminator yelled like the Enola Gay was about to drop an atom bomb. Sophia-Emma ran out first and started washing down at the kitchen sink, still full of dirty dishes from the dinner she'd missed earlier. The exterminator was now spraying horrible toxic chemicals throughout the house. The teen had to leave. She raced upstairs and put on whatever she could reach first, which happened to be dirty jeans and an Alabama t-shirt, and then sprinted the ten blocks to Miss Mildred's house, where she collapsed at her feet from exhaustion. She knew she'd never forget the look of horror on her mentor's face as she sprawled there in front of her on her front porch.

"My chile, my baby, calm down. You smell like bug spray. Before you tell me anything, let's take care of you, and then you can fill me in about all that's happened." Miss Mildred tried to speak softly and calmly. "Holy Moses, you stink, girl. Here, get in the tub, put some of this lavender oil in warm water and relax, I'm sure you'll be that sweet little girl I've always known in just a few minutes."

Her words of welcoming and concern made Sophia-Emma feel like she was an endangered species. She took her advice and nestled herself into the huge bathtub, all the while letting the lavender oil erase the smell and some of the memory of the ant attack and the putrid spray that followed. But once more she saw more ants—dead ones—floating on the surface of the bathtub's water. She also saw hundreds of inflamed welts all over her flesh from the six-legged varmints. Sickened by the sight floating around her, Sophia-Emma scrubbed furiously, wanting to rub away the welts. Then out of nowhere she kissed those welts her mouth could touch and yelled for Miss Mildred to call her mama and daddy.

"Tell 'em I'm here. I'm okay and ask if they're okay, will you please?"

"I'm on the phone with your mama now, chile," Miss Mildred yelled back. "Let me talk to her some more and then we'll put some special salve on you to make you as good as new before you eat breakfast tomorrow."

Sophia-Emma emptied the tub filled with dead bugs and then refilled it again. A few more dead bugs remained to float around her one more time. She shampooed her hair and still felt dead ants under her nails as she vigorously scratched her head and did another sudsing. The lavender gradually relaxed her till all she wanted to do was sleep and try to forget this night forever.

But she still had enough energy to tell her whole story to Miss Mildred. After that she would go to that entity called the Divine, a place that would hear her out. "Why pick on me," she'd ask. "Why send out the locusts to devour my beautiful dark skin? Did you permit the Angel of Darkness to have its way with me, right after I'd prayed to you in the church just minutes before?"

Miss Mildred opened the bathroom door ever so slowly. She'd dressed for bed herself. She put some clothes for Sophia-Emma to wear to bed out on a chair and brought over a cup of warm milk. The teen exhaled the remaining poisoned air from her chest, expelling it forever and breathing in fresh, hopeful, cooling, love-filled air. At last she was safe with a loving elder. She drank and swallowed relief and serenity. She became the baby Sophia-Emma, once more surrounded by her mother's breast where no one could hurt her.

As the last dead ant disappeared down the drain, she dressed in soft bed clothing Miss Mildred had left for her. The old lady was listening to some ancient church choir music, waiting for her on the parlor couch.

"Your mommy, she explained all that happened tonight, darling. Sometimes I wished that we didn't have to live down here in 'Bama where those damn ants rule the land and everything else 'round it. As if the crooked police weren't bad enough. At least the ants are gone now." She slightly coughed as she exhaled deeply. "I tell your daddy to be sure nothin' like this happens again to my little girl. He's still kinda mad at me for not tellin' them when you tried to run away a few days ago. But he'll get over it." She gave me her comforting smile. "Our spirit father and mother'll work on his soul, I do believe. Is there anything you want to tell me about tonight, darling?"

Tears fill Sophia-Emma's eyes. All that happened just hours ago now seemed like a bad dream, but she thought she had to get it out so she could deal with the experience and be done with it.

"Miss Mildred, my day had gone so well. I felt like I's in the palm of God's hand. I'd met with Moses Welch—we call him Bulldog—about helping us organize to get GED classes over here in Africatown. I visited Union Missionary Church and got approval to have two meetin's there in August and September. Then I had this supernatural experience, like I'm being' blessed and so happy. Everything was fitting together in my life. But when I got home the ants came after me. I never been attacked by ants or any bugs like this before. Now I 'fraid to step outside again, and I 'bout as 'fraid to even go back in our bathroom, or anywhere in our house."

She started to cry and used the borrowed pajama sleeve to catch her tears, while also wondering what else she could say to help all the pain go away.

"My child, I can't tell you why all this dern-right scary stuff happened to you tonight. I don't think God planned this. No, oh no. That wasn't God. But God rescued you, didn't he? He brought you to me tonight. And now I can rub oil on your feet, on your sores, just like that woman in the Bible did to Jesus. God ain't the referee or policeman up in heaven, but he can so often give you and me the courage to help one another. And I think when you go back home tomorrow and all that awful bug spray is gone, you and your mommy and daddy be closer. This a family affair. Y'all worked together to win over the locusts—even little Christopher. Your mama said he was the one who rescued you two by handin' out towels."

She reached over to tap Sophia-Emma on her shoulder. "*All things work out for the best for those who trust in the Lord*, Paul once wrote. And I think he right. Now, ain't you glad you's not off all by yourself when all this happened? And you certainly coulda been. What would you have done? So my chile, I don't think God makes bad things happen, but more often than not, he sends us to help one another when we can't handle problems by ourselves. Now don't go and get mad at God. Or the ants—they's just doin' what ants do, and rattlesnakes do what rattlesnakes do. But somehow we all learn to 'spect each other while we walk, crawl, or slither on this earth.

By now, Sophia-Emma was so exhausted she was about to doze off. "Thanks, Miss Mildred. I think I should already know everything you reminded me. You know, don't you think I'm a little weird? Like you sometime say, 'I have the word on the tip of my tongue, but it won't come out?' Then you remember it a couple days later, and everybody else has forgotten about it by then. If you were God tonight and this been a test, would you been proud of me or laughed at me? I feel a total mess. Do you think God 'member or forget all this?"

"You were a mess, darling. I don't exactly know what you mean when you occasionally say you were sent here for a special mission. Is that like you think you're an angel or a prophet, maybe a saint, starting your own church or what?"

"Aw, that's not so important now. I'm still young. Besides I don't know if I'm any of those things or somethun else. I know right here in my guts that I put here as part of some plan I had a part in putting together. I guess I'll find out someday. You'll be the first to know when I do. But for now, can I go to bed? I'm so tired."

"Sure, my chile," Miss Mildred blew a kiss her way and each went their separate ways to bed.

In bed, the puzzled teen asked her God to speak to her so she could one day tell Miss Mildred who she really was.

Chapter 11

No message from God either before dozing off or in Sophia-Emma's dreams that night. No surrestlistic hidden messages on dew-covered windows. Nada. Sophia-Emma was still perplexed, displeased, and depressed, so much so that she was in no mood to get up and continue her organizing work. She didn't even feel like going home and checking on her mama. Instead she wanted to stay in this safe and comfortable bed with eyes closed and wishing for a dream, a hallucination, anything but the reality of what was now in Africatown.

Miss Mildred finally knocked on her guest's door.

"Breakfast is served, Miss Sophia-Emma. Would you like it brought in on a tray, little princess?"

Begrudgingly, the *little princess* forced herself to put two feet on the floor and wrap Miss Mildred's robe around her much shorter body. She wondered what she'd wear when she left later?

Miss Mildred was a tall lady who was still wearing the same clothes today that she wore since her twenties. Her styles showed it, too. Sophia-Emma, on the other hand, was somewhat chunky and short. To her surprise, however, she now saw the clothes she'd worn when she arrived last night. This time they appeared fresh and folded perfectly in a chair. Miss Mildred must've washed and dried them last night.

Last night? She hadn't seen Little Guy last night at all. "Have you seen my puppy?" she asked Miss Mildred as she followed the breakfast scent into the kitchen.

"Why chile, can't say I have. If he's around, he's being mighty quiet. You musta' left him at home last night."

"I gotta go," she insisted as she slipped on her sandals in a rush. "Thank you for putting me up one more time. Don't know what I'd do if I hadn't found you."

"You not leaving looking like a lost puppy yourself," Miss Mildred fired back. "Now sit down. You young uns sometimes have no manners whatsoever. I want you to eat these eggs before you go anywheres."

She piled spoonful after spoonful of scrambled eggs onto Sophia-Emma's plate and added a bottle of ketchup next to the orange juice. "When you finish these, I want you to go into the bathroom, wash your face and run the comb through your hair. You're not a zombie, but quite a lovely young woman. Now act like one."

Not feeling like arguing with anyone this morning, Sophia-Emma inhaled the ketchup-soaked eggs and did the bathroom thing. She thanked Miss Mildred and bid her good-bye before starting her walk home, the entire time worrying about Little Guy. What could have happened to him?

Her daddy took him to the shelter.

He got lost.

The new owners came to take him back.

She wouldn't let herself get her hopes up and expect her puppy to meet her at the yard gate, wagging his tail in excitement while trying to climb up her pants leg.

But that's exactly what he did. At last some good news. And Mama was out in the yard to greet her, too. Not a single live fire ant was anywhere in sight.

"It's about time you're home, young lady . . ."

The blast of good news had ended. Sophia-Emma pecked Mama on the cheek and let her have her say.

"Bulldog has been calling here all day. Give him your cell number. Give it to all your friends. I got a show coming up next month and I haven't painted a stroke all morning. There're dishes for you to do, clothes in the washing machine and dryer ready to wash and dry. And don't forget, Christopher has to be at the pool by eleven-thirty."

Loving took a deep breath while her mama continued, "By the way, how're your ant bites this morning? Don't you ever bring those bastards back to this house again. That damn dog probably dragged them in, huh?"

"Mama, cool down," Sophia-Emma tried to speak in a relaxed tone. "I bet you didn't sleep well last night, right? Let me run a nice soothing bath for you. I'll put in some lavender oil, and you'll become the nicest mama on the block." If it worked for her last night, surely it'd work for her mama, she surmised.

"And no, Little Guy wasn't responsible for the ants. When I first saw them, they were heading from the porch steps toward me. Don't ask me how that happened, but Little Guy was asleep under the Magnolia when I got home. Let me call Bulldog now while you calm down. You white women! Always complaining," she said under her breath.

Bulldog clicked on his phone at the first ring. "What you want, bitch?"

"I'm hanging up," she responded. "Call me when you clean up your talk."

Sophia-Emma went on to load the dishwasher and unload the dryer so she could reload it with the clothes washed the day before. A text came through as she was immersed with the housework.

"Call me," Bulldog texted. "No one wants to get involved with your fuckin' project. Guess I'm out, too."

She wasted no time texting back. "Ur not out. Why u calling my house all AM?"

"Cuz I bored."

"Don't back out on me, man. C'mon."

The two went back and forth for ten minutes while Christopher shook dead ants out the towels his mama and sister used the night before.

"Kids, you've got only five minutes till you have to be at the pool. You're going to be late," Loving hollered to whomever would listen.

"We're out of here," Sophia-Emma yelled back as she forced Christopher into his only pair of shoes. With Little Guy, they all ran out the door and dashed the couple blocks to the Kitt Park Pool.

"Gee, the air stinks today," Christopher yelled as they got closer to all the chemical and paper plants. Her bro was her favorite mini man and he seemed to kind of like her, too.

"It might smell better if you'd chosen a diff'rent towel," she remarked. "Remember Mama used that one after we sprayed with bug spray."

Chris was a handsome kid even at his young age. His eyes reminded her of a full moon, steel wool hair, plus the neatest naturally sculpted fingernails. Sophia-Emma got lost in memories of the day Chris was born. She'd wanted a little sister so badly, but she got him instead. She'd long ago decided he was better than any sister could ever have been—most of the time, that was. Probably a little sister wouldn't have chosen the towel he used today.

When they got to within a block from the pool, he walked the rest of the way by himself. These days he was embarrassed to have his big sis leading him down to the pool.

While Chris was taking his swimming lesson, his sister scouted around for some older kids, spotting Harriet in the middle of a flirting session with some dudes by the snack bar. They waved. Harriet motioned for Sophia-Emma to come join them.

"Hey girl, I see you got kid duty today, too," Harriet teased.

"At least it's better than sweeping up dead fire ants," Sophia-Emma said and showed her and her homeboys bites on her arms. "Last night

I felt I was in a horror movie, *The Attack of the People-eating Ants.* You can't believe how they went after me and my mama. And they wouldn't die. We had to get an exterminator there on an emergency call. Never want to be in that flick again."

One of the bros, Jammer, got smart with her and asked her to pull up her jeans's leg to see more. She gave him the finger. He returned the greeting. They backed up from each other, but not because of fear. More like disdain.

"Sorry 'bout that, Soph. I was telling these dudes here—Bow Wow, Jammer and Da Vinci—about our get-together comin' up next month."

"Hey, y'all interested, ain't cha?" Harriet was making sure they were listening.

Da Vinci spoke first. "Yo, I'm tired of parking cars and scraping dishes for fat rich white folk. I wanna settle down one day with a hot chick like one of y'all, and I don't see it happnin' without some more learnin'. You know, I once was pretty good kid till I got labeled as a knock-off. Had to live up to it, you know. And then, ya know, I'm booted out of school flat on my nose. And no way I goin' back there—no way, man."

"Know what you sayin', bro," said Bow Wow. "As long as I's pullin' down the points in the baskets, I gettin' good grades, but when I broke my leg, my grades fell into like shit. But hell, man, I'm not goin' downtown for one of them GEDs. Forget it." He kicked up some dust and the rest of them brushed most of it off their clothes.

"So, y'all wanna' work with us to bring GEDs back to the hood?" Sophia-Emma asked.

The group looked around to be sure no one was watching them talk about school. When the coast was clear, they nodded their heads.

"Okay. It's like this," Harriet said. "We got a pizza planning meeting comin' up August twentieth, six o'clock sharp at Union Missionary Church. Bring some drinks, dessert, whatever, no dope. We'll look at strategy, who's our target, who does what . . . you know, like we're checking out the opposite team, getting at their weaknesses, avoiding their strengths. Then on September third, we bring our bros and sistas, preachers, the dog catcher, anyone we can pull out of the pool halls, and we hit hard at those powerful S.O.Bs, who have put their knees on our necks for too long. That 'portant meeting starts at seven o'clock. So get more leaders to come to the church fellowship hall to plan on the twentieth. Then before September third, get commitments from everyone else so they be there to hoot, holler, and hold a seat as we grill those fat butts in front of us—not lettin' 'em go till they commit to GED classes in the hood. I give you both our cell numbers. Stay in touch with your sistas here and all the dudes you gonna be talkin' this up to, okay?"

They give each other the Black Panther handshake—slide, click, and hands raised to shoulders. The guys left while Harriet stayed on with Sophia-Emma.

"Are you still on this religious kick, girl, or are you back with us in the human race? I still ain't shared what y'all told me, but I might if you get on your high horse again."

Sophia-Emma stared at Harriet, wishing she had her long eyelashes, her long shapely legs, and proud chin. Sophia-Emma wanted her confidence, too.

"I'm back, friend, just me, Sophia-Emma," she lied.

Chapter 12

Deciding to put her obsession with a spiritual mission on the back shelf for a while, Sophia-Emma did some research on what her full name said about her. She knew that Sophia meant *Wisdom* in Greek, but what about Emma?

Her mama had once told her about Emma Goldman, for whom she was named. She decided to read some of her quotes. From many attributed to her, Sophia-Emma liked this one the most:

"I began to speak. Words I had never heard myself utter before came pouring forth, faster and faster. They came with passionate intensity . . . the audience had vanished, the hall itself had disappeared. I was conscious only of my own words, of my ecstatic song."

Sophia-Emma decided she would model her life from now on this anarchist and female rebel for whom she was named.

Harriet seemed interested in her friend's new intended persona. "That's perfect, Sophia-Emma. I've always said you know how to talk from your guts by way of the heart."

"Yo girl, let's start a group of rebellious sistas here in Africatown between Magazine Point over to Three Mile Creek."

"There's already a group somethun' like that. It's called Connections," Harriet interrupted. "And boy, they need some of our type to liven them up. That's us, sista." Harriet pointed at Sophia-Emma and then back at herself. "We're *Young, Gifted, and Black,* as Nina Simone would say. Thank God, we're not *Mississippi, God Damn.* But Alabama sure is close."

"That awesome, girl," Sophia-Emma hollered. "But right now I'm thinking of what we gotta do in the next couple weeks, so we don't have to catch a bus downtown at night for GED classes."

Sometimes she didn't know how Harriet came up with her ideas, but she liked her gumption. "I'm not worried, Harr. You know you a terrific organizer, don't you? I saw you talkin' with those bros the other day. How many more can you get to? I need to dig up some dirt over at the Community Action Offices downtown. Think I'll do some volunteer work over there. Our bro Nico still needs to be contacted, a bunch of sistas, too. A'ight?"

Harriet's smile turned to a scowl. "Oh no, you don't, Soph. You don't dump all this stuff on me while you move around in air conditioning downtown, take coffee breaks, and eat lunch with big shot divas while I sweat it out here in the hood. No way."

Sophia-Emma had no comeback. She figured if she kept bragging Harriet up, eventually her ego would kick in and they'd have a fired-up team.

Meanwhile, Harriet's little sister, Sequita, along with Chris, shook excess water onto the sandy path as they ran over to their older siblings.

"Here come the little demons," Harriet said as Sophia-Emma reached out to her little bro, glistening like a fish out of water in the hot sun.

Sophia-Emma wanted some of that cool water on her, so she wiped him down with her bare hands and wrapped his wet still-stinking towel around her shoulders before starting their walk home.

Chris looked up at his big sister and pleaded to stay a little longer, but she wouldn't budge. Harriet faced the same pressure from Sequita. Both big sisters stood their ground. They were in charge, and the younger siblings would have to submit.

Out of habit, Sophia-Emma walked with her hands in my pockets, where she discovered some cash, probably put there by Miss Mildred earlier this morning. It was enough for all four of them to flag down the Sweet Dairy Truck for snow cones on the way home. Smiles showed up on all their faces, along with rainbow colors on their tongues. The temperature by now must have been in the upper nineties with no breeze or shade to give any relief. Sophia-Emma felt the burning sidewalk baking her feet through her sandals, like she was walking on hot coals.

"You know, Harriet, when I look around here and see so much falling down or boarded up around us, I wish I could be one of those little girls just after they got their freedom—fired up, mind you—gazing out over all these waters, the bayou, no bridges, lots of fish, and seafood begging to be dinners, I don't want to see what around us now—dirt, roads everywhere going nowhere for us, graves of dead ancestors facing east, chemicals in our air from oil, asphalt, freaking factories—do you think you'll always live here?"

"Not if I can help it," Harriet answered. "Me and Mousetrap, we goin' to Atlanta, live in Buckhead. We'll be famous rappers and I'll also be raising flowers and babies, pretty black raspberries."

"Dream on," Sophia-Emma teased, as she focused on two sticky sweaty kids beside her. "I'm never having kids, never."

Seeing Mama outside getting the mail, she said good-bye to Harriet and stopped at the mailbox to see what other jobs her mother had waiting for her. But first, she had to ask a question.

"Hey, Mama, remember when you gave me my second name of Emma, did that mean you wanted me to be like Emma Goldman, or what?"

Her mama glanced at the mail and then looked at her daughter. "You know, my old boyfriend Pete, 'fore he was killed the next day, made that decision. I liked the name, too. But I don't think that meant I wanted you to grow up and be her reborn. She was courageous, passionate, a *woman rebel.* Come to think of it, you're turning out a little like her. I can live with that."

"Cool," Sophia-Emma said. "Think I'm gonna put my efforts into activism and social change from now on anyway. This mission—God-stuff—ain't getting me nowhere. I hope you don't mind, think I'm gonna do some volunteering downtown this summer. Aw shucks!"

She paused and rethought where she was going with this. "Do you have a few minutes? I want to run my scheme by you."

Fortunately, both were now in a better mood than they'd been earlier. Loving said she could spare a few minutes while Chris played with Little Guy. After washing the ice cream off her and Chris's sticky hands, Sophia-Emma and Loving sat down at the kitchen table to chat. Sophia-Emma began to explain what she intended to do with her all-important life as a woman rebel.

Her mama's smile grew bigger as her little girl explained it all, bringing back memories from the time when she too was a woman rebel.

Chapter 13

Dressed in her best clothes, Sophia-Emma arrived downtown on the bus early just after the morning rush. She felt overdressed in a bright red, sleeveless blouse and a thigh-length, tight, navy-blue skirt But she'd seen tighter. Her mama did her hair, wrapping it on top of her head. She added sensible makeup, a soft pink gloss, and a smattering of bronze eye shadow and mascara. Harriet helped do her sista's cherry red faux nails last night.

Upon arrival, the volunteer wanna-be went to the front desk of the Mobile Community Action Center on Donald Street. She announced that she wanted to volunteer. The application was easy to complete, although she left the race box empty because she considered herself a bit of every race. An elderly, pudgy, black lady with no make-up and swollen ankles interviewed Sophia-Emma. Her name tag said her name was Carol Vogel, who chewed gum in time with a little tune under her breath. She looked over Sophia-Emma's completed application.

"Oh, I see you're from Africatown. How're things over there these days? I was fearful when they had that tar sands crude oil being pumped into those old pipes in your neighborhood, but I guess no leaks lately. Glad that most recent hurricane fizzled out."

"We've had some close calls. Of course, we're always last to find out." Sophia-Emma didn't mention that her daddy had constantly complained about the tar sands pipes for years.

Ms. Vogel nodded and scanned more of her application. "I see you're homeschooled. Do you miss socializing with other children who go to your schools over there?"

"No, Ma'am, my mama went to college. I think I'm learning more from her."

"And I assume you get a Christian outlook on things. I hate that we can't do that in the public schools. See you only want to help us this summer. We need help with the summer feeding program at our parks and . . ."

The young applicant interrupted. "Ms. Vogel, I love kids, but I was wanting to help in the office some. Your staff looks so busy. I could help y'all and improve my computer skills and refine my telephone manners. Plus I love social media. I noticed that your website could stand some updating."

Miss Vogel's attention seemed to perk up with that suggestion. "That would be fabulous. When do you want to start? And how much time could you spend with us in, say, a week?"

"How about Monday and Friday, two to five? Six hours a week? Maybe I could throw in a few more hours if you get short-staffed because of vacations, people getting sick or other stuff."

"Well, Miss Sophie . . ."

"Sophia-Emma," she interjected.

"Miss Sophia-Emma, welcome to Mobile Community Action. I'm sure you'll like spending your time with us.

"Yes, Miss Vogel." She reached over the woman's desk to shake hands, a surprise for her new boss since most teens she knew hadn't been taught such courtesies in recent years.

Position secured. Sophia-Emma was so proud that she had actually spoken like a real grown-up. As soon as she emerged outside into the hot smelly air, the new volunteer was on her phone with Harriet.

"We're in, gal," she nearly shouted. "I start this Friday at two. And get this: I get to work in a nice-smelling cool office. They'll let me do social media, update the website and answer the phone. Isn't that a'ight?"

"I'm jealous," Harriet answered. "But that's okay. The dudes I'm bringing on board are much better looking than the old bitches in that boring, just-as-well-be-dead office. Stay cool this summer while I win the hearts of the studs over here."

"I've only begun to fight, sista. I plan to go by the city library, before I catch a bus home. I need to get some info in its archives about how Mobile has taken more from us than it's given us. You know, stuff like that. When I get home, Mama's got work for me to do. Talk to you tonight. Can't wait to get out of these skin-tight clothes. Life out in the streets in these wraps must be the pits. So long, Har."

At the library archives, Sophia-Emma, in surgical vinyl gloves, dove into articles about the many times residents in Africatown would get new plants in Magazine Point, but not the jobs. The asphalt company overnight moved into the hood—with no permits. All they had to do was pay a measly fine after they got their dirty hands slapped. She also read about the high drop-out rates in the high school, and why the Community Action Center, which had helped kids get GEDs, was closed reportedly because of a tight budget. Her goal became one of finding the funds. Had they pursued grants, commitments from funders? Their group would show the hypocrisy interwoven into programs created to help poor people not be so poor. As far as she could see with her limited research experience was that the Community Action Center was simply a mirage to provide a few jobs for bureaucrats. Time would tell.

Of course, Sophia-Emma ended up staying downtown longer than she'd planned. Once again, she had a mama waiting at the front door, hands on hips, and a scowl on her face. She could tell she wasn't her mama's favorite person at this moment. So, she attempted to brighten her eyes by talking about the broken system they all lived in.

"I know I could have been home sooner, Mama, but I visited the archives at the downtown library, and you wouldn't believe what the system is doing to us over here. We gotta let them know we're not going to be stomped on any more by their racist policies. And, by the way, I start my volunteer work at the Community Action place on Friday."

Her mama continued to stand there with her stern look.

"Mama, you hear what I've been saying?"

The former anarchist rebel and matriarch managed a slight smile, but then broke out crying.

"Your dad . . . your dad . . . he got locked up again. He's gone and we have no money for bail. I don't know what I'm going to do."

Sophia-Emma ran over to her and hugged her as tightly as she could. Tears from her mother nearly soaked her daughter's best blouse. Surely, she thought, her daddy was booked on some minor act of civil disobedience. He crossed lines more than others crossed the street. If things were as bad as her mama seemed to think they were, they could call on her Grandma Foster, so rich and so alone on that big old plantation over in Dallas County. Perhaps this would be the way to melt that old bag's heart. But for now, she let her mama cry into her good outfit.

Their discussion tonight would be set aside. Instead they would talk about bailing her daddy out of jail. So while she cried gallons of tears, her daughter thought of bail.

"How much is his bail, Mama? And what has he done this time?" Sophia-Emma asked.

Chapter 14

Sophia-Emma made comfort food for dinner—boiled shrimp, corn on the cob and mac and cheese washed down with icy sweet tea. She even cleaned the kitchen afterwards and read Christopher a book before he conked out. Then she chewed on ideas for bond money. There was the house they lived in which really belonged to her daddy's mother, Ophelia. But she'd helped put up a bond for him a few decades ago, before he cut and ran to Sanctuary where he met Loving. What about the guys her daddy worked for? Maybe Miss Mildred could give some cash for her daddy's bond. And then there was the elephant in the room—Grandma Foster.

The teen laughed at the thought. Her mama wouldn't hear of making a plea to her mother. They hadn't spoken in years.

Perhaps there was more that Sophia-Emma's mama hadn't told her yet about why her daddy had been picked up and put in the slammer.

"You mean you hadn't heard anything yet?" her mama asked.

"No, nothing. I figured Daddy must have done some type of civil disobedience related to his work."

"How I wish that were so," her mama responded. "But it's more serious than that. According to news on the street, police had been watching your dad for months, and today they cornered him with some serious evidence, so they've said. Using and selling coke, heroin, meth, marijuana. You name it, he sold it. He now tells me money from selling has kept our heads above water for months. His job with Bay Clean Water was cut to halftime. And since he was already self-medicating after he'd fallen last year, he figured he'd start selling the stuff himself and finance his habit from his sales. I guess it worked, didn't it?" She looked at me as though I was part of the problem. "You got those clothes you wore today with drug money. We paid the exterminator the other night with drug money. His customers depended on him, as did dealers under him."

"So you're telling me that you've known all about this the whole time?"

Her mama shook her head in disgust and began to cry again for about the fourth time since Sophia-Emma had stepped in the house a few hours ago. "I knew, but I didn't know. Guess I was in denial. I liked the money coming in, but it was always in cash. I should have known better, should've confronted your dad, but I didn't want to break up the stream of dollars coming in."

"When can we see Daddy? This is going to be rough on all of us, Mama. And Christopher? No wonder he's so mopey tonight. He needs his daddy," she said as Loving wiped more tears away.

"And you know, don't you, that your dad's gotta be the fall guy. If he says where he got his drugs, all of us are game. That's how these messes work. You and me and Christopher are stuck. At least this house belongs to Grandma Ophelia. When he does get out, nobody can keep him out of this house, except his mama. She'd never do that. If we lived in the projects, he would be barred from living with us there. Convicted felons can never come back to live in HUD housing."

Mama blew her nose, gave me a slight smile, and went back to her painting. Now, more than ever, she had to make some big sales, and soon.

But Sophia-Emma hadn't mentioned another source of help yet. She took a stab. "Mama, there's always Grandma Foster. If you don't want to see her, I can take the bus up that way and talk her into helping us. You know I'm good at that kind of thing."

"No way, Sophia-Emma, and don't bring her name up again, you hear? What we're going to do is let the system do its thing. Your dad serves his time. You and I get real jobs. No one squeals on anyone. One day they'll let your dad out and I'll see that he never shoots up, sniffs, or smokes again."

This said, the mama she used to know—full of fight—was gone. She had moved to playing the doormat victim because she now had kids to worry about. Sophia-Emma knew that a parent couldn't get too daring when there was no one but them being the responsible one for their family's welfare.

She made up a lie that she needed to see Harriet about their gathering next week. Her mama, now at peace, but with no backbone, waved her arm Sophia-Emma's way, and she was then headed over to Miss Mildred's, whom she found swatting mosquitoes while she surveyed the setting sun from her front porch. Little Guy beat his owner and jumped on Miss Mildred's lap before Sophia-Emma closed the yard gate.

"Well, look at who the dog dragged in," she joked.

"Wish I in the mood to joke, Miss Mildred, but I feel that this weight on my shoulder is gonna flatten me any minute."

"Now that sounds like serious stuff, and right after I've been a hearin' such good things about you."

"Thanks, Miss Mildred, but there's not such good goin' on back home. Guess you heard my daddy got locked up, and he's taking the whole wrap. If he tells the cops anything . . ."

"Now, just hold on a minute, girl. What the dickens you talkin' 'bout? Your dad's locked up? Squealing? What's all this nonsense? Your daddy's a hard-working man taking care of his family . . ."

"That's what we thought." Sophia-Emma scratched Little Guy's neck as he leaned on her leg. "At this minute though, daddy's lying on a cot over at the county jail. He's admitted to selling drugs. The police had been on to him for a long time, and I guess today they decided to drop the net over him."

"Well, I'll be." Miss Mildred put on her surprised look. "This is about the worst news I could be getting right now. No one told me, guess 'cause I've been working outside all day. My chile, is there anything I can do to help?"

That was the offer her visitor wanted to hear. "All I want now is advice. I don't know where to turn. I shouldn't even be here now. Need to be looking for a job, preparing for our meeting to make Community Action open an office here, and meanwhile doing volunteer work over at MCA downtown so I can get some dirt on them. Now I have to add to all that attempting to raise money for Daddy's bail, watching Chris while Mama paints like crazy for her next show and . . ."

She stopped listing all she had to do simply to catch her breath. "All this is hitting me bad, real bad." She wiped away a stream of tears with her bushy hair. "I want to see my daddy. I'm scared for him. I want to hear him tell me what he did, How could he put his family in this predicament? I know one reason he spent seven years at Sanctuary commune was because he was afraid to go to jail. And what if he has to serve a long sentence, what then?"

Her uncontrollable crying prompted Miss Mildred to offer a clean handkerchief from her apron pocket.

"I'm so tired of being the responsible daughter, Miss Mildred. I don't want to play this good little black girl anymore."

There she'd said it again, claiming she was special or an angel or some type of overworked spirit. "I don't like this situation at all. I gotta get out of here."

Miss Mildred's surprised look turned into one that Sophia-Emma could only describe as weird. The aging mentor removed her glasses and wiped the dust off them. She didn't say a word. She only stared far off toward the bay.

"I'm afraid, darling, that your imaginary life needs to come to an end. I don't know who you are anymore. At times, I'm as proud of you as any grandmother could be, but other times—well, you baffle me, How much of this is the truth and how much is fantasy?"

Now it was Sophia-Emma's turn to stare. This wise woman, her mentor, whom she'd always shared even the tiniest of things, now seemed distant and peeved. She had to try harder to explain her situation.

"Miss Mildred, don't give up on me. Everything I've confessed to you is from my heart. It's too hard being human anymore. Tonight has made me wish I could run away and not bother with family or friends no more."

Miss Mildred abruptly stood up and walked into the house, seemingly abandoning her visitor. In a couple minutes, however, she returned with two tall glasses of Mountain Dew. "Here, take a long cool swallow of this. On a hot night like tonight, a cool fizzy drink will often bring me back to reality quicker than anything else I can think of."

And that's what they did as the crickets began to play their nightly tune. For the two humans on the sticky front porch, there was no talking. They looked at the Hawkinses walking their Doberman. Little Guy galloped to the fence and smelled the other dog separated from him by woven wires. He turned around in disgust and dashed back to sit on his owner's lap. They heard the little girls next door, the Collins twins, doing cheers for school. The sun had dipped below the flat horizon spiked with smoke stacks, tanks, and bridges. Looking in the opposite direction, the couple witnessed the moon moving in to take over the night guard. Everything and everyone seemed to be once more at peace with the world, which Sophia-Emma also longed for. But she also yearned for that advice she'd come to absorb from Miss Mildred.

"So, of all those things I've told you I need to do, what do you think is most important?" she asked.

"If I you, chile, as much as your mama needs you, I'd go visit your father. He's had some time to think now, I reckon. He needs to talk to you as much as you need to talk to him. Then assist your mama. Maybe you can do your father's job until he gets back. You like environmental work, don't you? You've got that wild little Harriet girl helping on your meeting. Remember, idle hands are the workshop of Satan. To tell the truth, I don't think you're going to have idle hands for a while. But I have faith in you, Sophia-Emma. Perhaps you're not God, but you sometimes have god-like qualities, so I can never stay mad at you for long. Tomorrow, see if you can visit your daddy first, okay?" She gave her mentee a wink and smile.

"And a reminder," she said as she collected both empty glasses, "I know some kids in this part of town have things a lot worse than you. So don't pull your hair out yet. Things'll get better."

And that was the extent of advice Miss Mildred had for her that night.

Sophia-Marie hurried to get home before it got pitch dark. When she tried to open the door, she discovered it was locked.

"Now that your father's gone, we need to keep the door locked," her mother lectured as she responded to her daughter's yelling and knocking. "There're mean people around here who, if your daddy says one word about them, we're sewer flush," Loving warned.

In her room, she called Harriet and filled her in on the new circumstances in her life.

"So what?" her friend responded. "Your family was about the only one in the hood with both parents living together anyway. Many of us depend on dealin' to pay the bills. The cops pull bros and sistas over by the dozens everyday. We got no money, none of us. Have your mama go sign up for welfare and SNAP. She won't get much, but y'all can survive, just like our people been doin' for decades. You're one of us now, sis."

Sophia-Emma suddenly felt that she'd just got accepted into a local gang.

After Harriet put her friend in her place, she updated Sophia-Emma on her organizing. "Let me share some numbers with you. I've got at least twenty coming to our meeting August twentieth. I suggest you butter-up that preacher friend of yours. He'll need to find some folk who'll get us some pizza and drinks. You want to run the meeting? I'm doing turn-out. You take it from there. And stop all this worrying. We're either goin' do this right or look stupid. Either way, I've met and flirted with some super cool dudes, and my summer is doing just fine. No complaints, hear me?"

Sophia-Emma guessed she had become upset about the cards she'd been dealt more than she should. But now she was mad at her mama. As a white woman, she seemed to assume that everything wrong would be fixed. Meanwhile, a bunch of people whose families had lived in the hood for more than a hundred years learned to accept and adapt. Maybe that was what her family needed to do. And if there was anyone needing to learn that now, it was her mama.

Chapter 15

Taking Miss Mildred's advice, Sophia-Emma decided to visit her daddy in jail. She went online to get an idea of what to expect and immediately discovered that preparations to arrange visits with the incarcerated were overwhelming.

Sophia-Emma would have to schedule ahead and certainly not just show up. Her daddy had to put her on his list of approved visitors and she needed an ID to prove she was the person on his list. Very few teens her age from the hood had approved picture IDs, especially ones like her who were homeschooled.

After scouting around the house, she found the doctored birth certificate her mama had a friend counterfeit when she was a baby. Then she scrounged up her Social Security card and actually took a bus to the Mobile License Commissioner Office to get a driver's permit.

That was just the beginning. Next step was to write her daddy begging him to put her on his list of approved visitors. She sweetened the deal by promising not to run away again if he added her to his list of approved visitors. More than a week later, everything came together and she boarded another bus to the Metro Jail. There she witnessed a whole new world.

First she noticed sudden obnoxious noises of clanging cell doors and angry people. Then there were the smells of bleach, urine, and sweat. Her eyes widened with sights of worry and sullenness. Her senses reached a saturation point because she'd arrived early and was forced to wait hours before being called to see her daddy.

Eventually her turn came. After being scanned and frisked, she was admitted into the visitors room. One hug at the beginning and one at the end were allowed. No touching any other time.

"Daddy, are they treating you okay in here?" Sophia-Emma couldn't help asking this because he looked like hell warmed over.

He looked into her eyes with his filled with tears.

"I never wanted to have you see me in here like this," he said. "You shouldn't have come. I'm a bad influence on both you and Christopher."

"But Daddy, that doesn't mean you've stopped being my dad. We both still love you."

"Well, stop it now," he abruptly shouted at his daughter and pounded the table. His daughter didn't know how to react. People in the big hall were looking over at them from all directions.

"I'm not your real daddy anyhow." He was now whispering so softly she had to read his lips.

"But you're the only daddy I know. All I came for today was your advice. You don't have to explain why you're here. I know, but I got some ideas I want to run by you. So pretty please, let me go on. I don't have much time left. I've memorized my questions, so let me rattle them off before you answer."

Her daddy begrudgingly leaned back in his metal chair, nodded, and started to say something, but Sophia-Emma cut him off.

"Do you think the group you work for would let me take your place with some pay while you're in the clink here? Can I bring you anything or help get a lawyer for you? What are some good sources so we can put up bail for you? And can Christopher come to visit you?"

Either due to his lack of sleep, bad food or worse, he seemed totally overwhelmed with all my questions.

She got the message. "I guess that's all for now."

Her daddy looked at her like she was a cracker from over in Fairhope. "I don't want anything from y'all. Wait a minute. That's not quite true. I want y'all to get on with your lives. I don't exist anymore in your mama's, your brother's, or your eyes. And don't come visit me anymore. I'm dead. Now, good-bye." He turned away, stood up from his chair, and motioned to a guard that the visit was finished. He wanted to go back to his cell.

"But Daddy, you didn't answer any of my questions," Sophia-Emma screamed through her tears. "He can't leave me here like this," she complained to the guard escorting him out.

"Daddy, don't go," Sophia-Emma yelled across the room. "At least hug me with your eyes." But by then he was gone and the door behind him had slammed shut.

Another guard without any emotion on his face led her out of the visitors room as Sophia-Emma bellowed out her frustrations, not caring what others around her thought. Her first thought was that her daddy was selfish, mean, and defeated. He didn't care about anyone in his family except himself.

While standing in line to take a bus out of this hellhole called jail, she continued to sob. A middle-aged white woman came up to her and looked straight into her red watery eyes. "I saw what happened in there 'tween you and your daddy. Let me ask you, was this your first visit?"

Sophia-Emma nodded yes.

"I could tell. Most of these men do the same thing, or something just as bad, like your daddy did. I know he feels horrible this minute. Can I suggest that you let him calm down a while longer? Write to him. He can read your letter day after day. Soon he'll feel loved and will be more like your real daddy."

Respecting the lady's good intentions, Sophia-Emma still was concerned about getting a good attorney or a psychologist for her daddy. She had some serious questions that needed to be answered. Maybe Ms. Vogel over at the MCA would know the answers. So far no one had been able to tell her who was representing her daddy at his upcoming indictment. Or had he already been indicted? Was he charged when he was arrested, or was that before police nabbed him? Sophia-Emma had always thought she was pretty smart, but today she'd discovered she knew nothing about law and legal procedures. One thing she did know was that her dad needed a good advocate, and she was going to find one for him.

When she got home her mama was asleep on her bed as though she'd collapsed there. It was only two in the afternoon. Christopher was out in the backyard playing with Little Guy. She thought her mama must be sick. Looking around the bedroom, her gaze landed on a cheap Yellow Tail wine bottle, tipped to its side on her end table.

Sophia-Emma asked herself if her mother now expected her daughter to play the family's mother, head of the household, money earner, cook, and housekeeper, too?

She angrily shook her. Her mama looked up and through her daughter. This time Sophia-Emma's hands were on her hips. Like mother, like daughter.

"You gotta drink some coffee, Mama, and then you gotta sober up." Sophia-Emma tried to speak with authority, knowing she was doing it poorly. "Mama, we have little Christopher here, just six years old, playing outside. Nobody's watching him. What in the freaking hell you doing drinking yourself into a stupor, and it's not even midday yet?" she scolded.

"I'm sorry, my Sophia-Emma, but I miss your daddy too much. Ever since you were a baby, he's been my strong arm. Now he's gone and I can't do all this shit by myself."

"Why didn't you go with me to see him this morning?" her daughter asked. "This drug charge and time in the slammer—a long, long time—it's not going away. We both ain't dreaming. If ever we need to fight together, it's damn sure now. So get in the bathroom, shower the booze off, and brush your teeth. I'll have coffee here waiting for you when you get out."

As Sophia-Emma brewed the coffee, she checked on Christopher one more time. He seemed oblivious to the turmoil going on inside the house. In this seemingly serene micro-moment, she remembered her mama's best friend, Chaos, who lived up in Virginia. She'd been an anarchist trouble-maker with her mama. Somehow Sophia-Emma needed to get in touch with her to see if she could come stay with Mama for a while. Loving never had many close friends in Africatown. She'd always homeschooled the kids and worked at her painting. But she'd never been a big drinker. Now, more than ever, her kids needed her sober, fighting for their daddy and the family.

A few minutes later, as steam was rising from Mr. Coffee, Sophia-Emma found Chaos's number among Mama's cell phone contacts. As she copied it on the palm of her hand, Loving emerged from the bathroom. Her dreads were dripping wet. Some drops landed in her coffee cup. She seemed to be focussed on somewhere beyond the four walls. Sophia-Emma wasn't sure she even realized who was there in the room with her. She brought her a second cup of the strong black drug with chicory root while her mama gulped it down like another glass of wine.

"Okay, Mama, time to talk." Sophia-Emma sat down next to her. "I think now we either fight this rotten system, or we can fly ourselves out of here. Another option, we can just freeze like opossums and pretend we all died.

"It's simple." Maybe the haze that seemed to be engulfing her was lifting, Sophia-Emma hoped.

"You get a job and support your brother and me. I'll do my art and sell my paintings. Your dad'll get out of jail and join us in due time. Then we'll all be back to normal again."

"Mama, listen up, I'm a kid. What do you want me to do? Work under the table? Sell drugs, too? Is that what you want?"

Now Loving's eyes glared at her daughter. Was she at last understanding what her options were as the only adult in the home now?

"Oh no, you can't get into this dreary mess. No, I'd kill you before I let you follow in your daddy's tracks. But you can clean house, watch kids, mow lawns."

"And you can go to hell," Sophia-Emma stomped out to the front porch and tried to reach Chaos, who picked up on the call while she was weeding her garden.

"This is Chaos. If you're trying to sell me something, all I can offer is chaos."

Put off somewhat by the strange response to her call, Sophia-Emma realized she had to forcefully speak up. "My mother, Loving–you might call her Amanda Foster–she needs you bad. We all do."

Chaos softened her tone. "Is she a'ight?"

"She's okay for now. But she needs help from old friends, like you. She's goin' through some tough stuff. I'm her daughter, Sophia-Emma."

"Well, my little Sophia-Emma is a big girl now. And I'll bet you got a little brother, too. Is that right?"

"Yea, that's Christopher. He's outside playing with our dog. Can I get to why I called?"

"Well, sure. Kind of busy now. Beans coming in. I'm gettin' 'em ready for farmers' market tomorrow."

So Sophia-Emma spilled it all out. "You see, my daddy, Pulsar, he in jail on drug dealing. Waitin' for his indictment and probably a trial later. No telling when that'll happen, but Mama got no good friends around here. I think if you to come see us here in Africatown for a little bit, she can get through this. The way she is today . . . I don't think she make it through."

Sophia-Emma had to pause so she could blow her nose and simply talk through the sobs. "Chaos, we need a level-headed woman here. I can't do it . . . just can't."

"What the hell you mean, that she can't make it through this? This ain't the old Amanda I once knew."

White women Sophia-Emma knew in Mobile didn't talk like Chaos, but she liked hearing what she was saying.

"She tough shit. Is she tryin' to take her life, depressed? I'm coming down there to see her if she's endangering herself or you kids . . ."

"Today I found her passed out from drinking a bottle of wine," Sophia-Emma shared.

Just then her mama came up behind her daughter and clicked off the call.

"You'd better not be reporting me to Children's Services, young lady," her mama warned. "So I had a slight set-back. You would, too, in my shoes. Now let's get busy and help me get ready for my show."

"I was talking to your old friend, Mama, You know, Chaos. She wants to come see you, maybe help you with your art show. I thought you might want some grown-up time with an old friend."

Her mama sat down beside her. She didn't say a word in favor or against the idea. Sophia-Emma wondered if she was happy or mad. Sometimes even her mama didn't know how she felt. But within what seemed like half an hour, her mouth relaxed and a smile brightened her face.

"Even more reason why we have to get busy," she said while she took my hand and led me into her little corner of the living room where she did her work. On the easel was the portrait of Pulsar in his fishing gear. She looked over to her mama, who again was mourning her husband's absence, their first time of separation since they fell in love back at Sanctuary.

"Go tell Christopher to come in the house with Little Guy now. We can't keep our eyes on him while he's out there in the backyard," she instructed her daughter.

Sophia-Emma was glad to see her mama as a mother again.

Later, as they started matting her mama's best pictures, and after Christopher fell asleep, cuddled close to a sleeping puppy, she asked the questions she'd been itching to ask for the last three hours.

"What now, Mama? Does Daddy have an attorney? When's his court date?"

She repeated all the questions she'd asked her daddy earlier, and didn't like most of her mama's answers either, which were either "no," "I don't know" or simply silence.

Sophia-Emma was convinced that her mama had reached the lowest point since her daddy's imprisonment. Her only hope was that she'd eventually come back to be the powerful woman her daughter had always admired. And with Chaos's offer to visit and assist, she'd receive the reinforcement she needed, now more than ever.

Sophia-Emma let herself imagine the two former anarchists brainstorming ways to transform *the system*, rehashing old victories, and recommitting to never give up. Never.

She called Chaos back, and found that she was already on her way.

Chapter 16

The next day Chaos knocked on the Jones's door. Almost immediately their guest could see that her old friend was a mess. So far, she hadn't lost herself in another bottle of Yellow Tail or any other pain-deadening brew, but not having her husband at home still tangled her thinking.

"I need your father," Loving seemed to repeat a hundred times a day as an excuse for everything she couldn't control.

Sophia-Emma hoped Chaos would remind her of the many times they were fine without men. She'd known for years that Pulsar worshiped her mama, who'd gradually relaxed in the comfort of having him take care of her and the kids. Now her man in jail needed a woman to be the strong one. Enter Chaos.

"Fuck! Y'all have really screwed up around here," Chaos jokingly scolded those who greeted her at the front door. What have you been doing lately besides drinking salty tear water?"

She edged closer to Loving and held her arms out for a long hug. She was disappointed that all she got from her old friend were tears.

"Worse'n I'd imagined," she whispered to Sophia-Emma. "Got any food in this hideout masquerading as a home? Young man," she addressed Christopher before she knew his name, "help your sister clean out my car. Please don't drop the eggs. First thing we're going to do is have a good ol' Virginia farmer's meal—salad with everything but the fence posts from my garden, hamburgers made from Creative Carnivores, and a bunch of blackberries for dessert." She noticed the children's faces light up with smiles. "We can do this, guy and gals," she cheered as she pasted an encouraging expression on her overwhelmed face.

Sophia-Emma took Chris's hand and discovered Chaos's car was filled to its ceiling with stuff for the family. Not just food, but detergent, clothes, self-help books, even anarchist literature. Big sister found the wheel-barrel and started filling it up, repeating the process two times. Then they had to find places for it all. Sophia-Emma couldn't help envying Chaos for how successful she and partner Craig must be, all the while resenting the poverty their little house seemed to scream out to anyone who visited.

Chaos moved on to look over some of Mama's paintings. She examined the prices the artist had put on them and scolded Loving again.

"What? A hundred dollars for this superior sunset? Change that to two hundred."

Sophia-Emma's mama had a fit. "I want to sell these pictures, not bring them home with no money in my hands. Don't you dare think you can come into my home and take over, ordering me and my kids around because you're playing Santa Claus," her mama stormed. "If you keep up this outrage of taking over, you can pack all the junk you brought and drive yourself back in your little freaking car and go right back to pulling tits on your goats. I'm not putting up with your sassiness now or later." Loving at last was showing a backbone. "I still run this house. You're here to help only. You hear me? Help only."

Chaos was in no mood to acquiesce. "My, don't you talk tough these days. It's all just a show. I know you better than anybody in the world. When you get scared, you try to appear mean. Okay, you've shown your toughness. Now be that woman who's falling to pieces. I'm not here to take your place. I want to put you back together again so I can go home and love my partner and admire my goats' tits. You know, we're getting married, right?"

"About time," Loving spit back. "And about time you had yourself a baby, too." Sophia-Emma saw a tiny smile emerge for the first time in days on her mama's face. Chaos followed with a shit-eating grin, or SEG, as Grandma Ophelia used to call it.

"Sophia-Emma and I, we'll fix dinner. You reprice your art, and we'll meet at the dining room table in an hour to eat till our tummies split."

Christopher looked at both women and me, wondering how he fit into this female-run household. Chaos noticed his confusion, as well.

"Young man, I need you to get the table ready, so you can set it, real pretty-like. That means getting your toys put away and making the table usable for plates, glasses, and silverware. Got it?"

Surprisingly, Loving seemed to start accepting that Chaos had the upper hand. She began putting new prices on her paintings, just as she'd been instructed. Sophia-Emma followed Chaos into the kitchen.

"Glad you called," the chunky farmer said as she shaped the hamburger meat into sand-dollar-size patties. She laid out the ingredients for the salad, ready for Sophia-Emma to toss together. From there, she made dressing by mixing ketchup and mayonnaise. Her mouth started to salivate as the mingled scents of fresh farm-raised foods made their way into her nose.

"Can you snap the beans and put them on to boil? I'll also do the cobbler." Chaos continued to direct the show. And that was fine with Sophia-Emma, who couldn't wait to gobble it all up as soon as it reached the recently set table. The family hadn't eaten a sit-down meal since the day Loving announced that Pulsar was in jail.

As the pair in the kitchen prepared the food, they discussed the woman who was changing prices on her artwork off in the other room.

"So how long she been like this?"

"Since Daddy left."

"So you've become mommy while she's been feeling sorry for herself?"

"You might say so. But then, I not doing much better."

"How's your father doing?"

"He doesn't want us to come by the jail. Think he's too embarrassed to be there. I went once and he yelled at me to never come back."

"Got yourself an attorney? Can you put up bond? When's his next court date?"

"I don't know answers to any of those questions," Sophia-Emma answered. "I've been trying to talk about all this, but nobody's telling me nothing. Mama seems to think it's all a bad dream. Someday she'll wake up and Daddy'll walk in the door, and life will all return to normal again."

Chaos muttered something. Sophia-Emma assumed it was something she didn't want anyone else to hear.

"What are you saying to yourself? Sophia-Emma asked. "I know I'm young, but I get this. I gotta grow up and do what's gotta be done."

Chaos walked closer to her fellow cook and put her right arm around the girl's shoulder.

"I've never seen your mother like this. If I were you, I'd get her to join a support group of women with partners in prison. She needs to do more than mope around here and let all your lives go into pause-control. Your mother is a mom and has to act like it, like when there were just the two of you. You probably know she was daring before she got you out of Selma, and she was great when she and your dad ran off to live here. She's got it in her. I'll work with her the next few days to help her resurrect that courage and toughness. I can do this. You guys should go about whatever you're involved in. Let me take care of your mama. You help Christopher stay occupied. If your dad doesn't want you around the jail, write to him—everyday, if you can. He needs to take control of this situation, too, not expect you guys to do it for him."

Then she muttered to herself again, calling Sophia-Emma's daddy a bunch of gutter words the young teen hoped she'd soon forget.

Later, as all sat at table, Chaos, who didn't believe in God, had everyone spend a minute in silence and to marvel at the food. Then everyone piled their plates like this was their last meal. Sophia-Emma noticed some color coming back to her mama's face. As she'd hoped, Loving and Chaos shared moments from the past, including how ferocious her mama had been in protecting her as a baby. She wished for that same lioness to come back. This was one of the funnest meals Sophia-Emma had ever participated in. Even Christopher was laughing, so much that food fell out of his mouth, there for Little Guy to lick up off the floor. Sometimes they'd laugh for no reason at all just to see who could laugh the longest before their stomach muscles all ached. These muscles had been dormant for way too long.

Chapter 17

The week Chaos stayed with the Jones family seemed to pass too quickly. She was magic. Each day Sophia-Emma's mama seemed to blossom more. She even decided to paint a portrait of Chaos in fatigues and a black bandana to take home with her when she left.

Sophia-Emma wrote three letters to her daddy, along with calling the jail almost everyday. They told her he'd received the letters, but they had to read them first for security reasons. In her letters, she kept telling her father the whole family was pulling for him and hoping he'd be home soon. Chaos suggested they be upbeat, but not act like they were having a blast without him.

The Virginia Genie (Sophia-Emma's name for her) remained a ball of fire, cooking and cleaning everyday, plus sitting for her portrait. She insisted, however, that Loving paint her slimmer than she really was.

Loving was finally fully prepared for her show at Inova Arts. Open house was Friday night. Chaos conjured up some finger foods for the event, while the gallery provided the wine. For a bright moment Loving's family felt as though they were moving uptown. They were becoming posers, of all things. But so what? If this show helped her mama shine, it was all worth the spotlight.

On the night of the big open house, titled *Home in Historic Africatown*, Sophia-Emma and her little brother decked themselves out in their best clothes and promised to behave themselves. Their mama also brought over her portrait of Chaos and marked it NFS—Not for Sale.

Harriet came with them to the show. She was amazed with all the recent goings-on at Sophia-Emma's home and with the changes in Loving. The two girls found some time to go over plans for the upcoming pizza party at the church and for the accountability meeting demanding the reinstatement of GED classes. Sophia-Emma didn't know what she'd do without Harriet, telling her over and over that she was a born organizer.

"I do the research. You turn out the people. Together we're going to win this thing, After removing that Confederate monument downtown, time is on our side." Sophia-Emma cheered a little too noisily for an art show, but she didn't care. "I've also been able to get our city council rep to come, the board president of MCA, even our state representative. The mayor's chair will be empty, but we'll have his name on a big name card staring out at the audience in his place."

Harriet asked about Sophia-Emma's daddy, which changed her friend's mood dramatically, leading her to weep in front of her father's portrait. Harriet moved over to stand in front of her, making her almost invisible.

Harriet whispered, "Geez, girl, sorry I asked. Most other friends just tell me, 'He's okay.'"

To get her mind off her daddy, after a few minutes of sobs Sophia-Emma shared with her friend all the dirt she'd dug up about MCA. She said that much of it wasn't the agency's fault, but Africatown and Plateau had often been treated like stepchildren of city and county leaders because they claimed assistance made poor people lazy.

Sophia-Emma saw her mother gesture them to quiet down over in their corner. Both simply shrugged and acted like they were talking about Loving's artwork.

"You know, I dread Chaos leaving after this opening," Sophia-Emma whispered. "Do you like our open house tonight? You wouldn't believe what we were able to pull off in this last week. Couldn't have done it without Mama's old cohort in crime, dear Chaos."

"I know. Your house now looks like something from *Southern Living,*" Harriet joked. "And your cupboards and fridge—a'ight. So good to have 'em full for a change." They exchanged high-fives.

"And don't forget, Christopher's learned about African history and some elementary physics." Sophia-Emma was still wiping away the last of her tears—this time happy ones. "That woman is an angel from heaven, although I wonder if such a place exists."

Harriet asked if she'd met any good looking homeboys lately. If not, she could line up a few who were out on the prowl.

"That's half the fun of organizing," Harriet said. "Hooking up with these young dudes off and on, that's normally hard work. But lately when I meet with them—all drop-outs, I admit—I find the ones not hooked or dealing, the ones who ain't two-timin' a baby mama. I even know who's a worker bee or a drone. At this moment, I can hook you up with at least three Obama types. They're yours because I'm such a good friend. If you don't want any, I'll pair 'em up with some other sistas. Speak now or they're gone."

"I'm not interested in any boys right now, Harriet. I hope there's nothin' wrong with me. I seem to be developing okay, you think? Five-five in height, a hundred-thirty-five pounds. But I seldom dress like most of my sistas. My favorite outfit is a loose pair of jeans and a hoodie, at least one size too big. Cat calls bother me. Some girls tell me that the calls make them feel sexy. Sorry," Sophia-Emma confided, "I'm more than a sight for a man to get a hard on. Nope, if any bros going come after me, he'd better have his head on straight and not down in his crouch. No way am I goin' to be some over-sexed stud's baby mama. Give me a break, please."

Harriet gave her a peeved look. "You weird, girl," she insisted.

"Mama's told me she wasn't interested in men either until this Pete guy came into her life up north," Sophia-Emma explained. "Because of him she got into all this anarchist stuff. Both she and Chaos mixed up in that. Most us colored folk didn't really go that route, and still don't. We're not against government. We only want a fair one that treats us like the humans we are." She paused to take a big breath.

"But back to the dudes, Harriet . . . I think Mama was first into Pete because of his passion for anarchy and his hatred of government, so she too became anarchist. And she loved it. Ruined her relationship with her mother, though. My other thought is that if Mama had been the kind of girl Grandma Foster wanted, I would probably now be a pile of scrunched-up bones out in their pasture. So I guess I need to see the importance of passion in a dude's life, passion beyond something that transcends family, religion, patriotism."

Tears all dried and on a roll, Sophia-Emma wondered if Harriet was bored with her idealistic talk. What was her story? But that was for another day. This was her day to talk.

Looking at her mama's paintings, she could see that when she quit running with the anarchists, she put her passion into art. There was Chaos with that smirk on her face and military fatigues on her body. Her daddy, fishing on a rich man's property, warning trespassers they'll be punished. Sophia-Emma saw a painting of Africatown protesters with a big banner calling for resistance. Now she realized that her mama's passion hadn't left her. It'd taken her in a new direction.

"I know your Daddy, Pulsar. But this Pete guy, was he black, too?" Harriet stared at the anarchists painting.

"No, Pete was white. Mama was with him for only a few years. But there was a life after him. When he was killed, she shifted her passion to me, my safety, molding me into knowing what love meant. And when Daddy showed up, the electricity in both of them was 'like the positive and negative charges physically igniting them in pure undeniable love'—Mama's words—'a love that gave them a strength they couldn't muster alone.'" Sophia-Emma looked over at her mama who was smiling as she explained her husband's portrait to an admirer. "I think Mama and

Daddy's love help them to speak on their feet and fend off most, but not all evil. Theirs is a love that isn't twice as powerful as each alone, but one like an elephant compared to a worm. Mama as a woman found a partner she loved and then integrated his passion into every fiber of her body. Now I understand why she flipped when Daddy went to jail."

By now, Sophia-Emma realized she was preaching to herself more than to Harriet. And like many preachers, she didn't know when to shut up.

"So Harriet, before I start becoming interested in men, I plan to figure myself out first, and then, with what I have left, I'll open my heart up to a man who allows me to be me. I'm not here to adapt to his passion or be his helpmate. Instead, I hope we can complement and respect each other's passions. You know I still have a long way to go."

With that, she finally shut her mouth.

Chapter 18

Sophia-Emma finally received a note from her daddy a day after Chaos had left. She tore the letter open and saw a too-brief note. With all the time her daddy had these days, she'd expected he would write more. All he wrote was:

Dear Sweetie (his pet name for her),

I'm sorry I wasn't nice to you on your first and only visit. I've been thinking about a lot of things lately. I still think you need to forget about me for a while. I'm not forgetting about you and the rest of the family, but you need to concentrate on your future for now. I'm fine, and I'll let you know if or when I want visitors in the future.

Love,
Daddy

"Well, I'll be damned," After she threw the letter on the floor, she told her mama who was preparing a gallon of sun tea. Loving picked up the letter and studied it. She said nothing and her face was just as non-expressive. Sophia-Emma was confused by both adults who claimed to be parents. She wanted to stomp, run around the kitchen table and yell like a baby.

"I need to know what you two are about. I can't live in this uncertainty any longer. Why did you two even bring me home the night I ran away? My life would've been better if you'd just let me go on my hike where I could have gotten away from all this drama that's happening now."

She rushed off to her room and slammed the door. Head buried in her pillow, consciousness faded away.

Suddenly she was in an institutional-like building. Not a smudge of dirt anywhere. She couldn't tell where a white cabinet ended and a white floor or ceiling began. There was a toilet the size of a casket. A silver handle along one wall controlled the flushing. She noticed a person dressed in white who welcomed her. One of the technicians, also dressed in white, pulled the handle down toward the floor. A person who looked dead was actually flushed horizontally into a tunnel that went through the wall. In its place clear water reflected the white ceiling above. Was she next?

Someone came over to her. She could feel the person's breath. It was warm, too close to her face. Now she knew it was her turn.

Sophia-Emma clung to her pillow. She wasn't going through that tunnel without a fight.

"Sophia-Emma, wake up. I don't want to hurt you."

The voice sounded an awful lot like her mother's. Was she in on this, too?

"Sophia-Emma, wake up." The voice was insistent, but kind. She hesitantly released the pillow and stared into her mama's face.

"Let me go," she screamed. "I'm not dead—yet."

"You're having a nightmare."

Her mama's grip on her arm is painful, but at least not as bad as being flushed away. "What? I'm not going to die?"

"No, you're not going to die anytime soon. I want you to know that I'm visiting your daddy tomorrow, and I want you to go with me. I think Miss Mildred can watch Christopher for a while."

"Oh. Sure. I see." Sophia-Emma was still barely awake. "But Daddy wants us out of his life. You read the letter."

"I think I know Daddy better than you, baby. I read between the lines in his letter. Basically, he's calling out to us. He's never wanted to be a bother, to cause anyone any trouble. But he's so lonely. The sadness he feels is dripping off the page. I think it's time for us to see him tomorrow. I'm calling Miss Mildred now."

"Okay," her daughter, still not convinced, said. "Are you up to this? He was damn cruel to me last time."

"Chaos and I talked about this before she left, and—by the way, stop cussing when you talk to me—she convinced me that we can't let things happen to us. We need to set the course, to encourage your daddy to take some risks, and fight like hell against all these forces that want to split up our family. I've been doing some research on lawyers. I remembered one who visited us a couple years ago. He and your daddy used to play ball together. He admired all the work your daddy was doing to keep Mobile's waters clean." Loving was back to her fighting spirit. "And he also does criminal law. I'm going to suggest that Daddy ask his old friend to represent him."

"Okay. Mama. I think it's a long shot, but what the hell, huh?"

Loving gave her a perturbed look again, but then put her hand over her own mouth, realizing she also had used *hell* just seconds ago.

What Sophia-Emma was more excited about was that her mama was again taking up the battle for the family. She was at last being proactive for its survival.

"I feel bad that I've dragged my feet so long." She stood up and looked at me with eyes like penetrating swords. "No more."

She kissed her daughter on the tip of her nose. "Now go to sleep. I'll need your quick thinking tomorrow. Good night."

But Sophia-Emma couldn't sleep the rest of the night. Little Guy jumped up on her bed and licked her wide-awake face. She was afraid to go back to sleep. Those people might still be waiting for her so they could flush her away. Maybe the one who was flushed before her had been her daddy.

Realizing that trying to sleep was a waste of time, she staggered out to the front porch, glass of milk in hand. The rich liquid brought her back to the nights as a baby when she'd suck the warm sweet liquid from her mama. They were skin-to-skin all night long until she moved into her own bed as a toddler. And deep inside she'd been lonely ever since. She finished the cold cow's milk and quietly slipped into bed next to her mama, who put her protective arms around her daughter. Her scent was the same as what she smelled as a baby. She was safe in her mother's arms once more.

Chapter 19

Loving got up early, and was able to finagle a way for her daughter and herself to see Pulsar the next morning. Usually, visitors had to schedule a visit at the Metro Jail a week in advance, but Sophia-Emma's mother had her ways to get her way.

After dropping off Christopher at Miss Mildred's, by eleven o'clock Sophia-Emma and her mother were heading to Emmanuel Street where the Metro Jail was located. She could feel her young body stiffening the closer they drew to the giant holding facility.

"Mama, I'm going to stay in the car. I can't go in there again, Sophia-Emma explained as her mother parked the car.

Immediately, Loving restarted the car and put it in reverse, saying, "I guess it was a stupid idea after . . ."

"Dammit, Mama. Park the darn car. I'll go in, too. But it's not a nice place."

"Sweet," her mama responded, "For nearly a decade I was in facilities like this on a routine basis, from Oakland to New York and here in the south. I know more about jails in my pinky finger than most people around here."

At least this time, Sophia-Emma realized she wouldn't be going through all the security checkpoints alone. Maybe this visit might be tolerable after all, but she still doubted it.

"I'm here to see Alan Jones," her mama said in a voice she'd never heard before. And very seldom had she ever heard of her daddy being called Alan Jones. When she'd visited, she'd called her father Pulsar Jones.

"My name? I'm Amanda Foster-Jones."

"And I'm Sophia-Emma Foster-Jones," her daughter said. No problem since most kids around Africatown had different last names than the men in their lives anyway.

As they waited to have their names called so they could visit her daddy, Sophia-Emma stared at her mama's face. Her dreads tickled the small of her back, while higher up they framed a serious, yet sensuous face. Her aqua blue eyes could travel through steel and back again. Her face was weathered but tight, surrounding a mouth that was neither smiling or frowning. Occasionally her tongue would pop out of her mouth and wet her lips. She's a tough mama, Sophia-Emma told herself. If there was any kind of blessing from Pulsar being in the can, it was how this ordeal had forced her to reach into her deepest toughness to rescue Amanda Foster, the sweet little curly-haired southern belle who would someday dream of beating the hell out of Scarlett O'Hara. But Amanda was authentic. Scarlett was a dreamt-up symbol of southern gentility who abused slaves and loved no one more than herself.

Ironically, the people of African descent were most of the tough men and women of that time. Maybe that's why long ago Sophia-Emma's mama decided to give up her fragile whiteness and join in their continuing struggle.

After a thorough search by jail guards, finally the two were ushered into the visiting room Sophia-Emma had sat in more than a few weeks ago. Her daddy walked in, a perturbed look on his face. Not a good sign.

Her mama did her best to attach a loving and sincere look on her face. She looked at Daddy and then shifted her gaze to her daughter. Sophia-Emma prepared herself for the worst to come out of her daddy's mouth. Loving started the conversation. There were no hugs or kisses.

"You're looking good, Pulsar," her mother said. "Are they keeping you busy here?"

"It's not too bad," her daddy answered. "Why y'all here? Is Christopher okay?"

"He's fine," her mama reassured her daddy.

"We need you at home, Daddy. Don't you want to come home and be with your family?" Sophia-Emma inquired.

"I told you last time I saw you, didn't I? I don't want to see you here again. It's not good for y'all. Go out in the waiting room while I talk to your mama."

As though ready, her eyes begin to fill with tears. She looked at her mama to see what she wanted. She nodded in agreement with her daddy. Sophia-Emma felt like that body she'd dreamt about last night was at last being flushed away, of no consequence to either of them. Inside she was being pulled in two directions. She could be the obedient child and leave, or she could be the individual she knew she was, hollering at both of them and insisting that they start acting like real parents. She did neither. She simply stayed where she was and pretended to be an innocent bystander. Her daddy gives her a threatening look. She pretended not to notice.

"Pulsar, we need to get you out of here." Loving broke the awkward silence. "I talked to your mother yesterday. She says you can use the house for . . ."

"I don't want that," her daddy bellowed. Once more she felt everyone in the room looking their way.

Her mama ignored his outburst. "Well, I also talked with your old buddy Prince Smith. Remember him?"

Daddy gave her a slight nod, but continued to stare at the door we entered from, as though he wanted us to leave.

"Just let me be, woman. I'm pleading guilty. I'll serve my time. I'll go with the program. To tell you the truth, I'm done trying to get out of something I deserve. I figure it's pay-back time. I ran away the last time. Not this time, okay? Now you can carry on with your lives and wait for me to come home, or we can split up right this minute. Sorry,

I want to be there to support you, but you don't want to be supported by dirty money, do you? I'm getting off this stuff if it kills me, even if I have to be in pain the rest of my life. You can sign up for welfare, food stamps, Medicaid. You'll be okay. Now, can we not discuss this anymore?" Pulsar took a tissue from his pants pocket and blew his nose. His expression was still mean when he put the tissue back in his pocket.

Sophia-Emma and her mama sighed simultaneously. The younger one wanted to punch her daddy, call him a chicken, tell everyone there that he wasn't her real daddy. Maybe she had no daddies, if they all were like him. But she still craved a hug from him.

But now that he had said what he'd been holding in his heart these last couple weeks, Sophia-Emma began to admire this brave and strange man she'd never really known until this moment.

Then he tried to change the subject. "How'd you do on your sale, babe?"

Taken by surprise, her mama looked back into his eyes. "Not bad. So far about five-hundred dollars, but the gallery gets nearly half of that. I may sell more as the month goes on. My paintings stay up till late July."

"Babe, you're a great artist. Keep it up, will you? And Sophia-Emma, I'm sorry I've lost my temper so much around you lately. Forgive me? Will you help your mama?"

I nod an unenthusiastic yes.

"Good," he says. "Now here's some advice I've got to give you. Keep low profiles for a while. Crazy Dog is watching me and y'all. If any of us snitch on him, I'm afraid I'm dead meat. But who I really care about is y'all and little Christopher. Don't make waves. Understand? Maybe when I get outta here on good behavior, we can disappear for awhile, not constantly being under the spies he has throughout the Magazine area, keeping track of our comings and goings. That's one reason we write only—no visits, no phone calls. You gotta promise you'll play along with me on this."

Loving didn't like to be hemmed in. Neither did her daughter. Nevertheless, looking at her daddy's worried look, they both assured him that they'd not mess up on this.

Sophia-Emma knew Crazy Dog, the biggest dealer in all of Southern Alabama. Lots of ugly crimes had been attributed to him and his gang, but none of 'em absolutely pointed to him. He was like a greased pig, slipping out of police hands in every attempt to nab him. He stayed free while he was willing to sacrifice one of his boys occasionally to keep the DA at bay. Some people said the police, the DA, big shot lawyers, they all were making money off of drugs. They had a thriving partnership.

"Now, it's time for y'all to go. Send me some more stamps with your next letters, okay? And tell Christopher I miss him. Let him know I made a mistake and that even daddies need to be punished sometimes."

Mama and Daddy sneaked a kiss between them. He and Sophia-Emma exchanged fist bumps. Visit over, the women walked out behind Daddy, like they were in a funeral procession. All of a sudden, her mama seemed weak. Her husband turned around and watched as they exited the other way on their way out of the clunker.

A veil of silence tightened its hold over them all the trip back to Africatown. As they picked up Christopher, they tried to answer as few questions as possible from Miss Mildred. But she was no dummy. She knew what the closed mouths meant. She knew Pulsar was selling and using, and she knew Crazy Dog had a monopoly on the entire town. She knew this better than anyone else in the community. They waved goodbye. All she could muster was a mysterious and worried look.

Looking at the dirty dishes in the sink, Sophia-Emma was rather glad she had something to do when she got home.

There was a knock on the door. When Sophia-Emma opened it, she saw only a plain white envelope with no one's name on it. She opened it and counted out a thousand dollars in twenty-dollar bills. She knew how it got there. She put it back in the envelope and put it into Mama's back pocket, who was in the middle of another painting and didn't immediately react. But about twenty minutes later her daughter heard a jubilant yell come from her little art corner.

"Don't tell me anything about what happened," she told Sophia-Emma as she wandered into the kitchen to make coffee. "I don't want to know."

Life soon began to become routine again, except there was no father in the home, no big deal in Africatown.

The three of them wrote Pulsar about once a week, and he responded in a few days. His court date had come and gone. None of those left at home were there to support him at his sentencing. Once he'd been sentenced to three years in prison, he joined a Narcotics Anonymous group. He wrote that he was hoping for a shorter sentence, but the DA found that Pulsar had jumped bail back twenty-two years ago, so no one expected much leniency from the parole board, or whoever made such decisions.

Sophia-Emma didn't have time to lament the loss of her daddy's presence in their home. Harriet and she joined forces to get a good turnout for the planning group pizza gathering at Union Missionary. They wanted at least twenty bros and sistas there. Twenty-five showed up. Of course, Sophia-Emma thought the idea of endless slices of pizza probably lured more drop-outs there than anything else. The two girls gave their presentations. First Sophia-Emma divulged all the dirt she'd collected undercover from her volunteer work at MCA. She also suggested names of who she thought their targets should be—the mayor, congressional delegates, the MCA director and the president of its board. Together they came up with demands and a timeline for action. Commitments from a couple high school teachers, the lady who used to teach the GED classes before she was laid off, and a couple students who couldn't get to GED classes downtown were all put on the program for the accountability meeting. Sophia-Emma had an attorney from the Mobile office of Legal Services Alabama coming, as well, to speak for them.

"We're going to be powerful," she told the pizza eaters as she finished the presentation.

Harriet followed up. "We have enough seating room in the sanctuary for two-hundred people. We'll get two-hundred-five in those pews. That means with twenty-five here tonight we have to each—I say each one of us—commit to bringing in about eight homies—moms, dads, aunts, uncles, teachers, bros, and sistas. You can do it," she demanded. "And the church choir will get us warmed up. Pastor Jackson will welcome everyone. But we still need an emcee. I say it again: We. Need. an Emcee. Who's going to volunteer? Sophia-Emma?"

The young girl wanted to. She wanted to so much that she had to bite her tongue to keep herself from speaking up. But she remembered her daddy's caution to keep their heads down. So instead she come up with an excuse that she was taking care of the logistics and research. Finally Bulldog raised his hand. Harriet and Sophia-Emma exchanged glances. Bulldog did have a good voice and passion. She started clapping her hands and then asked others what they thought. Everyone talked at once till Harriet broke it up.

"Com'on, Bulldog. I think you'll do great. Don't the rest of y'all think so, too?"

Bulldog joined Harriet and Sophia-Emma up front of the group.

"Do you have a suit you can wear that night?" Sophia-Emma asked.

"I'm not wearing a suit in this heat," he answered. "But I do have a tie."

"Great," she responded

Within a few minutes it seemed that everyone was naming folks they'd bring to the event. Sophia-Emma soaked up the joy as though she was watching a fireworks display. She looked around the fellowship hall and at Pastor Jackson. He stood and said how proud he was of all of them, finishing with the words, ". . . and a child shall lead them." But none of the young people there considered themselves children. Anything but.

After the volunteers had all left, Harriet, Bulldog and Sophia-Emma set about cleaning up pizza droppings and half drunk cokes. They sat down to review the night.

"I can't believe we pulled this off so well tonight," Sophia-Emma exclaimed.

"Bulldog." Harriet made a slight bow to him. "I think you'll raise hell for us. We'll come up with some questions and a timeline to get what we want. You can take it from there."

She looked down at her phone and changed the subject. "Sorry folks, I gotta go. Meeting a friend over at the park in a minute."

Bulldog and Sophia-Emma laughed as she grabbed her purse and checked her lipstick before rushing out the door.

Bulldog looked over the hall and gave it a seal of approval before they locked up. Outdoors he looked into Sophia-Emma's eyes. She froze. She felt her womanhood.

"You know why I volunteered, don't you?"

"I guess cuz you's the best for the job," she teased.

"Not quite, cuz you are."

She stayed frozen. What was about to happen, she asked herself.

"I'm just second best. But I want to see you as much as I can."

With that, Bulldog took her hand and laid a kiss smack on her quivering lips.

Chapter 20

Sophia-Emma didn't want to jump to conclusions. She'd said numerous times that she wasn't interested in developing a love relationship with anyone—boy, girl, or any other creature. There was too much to do without taking time to involve herself with a person she was romantically attracted to. Before she would know it, she'd probably start cooking for him, cleaning his messes up, thinking of sweet things to tell him, going to the movies, tickling each other, making love. Nope. She didn't have the time.

Life was already chaotic. She had Mama, Daddy, Christopher, and herself to worry about. The GED action was scaring her to death. She needed to keep her head on straight because Crazy Dog had his spies out watching everything anyone in her family did. Could even Bulldog be spying on her, be a stool pigeon?

Her mama had warned her about stool pigeons many times. They were "planted" into organizations, mainly as informants to report back to groups' enemies.

She decided instead of getting all worked up about one stupid little kiss, she would direct her attention to Bulldog as a possible informant. Did he ask more questions than most? Did he not quite fit in with the other members? Could he be part of the drug trafficking gang? Was he doing anything that could in the long run sabotage their campaign?

Into the night when Sophia-Emma should've been sleeping, her mind went wild remembering the few times she'd spoken with him. Why didn't he give her the run-around when she asked him to help? Why had he shown up when she hadn't even called to remind him? Was he playing on her sympathies when he talked about parking cars for rich white folk, while also telling her how smart he really was? And why did he kiss her? There had to be something not right about Bulldog. He was too nice, dressed too cool, drove a better SUV than most in the hood. One of her last thoughts as she finally drifted off to sleep is that she had to hash this all out with Harriet. She'd know. She got around like a cat after dead fish.

Before she could call Harriet the next day, Bulldog called. He'd come up with some questions to ask the panelists. Could she meet him for lunch and talk about them? Her suspicions grew larger, as though he was trying to pull her into a trap or was she now his boo? Red flags rising up, she called Harriet while riding the bus to get to her volunteer gig at MCA. It didn't help that Harriet was still half-asleep as she described her suspicions.

Trying to ignore her yawning into the phone. Sophia-Emma could almost smell her friend's bad breath.

"Hold on, hold on," she halted her diatribe. "It's early and I may not be absorbing all you're saying, but my gut tells me you're on the wrong track. He's as much of a stool pigeon, a spy, an informant, as I am. Maybe I'm a spy. Do you have any proof I'm not?" She giggled. "All I have to add is that Bulldog's into you for some reason. But that's just chemistry. I've known Bulldog since Headstart. If he's trying to lie or pull one over on you, he'll mess up. He's the worst at lying of anyone I've ever seen. Keep your eyes on his. He won't look you in the eye if he's going to lie to you. He'll get red in the face. And he knows all of this. That's why I say he's got no plans to sabotage us. He's no good at it. Now let me get back to sleep. It's only eight o'clock. Instead of worrying about Bulldog, get him to buy you lunch. That's all he really wants."

Nevertheless, Harriet failed to calm any of Sophia-Emma's suspicions. She needed more wisdom, so she called her mama and asked her how she could recognize a stool pigeon in her midst.

"What? A stool pigeon? Who? Don't tell him anything that may end up breaking your entire group up. But you know that, don't you?"

"Mama, I don't know what to think. Maybe I suspect people too much."

"The way our lives have been going lately, I can see why," her mama interjected. "But go on."

"You know Bulldog, right? The tall, good-looking dude that you said resembled *The Black Panther* star? Out of nowhere he's volunteered to be the emcee at our accountability meeting. He drives a nice SUV and dresses kinda sexy. Plus he's been trying to get on my good side a bunch of times."

"Yeah, go on," her mama said after a long pause.

"That's about it, I guess."

"Go look at yourself in the mirror, my girl, the next time you're in the bathroom. My gut tells me he's simply trying to have you be his woman, as folk say around here. I'm not saying your suspicions aren't valid. Maybe you're right. Try keeping your eyes open and your mouth shut around him from now on for awhile."

"I said I'd meet him for lunch today."

"No problem. Remember, eyes open and mouth shut. What does he want to talk about?"

"Some questions he's put together for the panelists on September third."

"Doesn't sound like a stool pigeon to me. Usually an informant wants to blend in, not raise any red flags. I think you got a lover boy on our hands. Personally, I don't think you're ready for that type of relationship yet. You know I didn't get into boys until I was in college. So go slow. I know you now look like a woman, but you're still far from mature enough to get into a loving relationship, no matter what Harriet may say. And don't think I haven't noticed her. The way she's going, she'll be a baby mama before she reaches seventeen."

"Mom, I didn't call to get a lecture. But since you've already given me all I need to know about that kind of thing, I'll remember it at lunch today. You know, he's kinda cute, strong, and cool. Don't you think?"

"Yeah, yeah, yeah. I don't think one word of what I said to you sank in."

"I'm at my bus stop now, Mama. See you tonight."

All morning as she updated the website, sneaking in a link about the September third meeting, she kept remembering Bulldog's kiss, everything leading up to it, the actual kiss, how it actually felt on her lips and the rest of my body, and how the two of them acted around each other afterwards. She replayed the episode over and over, wanting to frame the kiss, to hang it on her wall. If only she could also frame the feelings that ran through her body, like nothing she'd ever felt before.

She attempted to write a poem about it—something like:

You brought hope to my heart,
Longing to my life
Courage to my fear . . .

Reminding herself that she indeed was not a woman yet and her purpose here wasn't to be a baby's mama. She decided to ditch the poetry writing spree.

Looking up from the computer, she noticed a Middle Eastern-looking family come to the intake window. She overheard that they'd moved into a house in Africatown. At first, she wanted to tell them there was nothing for them in her neighborhood where only descendants from slaves lived. But, like us, they were a minority. Perhaps it was the hijab the mother and daughter wore. This occasion was enough to distract Sophia-Emma from her quasi-love life. Now she was trying to figure out what house they'd moved to in her neighborhood. How long had they been there? How old was the daughter? She looked about her age. Her parents were asking about how to register her for high school.

Sophia-Emma couldn't help but stare at this beautiful family with darting black eyes surrounded by stark whites and then again framed by dark long lashes. Mother and daughter wore bright colored clothing covering about every inch of skin above and below their necks. She wanted to welcome them to Africatown, but she reconsidered when she noticed they were having trouble speaking and understanding English.

Meanwhile the clock begged for attention and made her notice it was getting close to noon. Bulldog would be picking her up in his CR-V in just a few minutes. She finished the updates and went to the restroom to check her hair before going outside to catch a glimpse of her lover boy. No way she could miss it, she realized once she got outside where most vehicles seemed to have been manufactured in the 1990s.

Bulldog parked and escorted her into his vehicle. Overwhelmed at how high she had to step up to be seated, she touched his arm for support. She wasn't used to this kind of treatment. She'd heard that some dudes did this for some rich white women, maybe like Grandma Foster, but this is a first for her. Sophia-Emma couldn't wait to tell Harriet when she got back to work. Meanwhile she remembered her mama telling her to keep her eyes open and mouth shut.

Bulldog knew that she liked to talk. But this time Sophia-Emma was prepared to give her mama's advice a try. He asked her if Hart's Fried Chicken was okay for lunch. She nodded and listened to Bulldog talk as they headed over to South Wilson Street.

"I enjoyed our meeting last night," he said. "Did you?"

She nodded affirmatively again and smiled. She could tell by keeping her eyes open that he really meant the kiss at the end of the meeting. He put his big right hand with perfectly manicured nails on top of Sophia-Emma's left. An electric shock ran up her arm into the heart and then down and stopped where her thighs met. She returned his smile once more.

She let him order some spicy wings and a sweet iced tea for her. She sat across from him in a booth. It was luckily the only one empty at the back of the joint.

Feeling awkward, she took a long sip on her tea, as did he. They stared into each other's eyes and smiled. He handed Sophia-Emma a tiny piece of paper with some questions written on it—four of them. She read each of them with a critical mind. They were:

Why are we not offered GED classes anywhere in Africatown?
How can we help you get the MCA site reopened here?
What steps will you take to make this happen? and
How much will it cost?"

Sophia-Emma's vow of silence ended with the last question.

"I love your questions, Bulldog. All but the last. If you ask that question, it gives 'em—our target people sitting up front—a chance to make up excuses why they won't honor our request. How to pay for the re-opening, or simply offering GED classes, in Africatown is their concern, not ours. We're simply reminding them that this is our due as residents in the district MCA manages. Let's not use that question. Maybe instead we can ask if they believe in equal treatment under the law, no matter where we live in this city."

"I gotcha. Great idea," Bulldog responded. He seemed to care more that she was actually at last talking rather than that she was criticizing one of his questions.

Critique given, she nodded and smiled at him again and started eating her six spicy wings, savoring each bite this young man paid for. She wondered if he expected her to pay him back with another kiss when he dropped her off at Community Action. And for a while she thought she might comply.

After a good ten minutes of no speaking by either of them, Bulldog asked her age.

"Fifteen, give or take a few years," she replied. "I'm still pretty young. How about you?"

"Nineteen."

Sophia-Emma was stunned. Bulldog was nearly twenty years old. He'd probably had sex hundreds of times. Maybe he even has little Bulldogs running around somewhere. "Damn, you're much older than me. Why did you kiss me last night?"

"I just like you. Did you mind?"

"To tell you the truth, yes. And don't do it again," she added.

Chapter 21

The love affair was finished before it even started. Sophia-Emma had kept her eyes open and tried to keep her mouth shut most of the time, just like her mama had instructed.

Now Bulldog was looking at her like she'd just torn down the Lincoln Memorial. Sophia-Emma simply smiled, grabbed her purse, stood up and asked if he could drop her off at MCA. But he wasn't ready to answer her yet. He had to have his say first. So she prepared herself to listen.

"For a girl who's pretty smart, you sure know how to put a guy down, don't cha? I's not asking you to marry me, or even to shack up with me. I's simply said I likes you and if you cared that I kissed you."

"And I said I did mind."

"Are you a lesbian or somethin'? You and Harriet have a thing goin' 'tween you two?"

"Of course not. I can tell you she's definitely straight. You can't get straighter than Harriet. Maybe you might want to kiss her and see if she's more receptive. But me? I'm too young for you. You've been around. I haven't reached a point yet where I want to get involved with any man, especially someone four years older."

"Hell, my ol' man's ten years older than the ol' lady."

"And that's something else I don't like about you homeboys 'round here. Do you call your parents the *ol' man or ol' lady* to their faces? I don't want to hang out or hook up with disrespectful men no matter how good lookin'."

"Well, fuck you. Go find another emcee then and catch a bus back to that welfare hole."

Sophia-Emma had been flattened. No one had ever said anything like that to her before. And to think she'd lost an entire night's sleep and had obsessed about him all morning. She strutted out, head held high, no looking back.

Of course she was late returning to work and didn't offer any excuses, saying she'd stay later to make up the time. After all, she was only a volunteer. No stress needed. They couldn't dock her pay.

Sophia-Emma's afternoon was a drag. Gone was the connection with another human being, the electricity, the oozing chemical reaction. Now she felt alone, exiled to a distant planet with no friends. She wondered if drug withdrawals felt a little like she felt that afternoon.

Reminding herself that Bulldog used profanity in reacting to her, Sophia-Emma tried to convince herself that she had no other choice but to snub him and put him in his place. Plus he was the one who resigned as emcee and wouldn't give her a ride back to work. Men's pride! He was wired like her daddy.

On her break she told Harriet about her lunch catastrophe, from Bulldog escorting her to his CR-V to his dumping of her at Hart's. "At least he didn't make me pay him back for lunch," She caught her breath and thought of one more thing. "I told him to ask you out on a date. He thought we were lesbians."

Harriet laughed. "Sista, sometimes I wish I were. No pregnancy worries, soft whisker-free faces to kiss, no hard-ons to deal with, even better chances to win in fights."

"You mean some of the guys you've hooked up with hit you? I hope you dumped 'em right then. No man'll ever do that to me. I'd have to be dead first, not afterwards."

Harriet told Sophia-Emma she was crazy. "Dead? You want him to shoot or stab you before beating you? You're sick, sista. No, hanging with men can be a slippery slope. First, a gentle puppy love kiss, holding hands, passion, then the romantic words morph into 'Fuck you, bitch,' the slap, the punches, throwing you against the wall leading to rape, sometimes death. Perils of the game, you might say."

Sophia-Emma was speechless. There was only dead air between them.

Finally, Harriet changed the subject back to the absence of an emcee. "I guess you'll be the new leader, gal," Harriet says.

"Okay, I'll ask the questions and summarize my research. Could you call up those who want to speak? And we'll finish up together? Maybe even hold hands, making folks think we're lesbians."

"I'm game if you are. But you know we're really not, right?"

"Right," her friend said. "But getting back to men, I'm not ready to give up on all of them. All I want is to be treated with respect by homies about my age. Plus, I'm not a bitch out there for some dude to fuck."

"See your point, girl. But remember, aren't we s'posed to be gifts to mankind?" Harriet joked. "Don't get mad. Just playing the devil's advocate here."

Chapter 22

Sophia-Emma's talk with Harriet helped. She found peace in the thought of staying later than most of the office personnel.

"Just slam the door tight when you leave," Ms. Vogel said as she walked out to catch the bus.

"And, by the way, I've heard you're trying to get one of our satellite offices reopened over there in Africatown. Good luck with that. Folks have been trying to do the same for the past ten years. I'll be there in a second and clap for you."

Sophia-Emma was surprised that the old lady didn't seem at all mad or suspicious. "Oh, thank you, Ms. Vogel. I'll try to make you proud," she said, wondering if Ms. Vogel knew that one of their targets was MCA itself.

The quiet in the empty building was deafening. Bulldog was now only a bad dream. She walked way back into the guts of the compact building, back more than ten years ago when MCA shut down its presence in Africatown. Why Africatown, whose income was among the lowest in the Mobile area, where drop-outs nearly equaled graduates, where people were hungry and idle? She rummaged through file after file, old board minutes, annual reports, newspaper clippings. She turned on the copy machine and made a new file from the many old ones she'd just collected, putting all the originals back as she found them, and slipping her copied documents into her shopping bag. By now, it was dark outside. She exited and slammed the door soundly as Ms. Vogel instructed. This stuff would feed her mind and soul more than Bulldog could ever, even on his best days.

Sophia-Emma's phone rang. A disgruntled mama was worried that her daughter had run away with her new boyfriend.

"No Mama, no boys or men in my life—only papers. But they're papers that can do more for Africatown than any other single male would ever do," Sophia-Emma told her.

"Well, your supper's in the oven, your little brother's in bed and your daddy has sent us another letter. Plus, I found another thousand inside the front door tonight." Sophia-Emma felt her silent cheer.

Sophia-Emma's immediate inclination was to shout "Hip, hip, horray!" But she'd found out more about Crazy Dog who seemed to be the source of the money showing up at their place. She'd also seen signs that he was among others who pulled strings to discontinue GED classes in the hood. Her heart ached and she felt she would vomit. The uneducated were perfect customers for the likes of people like Crazy Dog. His strategy was to feed his bros and sistas just enough to enable them to breathe and consume, but he would take away what was truly more important—dignity. And that money inserted into their doorway tonight? Was it a payback for allowing her daddy to be the fall guy? Or an enticement to remind them to keep their mouths shut on September third? Pulsar had warned his family to keep their heads down while he was gone. What would happen if Sophia-Emma refused?

The ride home on the bus was full of tired and phone-addicted riders. Sophia-Emma wondered what dark thoughts were lodging in their brains and hearts.

She knew plenty such thoughts were haunting her. Which would come first—her family or community? She was too tired to even comprehend that question tonight.

Depressing thoughts followed her as she entered her little home, like the ants did a few weeks ago, and not any less pesty.

Her mama was at the easel again, this time in the middle of a portrait of Cudjo Lewis, one of the last survivors of the lost slave ship Cotilda, rescued back in 2019 under the waters of the Mobile River. The relic to oppression was currently being prepared for a later exhibition in the town's proposed new museum. As was her practice, her mama stepped back and smiled at the old man on her canvas.

"The community Center has commissioned me to do a portrait of Cudjo," she explained with a big smile on her face. "Pretty good, huh?"

"I'm so proud of you, Mama. Finally you're getting some recognition and respect around here. Can I read Daddy's letter now?"

"Sure, it's on the table out in the kitchen. Could you bring us both a couple cokes when you come back? I'm working up a sweat."

Sophia-Emma sat at the table and read the letter:

Dear Loving, Sophia-Emma, and Christopher,

I continue to miss each of you on an hourly basis. Some would say I'm settling into prison life here at Elmore quite well. As long as I don't pick fights, mind my own business, and try to blend in with the great orange wave, I wind up a safe guy with no one beating on me. I hope you're surviving okay. I think some friends want to help y'all get through the next three years. If Mama can keep producing and selling her work, and if Sophia-Emma can do a little part-time work, I think we can make it. Please visit your grandma Ophelia soon. Let her know that we're all doing well, even me. I promise to write her soon. Remember, as long as you keep your nose clean and don't cause any trouble there in Africatown, I'm sure we'll have another chance to start over–this time right.

I kiss you all and look forward to our reunion in a few years–maybe sooner–if they notice my good behavior.

With loving peace,
Pulsar/Daddy

His daughter read it again and again in order to catch those messages between the lines that her mama often read. She now knew that Crazy Dog and he had an agreement about the cash flowing under their door on a regular basis, but that it would discontinue if she got too big for her raisin', so to speak. She certainly didn't know what to do now. She would have to talk to her mama and Harriet.

First to her mama. She struck up the conversation about the letter as she handed her a glass of cold fizzing drink.

"It bothers me, Mama. You know and I know that Crazy Dog's giving us that cash. Is it hush money, you think? I also know I can't be quiet about that dope kingpin. He was also instrumental in getting the GED classes stopped here. I may have to speak up about this at our accountability meeting, unless I can just be a silent clog at the back of the room. Maybe Harriet can emcee."

"I thought that boy Bulldog wanted to do it," her mama said.

"Not anymore. We had a fight. He's out of the picture."

Loving gave her a sorry look.

"So you think I should ask Harriet?"

"I guess, dear. I don't like it any better than you. Hush money or not, we can't let it stop."

So much for Sophia-Emma's brave mama whom she'd always assumed would do what's right, not just convenient. With that, she knew she'd have to call Harriet and start to sweet talk her.

"Yo, don't cha know what time it is, girl?" Harriet scolded her friend when she clicked on her phone. You don't believe in texting?"

"Never think of it," Sophia-Emma said. "Besides I love to hear your assertive voice to set me straight every now and then."

"Then talk, sista! My time's worth big bucks."

"I'm in a quandary and think you can help me get out of it. It's kind of complicated. Can you bear with me for a few minutes, and then I'll let you get back to your sweet dreams?"

"I said, 'talk.' You're beating around the bush. You really gotta stop that. Say what you gonna say."

"Okay. Here goes then. You know Daddy's in prison, right?"

"Uh huh. Keep goin'."

"He's taking the rap for a big shot in the hood. But Daddy tells us to be careful. Keep our noses clean and heads down. Especially don't do anything that will make this dude mad. So, I'm doing more research today, and I find this guy is one reason GED classes were stopped here more than a decade ago."

"You're talkin' 'bout Crazy Dog, ain't cha, our king here. I could've told you that when we got started on this. Everyone knows. Where you been hangin' out all these years, girl?"

"Yeah, why didn't you tell me, Har . . . ? But that's not what's bothering me most now."

"Get to your question then so I can get some sleep." She was yelling by now.

"I need you to run the meetin' in September. You know we lost . . ."

"I know, Bulldog. Girl, you got no class when it comes to dealing with your man's pride. Couldn't you have waited just a couple weeks to disconnect from him?"

"No, I got my pride, too."

"If you ask me, you got nothin."

"C'mon, I can't be in the limelight at our big meeting. Our whole family could be knocked off. Someone could knife my daddy."

"Now, let me stop you right now. Think, girl." She paused. "I give you a minute. Think 'bout members of my home. Who's in and who's out?"

Sophia-Emma did just that. She knew Harriet lived with her mama. Her daddy was shacking up with an old lady over by the refineries. Been gone maybe three years. Harriet helped her mama take care of her little sister. Her older brother? Hadn't seen him for quite a while.

"Your big bro? Is he still serving time for drugs?"

"You got it, and who's he taking the rap for?"

"Crazy Dog?"

"I rest my case. And who do you think is helping pay our utilities and putting food on our table to keep our mouths shut?"

"You mean you and me, we're in the same fix? Hell."

"I see only two solutions," Harriet offered. "We call this whole thing off or you get your sweet li'l voice on your li'l phone, or maybe you try a li'l text to your kissy friend Bulldog and apologize for going off the deep end today. Ask him—I mean tell him—no one can do emceeing like him. Bargain with him. He'll eat it up. Tell him you think he's the smartest, most handsome man in this hood, and you be proud to be his boo, or bitch, or li'l Barbie Doll."

"I can't do that, Harriet. You want me to put all kinds of ideas in his head? I won't stoop down that low. I won't let both Crazy Dog and Bulldog corrupt my spirit."

"Then y'all chose the other option. I'll call all our leaders tomorrow and tell 'em it's off because you afraid your spirit is being threatened."

"Ain't there anyone else?"

"No one I can think of. Remember, most of us never finished school. We're drop-outs, huh? Now I got to go to bed. Sleep on it and we talk tomorrow."

Then she was gone. But Sophia-Emma remembered she could text her, or even do the same with Bulldog. Maybe she could say she was sorry and still keep her self-respect. After all, she was almost a woman. She'd heard that a man, if he thought you were worth it, would allow himself to be strung along up to a certain point. She wouldn't say anything that would make him think she was horny for him. Instead, she would aim for his intellect, not his dick. Brag him up. The new woman, if she was smart enough, could get guys to swim the dirty bay for her. But she had to play her cards right. She was ready to give it a try.

Chapter 23

All night sleep played hide-and-seek with Sophia-Emma. She laid there, closed her eyes, rolled to one side, then shifted to the other. She even tried playing restful music on *Spotify*. Finally she got up to drink some milk, and had to brush her teeth again. Still sleep eluded her, so she snuck into the living room to watch old black and white movies on TV Land. And she was still wide awake while sleep laughed in her face. Feeling creative, she attempted to compose short succinct texts to Bulldog in her head and onto her phone. She never clicked the send button, however. She didn't want to appear too needy. Maybe Harriet could contact him and be her go-between. That was it. So she sent her a text at half-past-three. Immediately Harriet texted back with simply "No."

Then something amazing happened. Sophia-Emma felt a presence at her side, something like a breath or a cooling freeze. She didn't hear a word, but felt lots of them, like: *don't be fearful; I'm here with you; grow up, girl; you asked for this; show your stuff.*

Chills climbed up and down her spine, even though it was still above eighty outside. She became consumed with confusion again, as though she wasn't the person people thought she was, or even who she'd assumed she was. But she wanted to be only herself–nothing special.

So worry stepped in to give insomnia a break. She played with her hair, like she always did before dozing off. At last her breathing slowed.

Her hair soothed and comforted her, twirling, braiding, untangling it, and doing it all over again. It's coarseness calmed her fingers. She glanced over at it against her cheek. Now she was tugging at it, wanting to pull it out. This wasn't her hair, she discovered. This hair putting her to sleep was red, too red. No way would she ever sleep again.

The darkness of the night turned into the pinkness of dawn. She began to hear her mama and Christopher moving around in the kitchen, She too got up and told herself that what had happened earlier was simply a nightmare, but she still didn't have the nerve to look in a mirror. She put on her bathrobe, the one with a hood, and joined her mama and bro at the kitchen table. And like her daddy commanded, she kept her head down.

It was like any other morning, she convinced herself. Her mama was talking about what groceries she would buy with her hush money while Christopher poured milk on his cereal.

"I wish I knew who drank all the milk last night," he complained as he shook out the carton's last few drops.

"Sorry. It was probably me," his big sister said as she sat down beside him.

His grumpy face turned toward Sophia-Emma to tell her how inconsiderate she was. But instead, he screamed, "Mama, look at Sophia-Emma. She dyed her hair red!" Then he forgot about the missing milk and pulled her hair, seeing if his fingers would turn red from the suspected dye, or see if the wig would come off. Neither happened.

"Her mama came around the table and pulled her daughter's hood down. "Well, I'll be. That's the same color hair my Grandma Gaines had when I was a little girl, but it was her natural color. Are you missing your relatives up in Selma, Sophia-Emma?"

"Mama, I didn't dye my hair. You saw me last night after I read Daddy's letter. Don't you remember my black hair then?"

"Well, I wasn't paying much attention. It was dark and I was tired. When I saw your hair just now, I assumed that was why you got home so late."

"What I gonna do, Mama?" 'Member that show you used to watch online? Was it *Twilight Zone?* I think I'm in it now. And last night, I felt some type of ghost-like figure telling me what to do about our upcoming meeting or something in my life. I didn't sleep at all. And when I finally thought I's gonna asleep, I glance at my hair that got in my face, and it seemed red. I gotta dye it back to black. Nobody can see me like this. It's awful."

"Well, I kinda like it, Sophia-Emma. Go look at it in the full-length mirror. It kinda gives you a mysterious quality."

"Mama, no way I gonna be a redhead in this hood. I'll stick out like a penguin on the bayou. No one know me any . . ."

"Go on," Loving prompted.

"Never mind, Mama. Ya know, like you say, it might be a good idea to be a redhead for while. Yo really like it?"

"Go see for yourself, Sophia-Emma. You look pretty, but smart, too. Wear your glasses and you'd be a completely new person."

"I understand, Mama. And it not even Halloween."

Christopher couldn't let the subject of Halloween get by without having his say. "Can I dye my hair white for Halloween? Boy, I be awesome."

Sophia-Emma took her mama's advice and looked at herself in the long mirror. She reached for her glasses, which normally she never bothered with. And her mama was right. She no longer was Sophia-Emma Foster-Jones, daughter of Alan Jones and Loving Foster-Jones. What should her new identity be? Maybe Gloria? Gloria Eagle? Not bad, she thought.

After a shower, she walked over to Harriet's, who looked at her not twice, but at least five times until something broke the spell.

"That you, Sophia-Emma?"

"Who she?" her friend jokingly asked. Then she noticed Little Guy had followed her to Harriet's home.

"I recognized your dog," Harriet said."But now I know your voice. Nice job. Is this part of your plan now?"

"Why I came to talk. Wait till I tell you my whole story, but this might be a solution to my problem. I don't know if I can pull this off, but what I have to lose?" Then she did think that she had everything and everyone to lose. She chased that thought away as quickly as she could.

She instead concentrated on telling Harriet the story of her makeover exactly as it happened. Harriet's eyes seemed to expand in size when she heard about the ghost part.

"I know you think I delusional when I talk about supernatural happnin's," Sophia-Emma said as she shook her locks and let Harriet marvel at her new, long, red afro.

"Nice way to explain it. I call it crazy," she said.

"But why my hair change to red, the same shade as Mama's grandma?"

"Level with me, Sophia-Emma. You mad at me last night and you went to the Walmart and got yourself some red hair dye. That your last resort."

"Okay, don't believe the real story. Go ahead, assume I dyed my hair. I don't care. But do you think I can pretend to be someone else, so Crazy Dog don't recognize that goofy redhead up front as Daddy's daughter next week? What I got to lose?"

She'd said it again, and realized she had a family, everyone she loved, to lose. She probably would hurt her family just as much as a redhead with glasses as she would looking the way had yesterday.

Sophia-Emma left Harriet's place with nothing solved, still clinging to a hope that she could deceive everyone in Africatown. She realized that her voice was still the same, She wasn't taller nor did she have a different shape. She told herself that she might indeed be delusional. Lots of women dyed their hair and people in no time recognized them.

So, Sophia-Emma and Little Guy ran over to Miss Mildred's place, but her friendly smile wasn't there to greet them. Her place was locked up tighter than a two-hundred-pound woman poured into a medium pair of stretch pants.

"She ain't home," a next-door neighbor, Miss Anderson, yelled from her mailbox. "She's in the hospital, over at Providence. She having chest pains, I hear. I always tell her to take it easy. She ain't no spring chicken, you know."

A pudgy golden skin woman of African descent, Miss Anderson had a questioning look on her face. "You a saleswoman or bill collector? If so, come back in a few days. I'm sure she be better soon."

"No, just a friend." Sophia-Emma had intended to tell her who she was, but remembered her little scheme to not let anyone know her real identity. "You know if she 'lowed visitors there?"

"Don't know. Call the hospital." Then, giving her a suspicious look on her face, she muttered something under her breath.

"Thanks," she managed to utter in a somewhat friendly voice.

Little Guy and his mistress walked toward home. She got on Richardson Street and I saw the Middle Eastern family painting the outside of their home. Waving at them as she walked by, she wondered if they owned the home or were just renting. "Welcome to Africatown," she yelled. "Hope you like it here."

They looked at her as though she were an outsider. Sophia-Emma wanted to tell them she worked at MCA, but that may have helped them remember the dark-haired version of herself.

But they did smile and waved back. She kept walking and waved again.

Sophia-Emma enjoyed the walk with Little Guy. For too long she'd been too busy to bond with him. Then she remembered yesterday. So much had happened in only one day. "Look at me, I have no concept of time anymore," she told Little Guy.

Then she remembered less than a day ago she thought she might be in love with Bulldog. It seemed like months ago when he told her to fuck herself. She still was intensely mad at him. Today she wondered if her mama had given her the wrong advice. The guy had put some questions together for the meeting's panelists. He'd been polite. Then she'd gone and stomped on his fragile male pride. She wondered how he felt today. She knew how she felt–sad because she'd blown a perfect opportunity. Maybe rather than try not to be the real Sophia-Emma, it may have been better to take Harriet's advice–to apologize and repair his damaged ego.

Then there was Miss Mildred. It was hitting home that she could be seriously ill with a weak heart. She decided to call Miss Mildred on her cell. Hopefully she had her phone right next to her on her hospital bed. Letting it ring for a couple minutes, the young girl realized she probably didn't, after all. Perhaps she'd just worked too hard. She did a search on her phone to get the hospital's phone number and called the main desk.

"Y'all have a Miss Mildred there?" she asked like a child. "Miss Mildred who?" the hospital staff asked.

Her mind went blank. She'd always just been Miss Mildred to her. Then, by some miracle, her name appeared out of nowhere.

"Washington," she said, patting herself on the back. That was close. Did anyone ever study the intelligence of redheads? She'd never known Miss Mildred's last name till today.

"Here she is," the male voice responded. "Mildred Washington, room 542."

"Is she able to have visitors?" Sophia-Emma asked.

"I'll check," the voice answered. "Let's see . . ."

There was a long annoying pause which gave her an opportunity to play with her startling hair again, braiding and unbraiding it with three fingers. So relaxing.

"Visiting hours end at eight tonight."

"After running home to tell her mama about Miss Mildred, Sophia-Emma boarded the bus to Providence Hospital, getting there in time to catch Miss Mildred as she looked over the lunch the hospital had just dropped off.

"Don't know why they can't hire god cooks in these places," she complained. But then she looked at Sophia-Emma, blinked, and looked again.

"Say something, girl. And who you think you are, scaring me like this? Why you go and color your beautiful black hair? It was so pretty."

"Go ahead and eat, Miss Mildred. I've got a lot to tell you about my hair and my life these last few days. You might say it all started with a little kiss a couple nights ago. But before I get started with my ramblin', what put you here? You scared me to death."

"Miss Mildred had her mouth full, but started chewing faster–surprisingly since she'd just complained about the food seconds ago. She swallowed the dry chicken with an effort, coughed, and started to talk.

"I had these horrible chest pains. Thought I couldn't breathe." She took a bite of mashed potatoes. "I couldn't sleep, so I called the ambulance. They came and got me and took me here. They been giving me some medicine to calm the pain while they run this and that test. Guess I get outta here in a day or so. Now, get on with your story, chile."

Still worried about her old friend, Sophia-Emma decided that Miss Mildred needed a distraction from her worries. She began by telling about her first kiss from Bulldog, followed by their fight the next day, when he used the f-word on her.

But she also confided in her about her fear that Crazy Dog was buying her family's silence with hush money and everybody thought her mama and her needed to not ruffle any feathers while her daddy was locked up with some dangerous folk.

And finally she got to the ghost breathing on her and then discovering that her hair had changed to red.

"If I'd been consulted," she joked, "I rather got highlighted blonde, but red really makes me look dif'rent, don't you think?"

"An understatement, sweetheart. I don't think I know you anymore."

"Aw hell. Miss Mildred. That's why I told you that long story, cuz I sure need your advice 'bout now." She attempted to pat Miss Mildred's hand, but the old lady pulled it away. "Let's not take any chances. This might be catching," she warned her young friend.

Sophia was shocked by Miss Mildred's caution, but she continued with her problem. "Harriet thinks I should tell Bulldog I'm sorry I hurt his feelin's and tell him we really need him be our emcee at our meeting next week. She says girls can get guys to do whatever we want 'em to do if we—you know—make them think they super strong, smart, handsome. You get the picture, right?"

"Oh, I know. I used that kind of charm on Martin more than once."

"But now I'm capitalizin' on my new image, maybe cuttin' my hair, wearin' glasses, puttin' on makeup, changin' my voice and name even. You like Gloria Eagle? I want to somehow get away with not lettin' Crazy Dog recognize me. So what do you think about that scheme?"

Miss Mildred said nothing.

Sophia-Emma assumed she was thinking as she nibbled on her tiny salad, but she couldn't hold her emotions any longer and started crying and blowing her nose on Miss Mildred's sheet.

"Stop that. Just because you in a hospital don't mean you can spread your germs all over my room. Shame on you. And stop that crying. I can't think when you so worked up." Out of nowhere her comforting smile came back.

"First the kiss—sweet. The breakup the next day?" she shook her head. "Don't listen to your mama's advice no more, you hear? White women don't know nothin' about our black men. Bulldog tellin' you to f-you? I would have put my foot down, like you did. But leave some way for you and your feller to come to an understanding of what's 'ceptable and not 'ceptable from now on. That's what I got to say about that."

Miss Mildred took a couple bites of her canned peaches while Sophia-Emma eagerly awaited more seeds of wisdom.

"Now let's get to the miracle in your life on that sleepless night. Maybe you definitely a messenger sent by God to lead us into an epiphany."

Sophia-Emma wondered if the doctors have given her any medicine that made a person a little nutty. "Miss Mildred, the Epiphany was when the Wise Men saw baby Jesus for the first time, I think."

"I know that," the old lady laughed. "But in another sense, I mean epiphany as somethun' amazin' or like a lightnin' bolt."

Sophia-Emma chewed on that comment a long time.

"Look it up on Google," Miss Mildred ordered.

She did. And the mentor was right again.

"Now, don't put that kind of weight on my shoulders." Sophia-Emma laughed for the first time in days. "I just a temporary redhead who maybe hallucinated last night. Could've been a weird dream. And you know, it may have shocked me so much that it turned my hair red. It could happen, huh?" Sophia-Emma unconvincingly explained. "Couldn't it? Say 'yes,' please."

"My girl, I tellin' you what I think from the information you shared. Take it or ignore it. I been wrong hundreds of times in my life, and God willing, maybe many more times before I die. But I also been right more times than not, especially when it comes to you."

"But what should I do about the meetin' next week? Can I take on a new persona and get away with it, while Crazy Dog still thinks I'm keeping my nose clean? Or do I eat dirt and beg Bulldog to please, please . . . be our emcee?" she pleaded.

"Let me tell you another little story. You mentioned Crazy Dog."

"Yeah, that bastard who think he own our hood, the monster everyone bows down to? Yes, I know of him. Haven't met him, thank God."

Miss Mildred didn't answer immediately like she usually did, but instead seemed to be absorbed in my comment. Finally she spoke up.

"Well, so do I. You may be surprised to hear, but he my boy."

"Naw, stop joking." Sophia-Emma was furious and her words showed it. "You never birthed that man. My daddy's in prison because of him. If he your boy, I'm outta here."

This time she didn't wipe her tears on Miss Mildred's sheets. Instead she soaked them up with her shirtsleeve. How dare she be the mother of Crazy Dog. She had to be crazy in her head.

"And he's too smart to not know who you really are, even with red hair and glasses. Sophia-Emma, I want to help . . ."

But by the time the words came out of Miss Mildred's mouth, Sophia-Emma was gone and didn't hear what she was saying. She had lost Bulldog, her daddy, and now Miss Mildred. Things couldn't get much worse, or could they?

Chapter 24

Looking up from the bus stop to where she thought Miss Mildred's hospital room was, Sophia-Emma grieved the news she'd heard from her mentor. How could such a loving old woman have a child like Crazy Dog? Of course, she hadn't given her much of a chance to explain what she thought of her son's activities in the hood. Maybe she'd tried to persuade him to reform. Or could they not be on speaking terms anymore. Was she the only one in the hood who didn't know about Miss Mildred and her son Crazy Dog?

"What the hell," she said as she left the bus stop and started to return to Miss Mildred's room. But it was of no use. She wasn't there. Upon checking with the nurses' station, she was told they expected her to be out most of the afternoon for tests.

"Well, at least I tried to iron things out," She told the nurse as she approached the elevator. "Can you let her know that Sophia-Emma came back to see her?"

The nurse wrote down the message and attached it to her file.

As Sophia-Emma walked down the hall back to the bus stop, three big men of African descent passed her in the hall. The one in the middle, the tallest and the only one with a shaved head, was telling the others what to do, like checking on a guy downtown, picking up an important package, while the other two seemed to be making notes on their phones. The short one with a limp asked a question,"But Crazy Dog, what if it's not there yet?"

Nearly falling over with shock, Sophia-Emma discovered Crazy Dog. He was probably on his way to see his mother. She realized that they must be on good terms after all. Of course, there was a slight possibility he hadn't seen her for years and he was on his way to make up. But if that were the case, would he have two side-kicks going with him?

Tempted to turn around and, like Little Guy, follow them, she quickly changed her mind. To tell the truth, Sophia-Emma was scared of being seen by these powerful men. It would be so easy to knock her off, throw her into the bay and no one would even know. So, being a coward, she continued toward the bus stop, staring ahead as if in a trance. Why was everything going wrong in her life lately? Was she being tested?

While waiting for the bus, she searched her psyche. Did she know God the Father and Jesus differently than the other people around her? Words and phrases seemed to flow in and out of her heart, like: *okay, you're on your own . . . your mission . . . human . . . not easy.*

Figuratively she took a vacuum she'd stored in her head somewhere and tried to vacuum the mess of words into the sky, but they fell back into her being like dust settling back on a piece of furniture she was trying to wipe clean.

She forced herself into reality again and noticed a Latinx mother telling a story to some young girls so they wouldn't dart off into a string of cars leaving the hospital. Then there was the old white man carrying a plastic bag labeled *Property of Providence Medical Center*. He looked like he'd just lost someone dear to him. Sophia-Emma fantasized that his lifelong partner wasn't doing well, or even worse, had died. A nurse in uniform was complaining to someone on his phone about his day. Sophia-Emma felt a wind messing up her red hair while sweat poured from her body like from a leaking faucet, making her clothes damp, clinging, and stinky.

It was only two o'clock, but this day seemed to have already gone on for thirty hours, maybe even a week. The teen wanted to go home and sleep till tomorrow came. Maybe she was in the middle of a never-ending nightmare. Could be she was dead, and this was what happened to people on their way to hell.

An hour later, still in her nightmarish state, she stepped off the bus at her corner and walked the rest of the way to her home. Once again, she wasn't greeted by a loving doting mother so glad she'd finally made it home. No, instead she saw a stern mama accusing her of running off and having fun all day with her friends. Oh, what she didn't know, and what she had no interest in learning from her daughter.

Loving snarled. "About time. Did you lose your phone again?"

"No. Mama, I know I should've called you mid-day, but it was a horrible mis-adventure from the time I left here to go visit Miss Mildred at the hospital. You remember me coming back to tell you, don't you?"

Her mama, after a minute of thought, nodded. "But usually you're not gone all day. Things can go bad for people who look like you in these times. I worry about you." She tied her dreads on top of her head. "I'm your mother. You're my responsibility, but you're off trying to change the world rather than pulling your weight around here."

"Mama, you got a phone, too. Can't you call me? Harriet gets calls from her mother all the time. You never call me. Why?"

"Now don't you turn this conversation around on me, my dear."

She stopped talking, just like Miss Mildred and Sophia-Emma did earlier.

Then something just hit Loving like an asteroid. She blinked over and over like she had gnats in both of her eyes.

"Oh no, I becomin' my mother," she whined.

While she was all wrapped up with this realization, her daughter slipped into her room, closed the door and pulled the shades before stretching out on her bed. Oh, relaxation. Every muscle in her body went limp, but not for long. Her mama wouldn't let up. She'd dealt with her realization and was back on her warpath. She stood in Sophia-Emma's doorway, right hand resting on her right hip, her favorite pose.

"Okay, we'll both call each other more. I'm okay with that. But I'm still angrier than those red ants were a few weeks ago. Why are you off to here and there, like you're on some type of a secret mission only you understand?"

Her mother then screamed so the entire neighborhood could hear, "You're driving me nuts."

"Mama, I know I'm strange, crazy, too. But I got to sleep right now. I am so tired that I can hardly finish a sen . . ."

After no sleep the night before, Sophia-Emma fell asleep. She vaguely remembered the door of her room gently being closed. But her sleep didn't last long. At twilight, her eyes opened again. Mama and Christopher had eaten. He had been playing with Little Guy and her mama was in her art corner, cleaning brushes and her palate.

Sophia-Emma sneaked in behind her mama and put her arms around the slim waist. "Can we talk on the front porch awhile?" she asked.

They spread themselves out on the porch, partly because they'd gotten so used to doing so for months, but also because Sophia-Emma needed a bath. The sound of children chasing and catching one another, dogs barking at each other, lingering smells from dinner, fishy smells like today was one of good catches all enlivened the pair's senses. They marveled at the purpling sky glowing over the graveyard. By habit, they tried to block out the industrial sounds and smells from the asphalt plant and other industries just blocks away.

Finally Sophia-Emma spoke first. "Mama, did you know Miss Mildred's at Providence going through tests because she was having chest pains? On my visit today she told me that Crazy Dog is her son. Did you know that?"

Her mama looked at her and nodded.

"Why nobody tell me? I'm finding out so much these days that I can't keep up, like hearin' Harriet's family is gettin' hush money from Miss Mildred's son, too."

Loving wouldn't look her daughter in the eye. Instead she focussed on the recently repotted plant next to them, perhaps wondering if it needed another watering.

"When she tell me Crazy Dog her boy, I leave her. Walk out is what I do. But later I tried to visit her again, after I'd left her room so pissed off. My luck, I run into three dudes going down the hall opposite me at Providence, and one of 'em is Crazy Dog, giving orders to the other two. I wanna follow 'em into the hospital, but I chicken out."

Her mama finally smiled, seeming to know that her daughter was about to lose her mind.

"I'm growin' up, but I feel like I know nothin, cuz everybody want me to know nothin'. I sick of all this. So, you too know Crazy Dog? Is there anything else I need to know about this guy?"

Her mama didn't answer right away. Sophia-Emma wished she'd go ahead and water that violet so she'd give undivided attention to her. But eventually she spoke.

"I know a few things about him. Wherever your imagination takes you, he's there. He's a charismatic man, even if one doesn't agree with his tactics. He's the godfather of all of us, in a sense. When someone's sick, a family member dies, a baby's born or someone's put in jail, he's at your door to help. The man some say might be a ruthless killer is also a confessor or a confidante when tragedy shows its ugly face. Why do you think so many here are willing to serve time in his place, to answer whenever he calls?"

Sophia-Emma wondered what would happen when she released information that he was responsible for MCA closing its doors in the hood. Would she then recognize him for the creep he was?

"That's dirty money involved with his gang we're taking from him. And with that money comes further damages to our hood."

Her mama responded, "Now from what I've heard from folk around here was that many of the industrial polluters that have taken over the Delta gave generous donations to Community Action from the 1980s on. Before that they were organized and controlled by local poor folk themselves. But poor folk began reaching into the causes of individual poverty, it being systemic poverty. This was threatening to big business and other good ol' boys serving on the group's board-of-directors. Eventually the U.S. government made it a rule that only a third of their governing boards could be the poor folk themselves. Later funding to these agencies was cut, big business got tax breaks and subsidies so they'd set up their factories right here. They hired our people to sweep floors—even college graduates—until they contracted that work out to temps. Wherever they needed some good publicity to offset a recent spill, or exceeding limits coming from their smoke stacks, or water releases, they'd give a few thousand to Community Action for such programs as GED training or feeding programs, using outdated books and food, of course. Now that's what I've been told. Seems to fit in with some of the stuff we discovered when I was active as an anarchist."

"So you tryin' to tell me that the guy Daddy's servin' time for is a saint? To me, that scenario don't fit at all."

"One thing you're going to eventually have to learn, Sophia-Emma, is that none of us are consistently good and none of us are consistently bad. I knew Miss Mildred worked hard to get that boy of hers ready to run a professional business. But even in the days when he didn't have a fiefdom here in Africatown, he was turned down for loans. He wasn't hired for jobs he was qualified for. Then he had a clean record. He'd even served in the Marines and left with an honorable discharge. He lived right, but was wronged by the government that sent him to Afghanistan and Iraq. One night he was pulled over by police driving his mother's car while black. He had no current driver's license, and his turn signals weren't working. They also found marijuana in the glove compartment."

"So? He shouldn't have had drugs. Isn't that what you tell me? But then he served his own time, right? He couldn't send anyone in his place."

"True. But in prison, that's where he learned from other crime professionals how to beat the racist system that keeps whites up and black and brown people down. He came out a different man. Before we knew it, we'd become his fiefdom. But as much as he was now a violent ruler, he was also a benevolent neighbor. He isn't giving us money to keep our mouths shut. No, we're keeping our mouths shut for your dad who chose to go to jail as penance for running away long ago. I've said my piece. Now you do as your conscience leads. Make up your own mind."

"But Mama, you telling me you ain't mad at Crazy Dog? Daddy's doing time for him. He expects us to find jobs. And on top of all that, now you tell me that because of principle, he was able to get GED classes stopped in the hood. Don't you think that was kinda cruel? We have young people around here selling dope for Crazy Dog. If they'd earned their GED, they coulda done work that wouldn't put 'em locked up. I don't even know if I want to hang 'round Miss Mildred anymore if she's raised a son like Crazy Dog. Plus, because of Crazy Dog's drugs, Daddy got hooked. Now he has to go through the pain of withdrawal."

"You know who got your daddy hooked?" Mama angrily asked.

"I know what you're going to say Mama. You'll say doctors at the clinic, right?"

"That's what I'll always say, but they get off like heroes. No, there're lots of folks out there responsible—Crazy Dog, the medical and pharmaceutical companies, his job, his friends, even us and himself. No one person is responsible for your daddy having to serve time."

Sophia-Emma was tiring of her mama's preachiness. She sometimes, like tonight, wished she'd left her out there in the Dallas County pasture where she'd found her. Tired of living here between the bayous, she wondered everyday who would shoot whom.

When her mama finally retired from her soapbox and went back to painting, Sophia-Emma visited with Little Guy and Christopher on the porch.

"So Christopher, I've not had a good old talk with you for a long time. You having a good summer?"

"It's okay," Christopher muttered as he scratched behind Little Guy's ears. "I kinda miss Daddy, though. How old will I be when he's able to come back home?"

"Can't say, buddy, A lot has to do with how the guards, the warden and other folk think. If they think he's been a good guy long enough, and that he'll be a good guy back home, they send him home."

"Well, I don't get it. Don't you think Daddy's a good guy? He doesn't hit me when I'm bad like Andre's daddy does, and his dad's not locked up."

"Know what you mean, Chris. Are you praying for Daddy every night when you go to bed? That kinda helps me feel closer to him. Maybe we could write him tonight after we eat a bowl of Sprinkles ice cream."

He bounced off the swing and ran into the kitchen. By the time his big sister had joined him, he was up on a stool reaching into the freezer.

Sophia-Emma's cell rang. She answered while at the same time trying to maneuver dishing rainbow dots immersed in vanilla ice cream into two big bowls. Christopher added two spoons to the bowls and ran outside with his so Little Guy could lick the bowl.

"Don't feed it all to Little Guy," Sophia-Emma hollered. Then she answered her call. She was curious because it was a call from a number she'd never seen before.

"Is this Sophia-Emma?" a gruff male voice asked, one that sounded like the one she'd heard today giving orders to two other homies at the hospital.

She definitely didn't want to talk to that crook, so she ended the call without a word.

A few minutes later, a black Silverado pulled into their driveway. A bald guy walked up the sidewalk. Sophia-Emma's heart was pounding. She ran into her bedroom and hid in the closet.

Her mama answered the door after about five minutes of heavy knocking. Sophia-Emma could hear the two of them talking. She actually offered Crazy Dog a beer.

Sophia-Emma strained to listen to everything they said. Crazy Dog was telling her mama that Miss Mildred suffered a major set-back and more tests were required. They'd put her in ICU about mid-afternoon today.

She gulped and started to sob. Pulling down a blouse hanging above her, she wiped her eyes and nose, trying to keep the bawling inaudible.

Loving told Crazy Dog that her daughter had always adored his mother. "She has a very good influence on her," she said.

Sophia-Emma knew she was buttering him up. The family couldn't survive without that hush money. The tears were gone now. They'd been replaced by anger. She burst from her closet out to the kitchen and ordered the man out of their house. In her opinion, he was dirtying it, like the fire ants did when her daddy was home, saving her mama and her from hoards of the pests. But this man was the worst of all pests.

"I can't stand you. We never asked you to come to our house, and now Miss Mildred's about dead. What did you do to her today?"

"Are you Miss Sophia-Emma?" the surprised man asked.

"I sure am, and I'm not into what you sell, and if I ever see my little brother selling your dope, I'll turn you into the police myself and work to keep you locked up to your dying day."

"Sophia-Emma, this isn't how we treat our guests," her mama said, trying to cut the tension in the room.

"Mama, how can you even look this guy in the face? Daddy would be here with us if it weren't for this monster."

"Wait a minute, young lady," Crazy Dog interrupted. "I ain't come here tonight to talk about what I do for a living. That's my cross to bear. I came here to tell you my mama is real sick, on life support. And she wants you to visit tomorrow. Can you do that?"

Sophia-Emma sat down close to Loving. She was scared, but she had to appear strong for Christopher's sake, who was currently licking the remaining ice cream out of his bowl and about to start on hers, which by now was more like whipped cream.

"Can I have yours?" Christopher shouted to his sister?

"If you go eat it out on the porch," she answered.

Out he went, thrilled to be starting his second bowl.

"Now, do you promise you'll visit my mother tomorrow?" Crazy Dog asked in a quiet voice. "I can pick you up."

"No way, I'll take the bus," she insisted. "Did you make her get sicker when you showed up today with the other druggies? Did you drop your guns off at the front desk before you went in to see your mama? How can you be a son to this woman who's been like a granny to me?"

"I agree," he said. "Little lady, I not here to argue or try to change your mind about me. We happen to love the same woman, and she wants to see you and me tomorrow. A deal? And for your information, she had a setback before I even got to her room today. I talked to her after they moved her into ICU."

With that, he finished his beer. "Thank you for talking to me tonight, Ms. Foster-Jones and Sophia-Emma. Hope you gettin' along okay with the small help we been sendin' by."

"Tell your mother, I be there as soon as they let me in tomorrow," Sophia-Emma said as she stormed back to her room and slammed the door behind her.

She fumed there, walked around and peeked out the window. He petted Little Guy and shook Christopher's hand. Sophia-Emma wondered if he saw him as a future dealer in ten years or so like his daddy.

"Over my dead body," she whispered to herself.

To be expected, her mama knocked on her door and let herself in with one of those mad looks on her face again.

"I hate to tell you that you were very discourteous to Crazy Dog in the kitchen just now. And to think we'd discussed his life just a few minutes earlier."

"And may I also tell you, Mama, how disappointed I am with you?" her daughter fired back.

That was enough for her mother. She walked over to Sophia-Emma and planted a stinging slap on her right cheek, shocking her daughter, whose face felt like it had been set on fire.

"How dare you act so holier than thou with that man or me. Yes, he's done some horrible things, but I have faith that in the end his mother's influence will win out. However, I wonder if my influence on you will win out." Her mother's face was redder than Sophia-Emma had ever seen it.

"How can you always tell me you're here on a mission from God, but then you come off so judgmental and cruel? I want you to do some real soul-searching tonight when you lay your head on this pillow. I don't want to see you out of this room the rest of the night."

Her accusations made the young teen boil with rage. Her cheek still stung as she sassed back.

"Mama, I'm embarrassed by you. Here you once fought for justice and righteousness against big business and government, but this guy's responsible for your husband becoming an addict and a dealer and now a jailbird. No one knows how many murders have been dictated by him. Aren't you worried about your kids even being within spitting range from him? Plus, I don't want to do our housework or do our laundry so you can stand around and paint your day away."

Her mama had contempt written on her face. She knew her daughter had lost all respect for her.

At that moment Sophia-Emma decided she would go visit Miss Mildred tomorrow and prepare for the accountability session, but then she'd be gone. This time no one would find her. She was sickened to even look at her mama. Crazy Dog was poison to the hood, and Africatown could just sink into the gulf for all she cared. But there was also her daddy and Christopher and Little Guy. They were important to her. She'd take Little Guy with her, but she dreaded leaving Christopher behind. The way she felt at this time, she couldn't trust that her mama would give him the care he needed. Maybe she'd again pass out drunk or slap him like she'd hit her. But still she had to be out of here after September third. And she was going to proudly stand up there with the panelists, exposing Crazy Dog for all the slime he was. And if he was there, she would dare him to pull a gun on her. She hoped Bulldog would be there and weep because he, too, was an abuser with his filthy words.

Sophia-Emma yelled out the window for Christopher to come in the house. He wasn't within sight. She called for Little Guy. No responses. As much as she didn't want to, she found her mama in her painting corner. To get back at her for the slap, she told her that her only son was missing, and it was all her fault.

Loving went berserk and ran past her daughter, yelling Christopher's name door after door. Sophia-Emma was right behind her. Finally Christopher answered in the dark smelly air, "I'm over here playing with Amala," he yelled back.

The Middle Eastern family smiled at the two frantic women. For a moment, Sophia-Emma wished that her family could be like theirs. Then she remembered; it had been just a few weeks ago.

Her mama, relieved that she'd found her son, thanked them for letting him visit. But they seemed to want to spend more time with their visitors. Maybe a conversation with new neighbors was just what her family needed after too much fighting back home.

"Come in, please," the husband pleaded. "We like to share some tea with you."

They entered their sparsely furnished, but spotless home, expecting a tall cold glass of sweet tea, ice cubes clinking on the glass and sweat beads of condensation racing down to the base of the tumbler. Instead, upon sitting on a rug on the floor and passing hand sanitizer around, the wife gave them tiny clear cups with handles and filled them with a spicy hot overly sweet tea, which she continued to fill over and over.

Sophia-Emma saw the family put something like a sugar cube in their mouths as they sipped additional cups of the hot liquid. Finally, the father turned his cup upside down, which seemed to mean that he'd had enough. The others did the same.

They were also treated with sugar coated almonds and toffee which the hosts called chocolate. Christopher gobbled them down like popcorn at a movie. Her mama was in conversation with the adults about the nearest schools, neighbors, history of the hood and other local matters.

They discovered that the family was from Afghanistan. After a decade of trying to get visas to work here, they had finally been approved. Their names were Jamil, the father; Nairem, the mother. Their daughter was Amala. In turn, Sophia-Emma and her family introduced themselves. Her mama told the family that she changed her name from Amanda to Loving when her daughter was a baby; that Sophia meant *Wise Goddess* and Emma was a famous American activist. Of course Christopher was named for a legendary saint who blessed journeys. Their father, named Pulsar, was legally Alan Jones, who descended from the original settlers of Africatown. He was currently serving time in Elmore State Prison now, but that he'd be home soon because of his admirable behavior.

The hosts seemed startled, and Loving noticed. "You have surely discovered by now that most of our residents in this area of Mobile are people of African descent. Many fathers, some mothers, and even children are in prison, have been in prison, or are on probation. We live in a racist country, even though black people are still a minority in our country, they seem to make up much of the prison population."

Her mama was on her soapbox once again. "For example, my husband hurt his back a few years ago. A doctor gave him oxycontin. Then the doctor stopped the prescriptions. But by then, he was hooked. Now he's in prison getting off drugs. We'll be so happy to have him home again. Tell me what made you decide to move here?"

Jamil and Nairem looked at each other. Nairem nodded for her husband to speak.

"We come here because we could afford the rent. I also work close by at the asphalt company. I don't know how long we'll stay, however. You're the first to come visit us. I was a teacher in Afghanistan and would like to teach in America, too."

"Just be patient, my friends," Loving encouraged them. "People here tend to be stand-offish at first, but when they learn they can trust you, they'll visit and welcome you into their homes. As you can see, I'm a white woman who chose to live here rather than move out in the country near Selma, where my mother lives. I know we have some horrible smells around here and more pollution than I care for, but we residents are proud of our hood—neighborhood—that is."

Christopher looked over at his mama across the rug from him and said, "Mama, I think I ate too much candy. Can we go home, please?"

"He's being paid back for gobbling up all your terrific treats," Loving said while the three of them stood up to leave. "We'll have to invite you to our humble abode, someday soon."

"Khudafezi," the entire family said. Loving's family tried to respond, but they all laughed instead. The daughter, Amala, came over to Sophia-Emma as she started to leave with her family.

"Could you introduce me to some of your friends?" she asked.

She was beautiful. Sophia-Emma also guessed she was living under strict parents, as well. She wanted to tell her that she probably wouldn't like her friends. But the girl looked so lonely that she decided to introduce her to Harriet soon. Then she remembered the upcoming accountability meeting. They needed as many as they could get to attend.

"And please come to this big meeting we're having September third at seven," she urged. "It'll be a good way for you to understand how we let our leaders know what we need here."

"Yes, I would like that much, but my father will have to come with me because young women are not allowed to go out at night without adult supervision. Maybe once my parents adjust to customs in this America, they will change their minds. I get tired of staying in this little house so much."

"I understand. I feel the same way. Hey, I'm visiting an old lady tomorrow morning and then going to the Community Action place where I volunteer, but how about getting together with my friend Harriet and me sometime later. Hopefully we'll see each other soon."

"That is—what you say? Awesome."

"Yes, good word," Sophia-Emma agreed.

The three of the Foster-Jones family walked home as though their lives had received a dose of respect and reality.

"Mama, sorry I so nasty tonight."

"Well, Sophia-Emma, guess I need to apologize, too. Let's try to be kind to each other for a few days. Work for you?"

The two hugged and giggled like they had when Chaos was with them. "Hey, I'm tired of being so grouchy lately," Sophia-Emma said.

Christopher, still rubbing his tummy, added, "I know, you want me to apologize for going away from the house and not asking, right? But Amala is so pretty and nice to me. I hope she becomes your good friend, Sophia-Emma. It would be fun to have her come to our house. Maybe tomorrow?"

"We'll have to see what her parents say," his mama said. "I think your sister and Amala are talking about getting together soon. In the meantime, young dude, never leave our yard without telling us. I get scared when my young-uns are gone without telling me."

Christopher looked up at his mama, and with a smile, opened his mouth and spewed out puke, landing on Loving's sandals and feet. Everyone laughed anyway.

"I'm first in the shower tonight," she demanded as she ran the rest of the way home.

"You're second after Mama," Sophia-Emma told Christopher. Little Guy, meanwhile, licked up the vomit and displayed a pleased look on his face.

That night in bed she reviewed her long day, from red hair, Harriet, Miss Mildred, Crazy Dog, her fight with Mama, and the fun tea party with new neighbors. She didn't know what to empathize in her prayers—sadness, regret, fear, hope, happiness?

"You know, Father, I messed up a lot today. A lot. I don't know what I once promised you I would do. It's rough, really rough. Got any extra angels you can send my way? After all, I'm still only a kid."

Chapter 25

As promised, Sophia-Emma was up at dawn, preparing herself for another long day.

It didn't start well. She nearly missed her bus heading to the hospital. As she rode the elevator up to ICU where Miss Mildred was being monitored, she worried about what to say to this old woman who'd always been such a fine example of strength for Sophia-Emma to follow. In addition, she was still carrying a grudge because Miss Mildred had never told her that her son was Crazy Dog, who happened to be facing her in the hall outside his mother's room at this moment.

It was hard for Sophia-Emma to pretend she didn't see him. She couldn't help but notice that he was dressed in an attractive gray sports coat and that he was walking toward her in new Jordan wing tips. Flaunting his drug sales, she told herself.

"How're you, Miss Sophia-Emma?"

"I'm tired. Wish I could visit Miss Mildred at her home rather than in a place that smells like chemicals and where she's hooked up to tubes like wires plugged into surge protectors. Wish I was here alone, too. But she your mama, so why don't you go in first? I wait till you're done visiting."

"No, I checked with the nurses out here and they said both of us could visit at the same time." Surprisingly, he started tearing up. "I think we need to be quick though. They talkin' about doing more tests.

She immediately felt tears forming in her own eyes, but attempted to blink over and over, telling herself to be strong for Miss Mildrid. A nurse stood blocking the entrance into her room. That's when Crazy Dog put on his mean demeanor. He pushed her aside and grabbed Sophia-Emma's arm as they both went into his mother's room.

The young teen knew that time was precious. They'd physically be removed from Miss Mildred's room any minute. Seeing a box of surgical gloves on a shelf, she hurriedly took four out of the box so both could wear them.

Amidst the tubes, monitors, and machines performing their medical dissonance, the old lady seemed to be sleeping through it all. Probably loaded with sedatives, Sophia-Emma assumed.

Crazy Dog stood closer to his mother. He planted a kiss on her forehead, no matter what the risks. After all, his entire life was built around risks. Miss Mildred opened her eyes and managed to smile at her son. Sophia-Emma could see the love between them even though they were so different. She wondered why he couldn't have turned out differently. Surely, this situation would have been a lot easier on her if he'd been a barber or a minister, not a drug kingpin.

"Mother, I was able to convince Sophia-Emma to come here this morning."

The old lady touched their hands. Miss Mildred's grip still felt strong, Sophia-Emma thought.

"Oh, my two favorite children. I love you both. I . . . I do hope you can reconcile and see the good in each other before I have to leave this world." She stopped and took a number of labored breaths.

Crazy Dog and Sophia-Emma exchanged glances at one another. He managed a smile. She didn't.

"Miss Mildred, I so sorry for how I left yesterday in a huff. I've been doin' strange and mean things to people I love lately. Will you forgive me for not treatin' you with respect?"

She took some more labored breaths and spoke. "Chile, you know you can't . . . do anything to make me . . . stop loving you. You are like . . . my own granddaughter." A surge of coughing made her stop talking. The oxygen tube in her nose slipped out. Crazy Dog did his best unsuccessfully to ease the tube back in. Sophia-Emma told herself that if by some slim chance Crazy Dog ever decided to give up selling dope, that he shouldn't try to get into medicine.

"Sophia-Emma, I want . . . want you to know that I'm proud of Bernard, my son. I know ma . . . many in the hood think he's a . . . a crook, but I want you . . . you to know that he'd give his life for any of us."

Just to not upset her mentor, the teen half-nodded in agreement, thinking that all mothers loved their children. And sometimes mothers lived in denial of the harmful things their kids did.

The nurse whom Crazy Dog had shoved out of the doorway came back in the room with a guard, ready to remove both visitors from the room. Miss Mildred was calm and seemed to be resting from her speech.

Sophia-Emma noticed that the nurse's name tag said *Amy Marrs*. With the support of the guard, *Jerome Lyons*, she took charge of their visit.

"You two must leave now," she commanded. "Mr. Lyons will escort you out. Please leave now."

Miss Mildred smiled, trying to be the peacemaker one more time. She was more beautiful than Sophia-Emma had ever seen her. But then everything changed. Her whole body seemed to go into a seizure as she started coughing uncontrollably. The monitors and other machines began to seize the moment with loud alarms and buzzers.

Simultaneously Sophia-Emma felt something—like a lightning bolt—energize her entire body. It shot through her fingers. Not thinking of anything but the healing of Miss Mildred, she bent down and let that energy pulsate through herself and flow into Miss Mildred. She hugged her until all the energy had left her body and was now flowing through the sick woman who, seconds ago seemed to be in shock. Color came back into her face. Her ashy skin had turned to a vibrant rich brown. She threw the oxygen tube off her bed and propped herself up to lean on the pillows behind her. All in the room were stunned, especially Sophia-Emma. While Miss Mildred's true self was returning, the teen healer grew immensely tired. She yearned to lay down in the bed and sleep beside her old mentor like she'd done so often as a child. But she knew she couldn't.

Everyone in the room—Crazy Dog, his mother, the nurses, the security guard—they were all looking at her as though a miracle had happened.

Sophia-Emma reacted as many other multi-race teenage girls who wanted to be normal would. She lied, even to herself.

"Miss Mildred's medicine simply kicked in at the moment I was hugging her," she insisted. "That's all. Why y'all lookin' at me? I don't do miracles."

"Well child, you did it." Miss Mildred seemed to want to tell the world. "You found your mission." She laughed and squealed so the entire floor could hear her.

Sophia-Emma rushed to put her hand over the old woman's mouth. "Please don't say anything. That just a coincidence," she whispered to her.

Meanwhile Ms. Marrs simply stood with the oxygen tube in her hand, looking at Sophia-Emma and then at her patient. The pudgy thirtyish care-giver with a wedding band on her right hand, drowsy blue eyes, and freckles splattered across her white face, took her phone from her pocket to report the incident to a higher-up. She dismissed the guard, who walked away in a daze.

"Please, Ms. Marrs, don't call anyone. Please. I need to go right now."

She hurried to find the closest elevator that would spit her out at the nearest exit. Along the way, people looked at her as though she must have shot the place up.

"No one else must know I did this," she muttered over and over as she ran toward the hospital's front doors. Seeing a security guard, she slowed down to a walk for a few seconds, smiling innocently as she eased past him. Once outside, she again went into a fast walk mode until she was beyond suspicious eyes, She stopped at a grove of trees, hiding behind a fat old Magnolia and planned how she was going to avoid any media over this healing.

She wanted to call Miss Mildred, but then hospital folks would get her number. No, she'd have to go incognito for a few days, maybe dye her hair back to black or do a bleach job on it. No matter what, being recognized could not happen. No way would she go to the MCA today. Here she was again, running away. But what the hell, she thought. Sometimes you just gotta do what has to be done.

"I'm not ready yet, Father," she confided to her higher power.

The monumental reality of what happened through her hit harder. Yes, she was running from that hospital. Yes, she was thrilled that Miss Mildred seemed to be healed. But she was running beyond all that. She had to run to a quiet spot where she could come to terms with what was going on in her life.

"Father, not now," she pleaded in prayer. "I've got lots of important business to do. Now in a couple years I might be available, but really, I'm booked till I grow up. Can you go fishing for a while and check back when I get my life together?"

Sophia-Emma's heavy breathing slowly subsided. Time for another hair color change, she lamented, and some important calls. Then she'd be out of this town called home.

Chapter 26

Finally, Sophia-Emma was at the bus stop and hastened to board it before the driver put his foot on the gas. She'd made it just in time. No one seemed to recognize her as the miracle worker. To the other riders, she was simply an average poor teenager with survival of her family on her mind. But she knew her only goal at the moment was to get out of town ASAP.

First she'd call MCA to tell them she had a family emergency and couldn't volunteer today. Next, a more challenging task: calling her mama to let her know she'd be gone for a few days while she sorted out some things. She knew she'd be mad again, so she prepared ahead what she would say.

"So Mama, please, please, I'm beggin' you please, try to understand my situation. People thinking I cured Miss Mildred—and maybe I did. But I can't become the magic healer—not yet. All I want is to live as a kid for now, nothing more. Can you go and tell Amala I won't be in touch with her today like I'd promised?" The only response she heard was silence. "I'm gonna pick up chemicals to bleach my hair—already I'm known as a redhead—and will try to get Harriet to help me. Then I'm out of here for a time till the news story fascination dies down, Can you also drop my phone charger at Harriet's? I'm calling her now."

Her explanation did little to convince her mama of the wisdom of her plans. She blew her top, told her that she was being disrespectful and that she had no concept of the trouble she was getting herself into just wandering off to only God-knew-where. In a sense, she was as guilty of Crazy Dog himself, especially during these dangerous times. There were white supremacists out there who liked to kill black and brown people.

"Okay, okay, Mama, I know you speak the truth. But so do I. You can discuss all of this with Miss Mildred if you want—and please do—but no one will find me for a few days. You know how once Jesus went off by himself to fast and pray on top of a mountain. That's something like what I want to do. I'll be in good hands, I promise."

Sophia-Emma's part of the conversation was over, so she disconnected while her mama was still accusing her of being a stubborn delinquent. She wondered how she ever stayed alive this long considering her mama's efforts to drown her in warnings her whole life.

Seeing a CVS pharmacy, she pulled the cord on the bus so she could get off and find some bleach powder and other ingredients for her next hair color change and to call Harriet.

Fortunately, her friend was stuck at home with her little sister. Sophia-Emma told her the unbelievable tale of healing Miss Mildred. Harriet wasn't a willing participant in her friend's plan, but after she did the "*a real friend would trust me*" routine on her, the two of them got into the actual process of striping Sophia-Emma's hair of all its color. A good distraction, her hair took center stage pushing the miracle to past news.

It turned out beautiful. "A professional hair-dresser couldn't have done better," Sophia-Emma raved. Next step was to cut it short, very short. Anything to hide her identity when she attempted to skip town today. No more absent-minded braiding of hair for a long time.

As she examined her new haircut in the mirror, and added the glasses from her purse, Sophia-Emma dropped one more bomb.

"Oh, by the way, as you can probably see, I can't come to our session September third. Could you and Bulldog do it?"

For the second time today, she ran out of another building. This time it was Harriet's home. She split so fast that she forgot her charger. She turned around to fetch it, deciding midway that she wouldn't miss it since she probably wouldn't have access to any electricity while she was gone anyway.

The new pixie-cut blonde looked like a tourist with her blue-tinted glasses, plus some new duds—a mid-thigh, baby-blue skirt and darker blue top—that Harriet lent her (before she asked her to take over the accountability meeting). She was convinced that even her own mother wouldn't recognize her. The result was just what she needed. Plus she had some cash saved from the night she broke into the piggy bank on her first run-away attempt.

Still it seemed like she'd forgotten something. She didn't have time to ponder what. Sophia-Emma had to get to her destination, the shores of the Alabama River outside of Selma. But she wouldn't be visiting Grandma Foster. No, she had to be alone with the Creator and some old waiting souls buried in the Promised Land slave cemetery. She wasn't taking food or even water. All attention was directed on being alone to see what in the hell was going on in her life. She felt like she was wading into the dark with hopes of coming into some type of light that would finally reveal her path for life.

When she arrived at the Greyhound Bus station, she remembered what she'd left behind, Little Guy. At first she felt like she'd deserted her truest buddy. But then she also remembered Christopher, who loved him about as much. If both she and Little Guy were to disappear at once, little bro would be devastated. Probably her forgetfulness did some good this time. One more benefit: Without a dog, she could board the bus. She needed this bus, after discovering how she'd messed up the first time she ran away with the pup. After all, it's not like she'd never return. At least she hoped she'd come back.

Ticket purchased, she finally boarded Greyhound that evening, due to arrive in Selma in the wee hours of the next morning. She had nothing but her handbag, the one she'd taken to the hospital to see Miss Mildred. Her mama tried once again to convince her daughter not to leave. "You can die out there on the river bank and no one will know where to find your body," she warned again.

Sophia-Emma knew she didn't mean to predict her outcome quite the way she heard it, but it sounded like she was more concerned about finding her daughter's body than whether she would live through this journey. She lamented her daddy being locked up. But at least because of imprisonment, he wouldn't be pulling her off the bus any time soon.

Trying to persuade her mama to trust what she was up to, she even promised she'd be back in just a couple days. "Let me go," Sophia-Emma pleaded. "I need to get to Promised Land." That set off another barrage of warnings and threats from her mother. She was not very *loving* lately, her daughter accused.

Loving had once told her to never take a Greyhound. Now she knew why. This one stunk and was dirty. Staff were uncaring and snacks from their vending machines were outdated and not suitable for human consumption. Nevertheless, Sophia-Emma was grateful. Once more no one seemed to recognize her as that strange multi-racial redhead who could heal with a hug. She asked herself if someone would collapse on the bus station, would she try to heal that person, or would she look the other way? Or what if she tried to heal someone and nothing improved? She decided if that happened, like everyone else, she'd scream for a doctor and cross her fingers. She could also pray silently. Good idea, She told herself.

The hours on the bus passed slower than a sloth trying to get from one part of a tree to the ground. Sophia-Emma discovered that she'd brought her portable charger after all, so she used her phone, quietly calling a dozen people, first being Bulldog. She apologized for how she'd treated him the other day. She waited for his apology, but it didn't come. Her pride told her she'd been right to dump him, but she knew Harriet needed him as emcee next week. Africatown needed him. He was playing hard-to-get exceptionally well. All the more reason he needed to be the emcee. She didn't even care if he yelled at her, but he simply said nothing after her apology. Waiting for some kind of response, she checked her phone to see if it was working. Sophia-Emma hated this kind of silence, especially from a guy who had kissed her only a few days ago. Finally she gave up.

Then he called back within a couple minutes and told her he'd get in touch with Harriet as a favor to her, not Sophia-Emma. Then silence again and he was gone. Sophia-Emma's love life was truly over. Thank heavens she didn't have to worry about that anymore along with her other problems.

With closed eyes, she tried to envision her Creator, or whomever she was trying to hook up with. All she saw were colors—yellows, blues, reds, purples. At first she thought the Divine One was ready to establish communication. But instead only darkness replaced the colors. She thought she must be experiencing a *dark night of her soul*, a phrase that had been filed away when she read about saints of long ago on Google.

Miss Mildred entered her thoughts, reminding her to be sure to check on her soon. Yes, she was running away again, but she was going to succeed this time. Sophia-Emma also wanted to know if her health was continuing to improve.

No one answered Miss Mildred's phone. She assumed that Providence must have kept her another day for observation. Or maybe she didn't have access to her phone yet. A small aggravating suspicion haunted her. Maybe she wasn't healed. Did she herself believe? Maybe Sophia-Emma would never have a chance to say good-bye. Guilt overwhelmed her.

Instead of calling her mama, she texted her. "Mama, will u ck 2 see how M Mildred doing?" Click, it sent. She sent another "Love U & Chris xxx."

She dug an old receipt from her bag and wrote her daddy a short note telling him she was seeking enlightenment, and she loved him, too. Searching for a clean piece of paper, she fashioned a make-shift envelope, using a sticky cough drop as glue to put the old wadded-up receipt in. She added a stamp and tucked it back into her purse, hoping she would find a mailbox somewhere in Selma.

She smugly nodded to those around her and noticed the sad faces glued to their phones. Her mama texted back. "Get home. Mildred relapsed."

"Damn," she hollered. Too many faces looked up from their phones over to her. She tried to apologize by saying, "I'm good. If you smell anything, it's my fart. It came on me so fast. Sorry."

A small boy sitting across from her looked at his mother and laughed. "She farted. See, it's okay."

The riders laughed, too. Sophia-Emma shrugged her shoulders and smiled.

Looking outside, she saw a half moon, maybe her protector. She decided to take a nap, but couldn't take her mind off her mama's last text. Both she and Miss Mildred needed her. What to do now? Her heart told her to take the next bus back. Her guts told her to keep going. She couldn't back out now. She'd done all she could do, hadn't she?

So she made another attempt to nap, but now the smell of old vomit on her seat sickened her. As if some music would distract from the putrid odor, she put earbuds in her ears, closed her eyes and prayed for Miss Mildred. She texted her mama one more time. "Sorry. Going anyway. B back soon . . . hope."

Now she was missing her comfy bed, but she finally did slip into sleep, deep enough to envision her journey tomorrow morning along the Alabama River where it intersected with the Cahaba. Something told her to be aware of sink-holes. Her mama and she had never discussed Alabama's geography to that degree. Sophia-Emma couldn't understand where that thought came from. She decided it was just part of this crazy person she seemed to be turning into.

After an uneventful eight-hour quiet ride and numerous stops, Sophia-Emma was dumped off in Selma. The sky there was still dark with dainty glittering stars dappling an unending expanse.

Watching the other riders walk past her made her wonder what mission each intended to accomplish in their own lives. The young white woman, the one whom she saw crying, was she planning a funeral today for a loved one? Or the mother with a child, still half-asleep, was she coming back home after her partner gave her the black eye? Then there was the muscle-bound dude, was he here to settle a score with another just like him? Did he have a gun packed away in the baggage compartment? She realized that she was on a *first world* mission here. Her continued survival didn't depend on whether she found mere survival here. But since she was drawing near to her destination now, she certainly needed to carry on and find some answers to her countless questions.

The bus café was closed. Outside she looked up and down the street. No flickering *Open* signs signaled a hot cup of coffee to help her wake up. She lingered at the only place that would have her, on the curb outside the bus station.

Sophia-Emma tried to meditate again. Would she meet up with her Creator today? Would she find out who she really was? She didn't know how to converse with a God? Would this reunion with the Divine tell her what had truly happened in the past that had brought her to this place?

Thank heavens it was still officially summer. Soon daylight would be here. The stars were dimming. Looking east she thought she saw the horizon lightening. A bird or two started their mating baiting. Sophia-Emma wanted a coffee even more.

But still no human anywhere. Selma, the city with the famous Edmund Pettus Bridge that had attracted so many aggrieved people and their enemies more than fifty-five years ago, now asleep in their beds or graves. People black and white, immigrants, some still asleep, others making morning love, or dressing for work at the hospital or convenience store, would soon be filling the streets of Selma.

A light started to flicker down Broad Street towards Arsenal Place and Water Avenue, which Sophia-Emma intended to follow along the great Alabama River, the river of her people, calling today.

Chapter 27

Sophia-Emma opened the worn screen door leading into the Rebel Café, where a small world of morning people were either winding up or down. A few old white men sat in the last booth near the kitchen sipping coffee and talking politics. A cop was scrolling down on his phone, and some young white boys—older than her—were at the big front table by the window sharing bragging rights of their recent conquests. Sophia-Emma was apprehensive to sit in a spot so near them. She felt like the new virgin in town, aware that she was now a bleached blonde with a short skirt on. Did she seem to be someone looking for trouble? She inconspicuously moved to a booth next to the women's restroom.

"Can I have a cup of black coffee?" she asked the sleepy guy behind the wrap-around counter. "And maybe whole wheat toast and jelly?"

The waiter was short and seemed to be from Central America.

"That's all you want, mi hermanas?"

"Yelp, that's it."

She sensed that everyone's eyes were on her. Were they wondering why a woman—okay, girl—would be here at this time of the morning? The naive traveler felt like her clothes were being stripped from her body. Were those young men not far from her plotting about how they could enjoy some *personal* time with this cheap blonde ho? She knew that many like those goof-balls thought black and brown women were disposable like a hamburger wrapper, especially in the rural south. The night wasn't over yet. Did they think this lone teen might be available for a few extra bucks so she could buy some milk for a bastard kid, or a fix so she could sleep off a wild night?

She was determined to stay and eat there even though eyes seemed to be peering through her blouse. But surely it was safer in this booth than it would be outside where the sun was taking its time to deaden the desire inside men's pants.

Sophia took a gulp of coffee. Just like at home, chicory was part of the blend. But this was about the worst cup she'd ever tasted. She wondered if it had been warmed up from yesterday. After spreading the grape jelly on her toast and chewing each quarter slice slowly, she moved to the other side of the booth so she could stare at an old-timey picture of Selma when cotton was king, and black men were used for loading cotton onto steam boats, probably heading to the Bay for later shipping overseas or upstream to a textile mill in the North to be made into clothing for maid and mistress.

"Oh, pretty girl, show us your face again," one of the young men hollered her way. Laughter erupted from their corner.

The cop put some bills on the counter and was walking out. "Now you boys, don't give that little girl a hard time, ya hear? We all have to make a living somehow."

Sophia-Emma too put some money on her table and walked out of the restaurant behind the policeman. "Oh, sir," she yelled. He turned around with a fake smile.

"Yes, miss. What can I do for you today?"

"I've just arrived in town to study bald eagles over on the Cahaba. What's the best way to get there?"

"Simple. Take the Interstate south and get off at the National Wildlife Refuge. Follow the signs. Guess you're up so early 'cuz most bird action happens in the early mornin', huh?" He talked while chewing on his dangling toothpick. "I sure didn't know you colored folk liked birding, too. Now, you're not going to be doing any hunting, air you?"

Sophia-Emma played along. "Oh, sir, no way, sir. I been studyin' birds at school. I want to be one of those professors who give classes on birds to little chil'ren someday. Selma folk here, especially the white folk, don't seem to tolerate me much, and the black folk, they say I over my raisin', so I go out and talk to the birds. Listen real hard. I think I hear a meadowlark, ya hear it?" She cocked her head sideways and looked up into the trees over along the river, not far away.

"Well, be careful, young lady," the cop said as he walked over to his cruiser. Then he was off on his way. But the young white dudes were still looking her way.

Sophia-Emma took off walking, quickly reaching Arsenal Place. She turned right. The sun was promising to give her a hot day as she focused on a sense of serenity and expectation before reaching an intersection at Mabry St.

Suddenly she was aware of a car not far behind her. Was it following her? To play it safe, she looked for another open business to rush into. No such luck. The driver was just wanting to give her a hard time, she told herself. So she kept walking as though life was fine for a morning stroll.

Soon she realized that her morning stroll was in a danger zone. A vehicle loaded with young men pulled ahead of her and stopped in this deserted part of town. Four ran over towards her. One—the shouting one—was staggering and fell to the ground. Probably still drunk from partying last night. The others laughed and called him homo.

Now Sophia-Emma was running as fast as she could. To her horror, Water Avenue ended abruptly. Should she go right, up Church Street or continue to head straight along a worn path along the river? The town was still asleep. She rushed straight into a dense growth of trees and briars along the river, her river. She told herself that her river would protect her. She saw a slight slope that ended at the river. More trees, big ones. They would protect her, hide her. She slipped in the dew-covered weeds and stumbled over roots and fallen branches. Repeatedly she got back up quickly. Blackberry, mock-rose bushes, all were grabbing, capturing her, tearing her skirt, serving her up to the boys—the so-called men—at her heels.

The fastest, the one with the biggest most vile mouth, was the first to tackle her. For a split second she thought he'd release her from the thorns of all those bushes that had clung to her as though she were a trespasser or bloody food.

The man—the one who harassed her in the café—was now pulling the scared teen feet first from the bushes and pushing her down to the ground out of the thorns. He became a wild dangerous creature on top of her body. Sophia-Emma cried, screamed and smelled sweat mixing with dead fish, oil, and raspberry jam. He was ripping her blouse, pushing up her bra to expose her breasts and pushing up her short skirt. Always assuming that she was strong, she attempted to wrestle him away. She squirmed her body in every direction it could move. Then she resorted to biting, spitting, pinching, and pulling hair. No matter what she tried, just like with the ants, she couldn't get away from this terror. So she scratched and kicked. She tried to choke the burden on top of her. Lastly, she turned her head sideways toward the ground beneath her and cried bitterly. He was a prowling growling animal who pushed her face further into the dirt. He didn't want to see her pleading angry eyes. Her cries were heavy metal music to his ears. As though he hadn't already beaten her enough, he slapped her across the face over and over just as he was about to come.

Then she grew silent. In her half-conscious state, the scene replayed over and over and . . . she was helpless. It's as though she'd slipped into hell and Satan was fucking her. He was changing disguises, from wolf to bear to lion to bull, slobbering bile all over her, smearing semen on her thighs, on her lips, treating her flesh like dung, pants zipping down and up and down, laughing like wicked conquistadors, overseers, criminals. Sophia-Emma begged to be shot, stabbed, lynched . . . anything to be done with this cruelty. No, they wouldn't do that. Instead, they zipped up their pants, tucked in their shirts, combed their hair. They exchanged hoots and hollers, slaps on the backs. One spit in her face and cursed her for talking to the cop before catching up with the other three running back to the car. "Black Lives Scatter," he yelled just before a car door slammed shut.

Sophia-Emma knew they were gone when she heard the souped up muffler powering them away. But one remained. In a few minutes he was lifting her up, brushing off dirt and dead weeds. She opened one eye; the other hurt too much. The damaged girl wanted to get away, but her body could hardly move.

Just moments ago she'd been a virgin. She was clean, proud of who she was. Now she hated those crackers. But worse, she hated herself.

All she could do was nothing–just lie there–bloody, bruised and too weak to react. She felt like a dentist had taken his drill from a pile of shit and turned it up full power inside her vagina. And not just there, but all over her body. Her head was like a sticky balloon that was about to pop. She tasted blood dripping from her head into her mouth, joining the blood and semen already there. Sophia-Emma felt as though her entire body was swollen and ruined. Harriet's blouse was in shreds and everything else was painted with drying blood. Black and blue bruises from the gang rape, with red rivers of scratches flowing over them, made her look like a horror movie character. She passed out again, where the dirt, the blood, the hurt and hatred, the abuse all become silent. In such a state, she damned this river. It was supposed to protect her. It had failed miserably.

Chapter 28

When Sophia-Emma regained consciousness, the remaining young man who'd staggered by the car was standing above her, She shuttered uncontrollably, attempting to protect herself by crossing her arms over her face. Then she began to crawl away through the thorn bushes, trying to get as far away as she could from any male. She assumed, because her vision was still blurry, that he too was an animal, exhibiting a wild look of violence that she swore she'd never forget from the other four.

But this one's speech was soothing. She blinked and started to cry, a cry of hopeful relief. Like a newborn baby, she stared into his eyes. She rubbed hers, trying to focus through the blood and tears.

"Now lie still. The bullies are far gone," the young man whispered.

Was he an angel put here by her Creator? Had she now been baptized in blood or desire or the fire of lust? Had she now found the limit she could withstand before the mercy of death?

This seemingly kind man by her side was short and lean. Yet he had blood vessels bulging under his skin like blue river canals beneath layers of silt. His skin had a reddish rough tone. He didn't seem to be a sunburnt white man, more like an indigenous man. A pail of water rested on the ground between him and Sophia-Emma. Near the pail he had a small collection of various leaves and roots. He saturated them in the water that was left after washing her body.

“Remain calm,” he repeated. “I’m not here to hurt you, but to heal. You’ve been badly assaulted by men who don’t know yet about the sacredness of woman.”

Sophia-Emma managed to speak. “But you with ’em. If you so sure of my sacredness, why didn’t you stop ’em?”

“I tried,” the little man said. “They knocked me out. I came to as they were running back to the car. My neighbor, who usually gives me a ride into town where I work, kicked me away from the car and left me on the roadside ditch as the rest of the bruts spurred away. I wanted to stop them, but I fainted.”

“Go on to work,” Sophia-Emma said. “Thank you for cleaning me and doctoring me up. Can you reach into my bag and get my water bottle?”

“I’m sorry, Miss, but they done took your bag with ’em, it seems.”

That is when she swore, saying “God-damn them, those bastards. Those fucking filthy motherfuckers.”

The reddish man stared at her, thinking perhaps that she’d go after him now to get even with the other guys.

“I know where my neighbor hangs out during the day. He goes to Bryson’s place to play video games. I go by there and try to find your bag.”

“Thanks, but by now, I’m sure they’ve spent what little money I had, and they’ve probably smashed my phone, so I just as well let it go. My biggest disappointment is that I had a stamped letter to send to my daddy in prison. They’ll laugh when they read it. Those sons-of-bitches.” She tried to set up, but was too weak. “Holy maloney, my body is so weak. Just leave and let me die. Go, now.”

“Miss, you must get another top to cover your bosom. I will buy you one downtown. I’m fast. Just stay. You will not die.”

He leaned over her and his hands pushed Sophia-Emma’s shoulders down till they touched the bare ground. “Rest,” he commanded. “The herbs I’ve put on your body will clean and refresh you. But you mustn’t move till I return.”

Her desire was to get away from this spot as quickly as possible, so she resisted. “I can’t lie here. What if they come back to rape me again? I’ll kill myself before they attack me a second time. Do you carry a knife? Please leave it with me. Then at least I can pretend to be strong.”

“No, no knife. Don’t have one, and if I did, I wouldn’t give it to you. I’ll hide you. Let me scatter stems and scrubby bushes to conceal you. You be safe while I’m gone.”

His assertiveness gave her the courage to do as he said. Within twenty minutes Sophia-Emma had been tucked away from traffic driving by. She could see through the limbs and grass everything passing by. The man told her, however, that no one could see inside the hide-out he’d constructed.

Sophia-Emma threw up. Now vomit had mixed with dried semen and blood. The smell sickened her more.

Nevertheless, her body slowly gained some strength. Her brain was coming out of shock, trying to calm fear and hunger for revenge. She could detect a part of herself pitying and praying for the rapists. She sassed back to her *enlightened soul,* telling it to go to hell. Then she fell asleep again.

The red man shook her shoulders until she awoke again. He’d brought her a colorful, beautifully embroidered puffy white blouse that made me look like a Mexican folk dancer.

“Would you like to go to hospital and police station about this now?” he asked.

“I’m thinking about it,” she said. “But for now, I want to know what to call you and then I’ll tell you who I am. Agreed?”

“My name among Anglos is Steward,” he said. “But my Indian name is Chitto. It means Brave.”

“Perfect,” Sophia-Emma said. “My name is Sophia-Emma Foster-Jones. Sophia was a legendary goddess of wisdom.”

“I like that,” Chitto responds. “But I now think you must report this crime and be tested at the hospital.”

"Not now. Maybe later. Look at my color. Look at the color of the men who raped me. Look at the color of the witness, you. Do you think we'd be believed over some of their favorite sons? I don't."

Chitto pondered what the girl had said. He seemed to agree.

"Say, I have some important things to do today. Looks like you missed work, as well. Can you go exploring with me today?"

Chitto looked at Sophia-Emma for a while, pondering once more. "Miss Sophia-Emma, I will go with you. One of my nation's traditions is to accompany the stranger on his or her journey. May what I lose by guiding you on this road be less than what I gain."

She extended her arm up to Chitto, who was still standing. He pulled her to her feet and helped steady her for a few minutes and then told her another fact about himself.

"Do not worry while I am with you. I am homosexual. I don't react to women the way the men who harmed you did. But I can guard you better than any straight man."

"Thank you, Chitto," she said as she brushed off parts of the ground that were still on her. Then she washed off her vomit and the remaining blood from her body.

Standing on her own now, she said: "Now let me tell you about myself and why I came here from Mobile. For the next hour or so, they moved on. He walked and she hobbled, slowly at first, southwest along the Alabama River. No longer did she have a romantic attachment to the river of her birth. It had turned on her like Judas. It was no more a trusting guide, source of her embryonic fluid. It was only another dirty mean river regurgitating anything that got in its way.

Thankfully the couple walked under scattered billowing white clouds. Sophia-Emma carried nothing. She was now stripped down to only the few duds Chitto had found to put over her bare bloody and bruised body. Chitto had a Quaker Oats granola bar, which he ate about seven miles into their jaunt. Sophia-Emma told him she was on a fast until she got some guidance.

They stopped at camp grounds here and there, and found some empty bottles that they washed with crushed yarrow leaves the best they could.

Chitto became hungry at about mid-day, so he dived into some dumpsters in a couple convenience stores along the way. Sophia-Emma refused to take a bite of the apples, the cupcakes, even the jerkies.

"I want to be empty until my Creator fills me with wisdom about my mission. I also want answers on why I was abandoned back in Selma, why I was made into dirt and humiliation."

"Among my people," Chitto shared, "both of us, the girls and boys, we look for guidance in our dreams, usually when we're moving from childhood into young adult. We sorta adopt that special animal or element that appears in our dream as an item that is part of us or guides us in our decisions."

"So what special item is yours?" Sophia-Emma asked.

"An eagle appeared in my dream, so I'm modeling my life after the eagle," he replied.

Sophia-Emma gasped. "The eagle is also my guiding force. Remember how I told you that the eagle has always soared over me at critical times in my life?"

"Maybe we sister and brother at heart," he joked.

The pair relaxed in their walk, paying attention to smelling and hearing nature along the way. They let seep into them visions of hardwoods, toxic factories, warblers serenading their path, At times they had to avoid walking along the river because of thick underbrush. Sophia-Emma had already suffered too much for one day in a bed of briars. Her body, nevertheless, empowered her to move away, to not expose herself to more thorns opening old wounds, both physical and emotional. So Chitto and Sophia-Emma picked up their walk onto Dallas County roads. What she'd give for a shower to completely wash her vomit and pain and memories away.

She began to fall into the old questions she'd always asked her parents. "How long till we get there?" she asked Chitto.

"Probably about three miles," he estimated. "You know, walking alongside the river, especially the Alabama, makes for lots of extra steps. This river meanders about as much as any river I ever saw. But even it eventually wanders down to the Bay, losing its name when it marries up with the Tonnbigbee, and then downstream it becomes the Mobile River and, lastly, part of the Bay itself looking out into the Gulf."

She thanked him for his review of the Alabama river system and trudged on, hoping to get to the confluence of the smaller Cahaba by midday. As the journey moved on, the physical trauma of her rape was slowing and depressing her even more.

"I wish I had an Ibuprofen 'bout now," she complained. "Walking all this way for a girl used to buses and not used to gang rape is making me mighty sore and raw. I don't know if I can make it much further. Next place we see some people, can we stop to see how we can get some pain medication?" she asked.

"You've evidently caught an infection from those conquistadors earlier," Chitto commented. "You need some antibiotics. You rest here, and I'll go on a search for something to help you. Don't move. Stay put."

"Okay, I'll sit down here," Sophia-Emma pointed to a tree stump with some gurgling water near it. She assumed the water was coming from a spring. Taking off her shoes and feeling a refreshing sensation as her feet soaked up the water beneath them, she had an urge to sit in the pool of water, clothes and all. Oh, how whole and cool it felt. Her body responded with delight, like she was in heaven.

As soon as that thought filled her head, Sophia-Emma began to sink further into the hole. It was swallowing her, it seemed. She noticed she'd sunk now up to her chest. This wasn't right. She wondered fearfully if the earth was swallowing her into its bowels. She attempted to climb up and out of the hole before she drowned. But her energy was gone. To even lift a foot or an arm exhausted her more than she could have ever imagined. Suddenly something told her to not struggle, but to let go.

There she was almost submerged in this cooling pool. Her mind reviewed her day, arriving in Selma, making up stories of the struggles other bus riders were facing in their lives. Now she realized that what had been ahead for her ended up being more horrifying than any of the scenarios she'd imagined for them. The only good thing about the day was hooking up with Chitto after the horrifying rape. But now, here she was dying alone, sliding further and further into this soothing cool liquid. Ironically her tiredness allowed her to relax and enjoy parting from life as she knew it.

After letting go, she found herself in a water-filled cathedral constructed in another world of materials she'd never seen before except in dreams or in star-studded skies on moonless nights. She didn't miss oxygen and carbon dioxide exchange that normally filled her lungs. Whew, she wasn't dying or in hell after all. This was too beautiful. If it maybe was hell, it certainly wasn't like the place she'd expected—one of consuming fires. Not so here. She saw no one, but, if she let go enough, she could feel some familiarity with the ambiance around her. Verbal communication turned into what she called spirit talk. She now sensed her partners speaking. When she quit thinking and wondering and analyzing, a new voice welcomed her into this underwater paradise.

One entity said, "Do you remember now? We agreed with you Spirit Lady, that man had made earth a patriarchy. Women, however, were beginning to seek their own power, but they were finding it difficult to be in equal relationship with the male-based way of looking at life."

A second voice took over. "And remember, you offered to become a woman child on earth. You insisted for human centuries that humans needed a feminine aspect of God. We saw what they'd done to myself—killing me in a most hateful manner. We feared if you incarnated as a woman you would—what do humans say? Have two strikes against you before even starting your mission."

The first voice spoke again. "Finally, just to shut you up, the two of us agreed with you that you should go down to earth, with one rule.

You'd have to experience human-ness while not aware that you were a person of God. Of course, we couldn't remove all your Godly attributes—thus communicating with your eyes and the partial healing of your holy woman."

"Stopping the hurricane was a splendid idea," the other voice added as an after-thought.

Sophia-Emma agreed with the remark about Abram. But she was more concerned about Miss Mildred. "I need to get back to her," she pleaded as the Spirit she was. "We need to heal that woman, Let me do it, please."

"Are you ready now to take on all your Godly duties on earth? If you think these past years have been confusing and trying, wait till see what humans have in store for you in the coming decades."

The other partner finished the conversation. "This is our official meeting with you to confirm that, yes, you are our feminine side, a true goddess. You do have a mission—to speak and act in a Godly manner, stressing peaceful cohabitation, nurturing, cooperation, harmony, and creativity. Men will rebel. Women at first will doubt you, be jealous or you and then become too dependent on you. But you'll empower them, be their advocate, help them to love the internal strength we mold within their hearts."

"Now go ask your first disciple, Chitto, to baptize you with this holy water surrounding you," the voices commanded in unison.

With that, Sophia-Emma gained her buoyancy once more. Chitto was peering down the hole, about to dive in after her when they almost bumped heads as Sophia-Emma returned to life with humans again.

Sophia-Emma saw tears in his eyes. She kissed those tears now, knowing in her soul her mission. At last. The two sat down on the log, holding hands. Sophia-Emma started the conversation.

"You won't believe me, but I visited my homies down that hole, a little like Alice in Wonderland, you might say. Now I know my mission—to be the feminine side of God as the Spirit Goddess. Will you baptise me with these holy waters that also healed me from my physical injuries from this morning and my fever?" She brushed her long dark hair from her face and exclaimed, "Even my hair has returned to its own length and color."

She could tell Chitto thought there was some alcohol in the sinkhole she'd just emerged from.

"Down that hole I was reminded by my partners, the Father and the Son, that because of my constant bickering, the three of us—some call us the Trinity—decided that I, the Holy Spirit, would come down to earth and infuse it with what that great psychiatrist Carl Jung called *anima*, feminine attributes."

Chitto could see that this girl with him was eager to explain her adventure more.

"You see, somewhere along the line, humans got the idea that men and women would have different ways of expressing themselves in society. The males had an internal feminine side, called *anima*. Conversely, the female had an inner masculine side, called the *animus*. Culture and tradition assigned certain strengths to men and women, however. Throughout most of human history, men were expected to be masculine only, and women to be feminine only. Now, with God's help, both are now invited to use both their feminine and masculine sides as they go through this journey called life.

"Since the beginning of the Judea-Christian-Islam eras, masculine energy and male-like gods have made rules about what was thought to be important on earth. We made God in man's image, for example. Some other civilizations didn't make their god in the image of man, and the three of us give them good marks. But those making their god into the image of woman have also run into problems. Too much into pretty things and not enough in small engine repairs. Now I begin my mission with my baptism."

"I be honored to baptize you," Chitto said. "But I will add some Muskogian words my grandfather taught me before he died a few years back."

The Spirit Goddess told him that she'd feel honored to be baptized by him as well, no matter what words he used.

"I know some words from the Creek Days of Purification. I'm prepared to say a couple lines from that," Chitto offered.

"Then we'll go with that," she said. "How about you use my requested motions, and say your words of purification?"

Chitto agreed and the two in unison prepared. Sophia-Emma knelt and submerged her entire head in the holy water. As she lifted her head and the water created streams all the way down to her toes, Chitto repeated the words of purification. Even though Sophia-Emma was part of the Godhead, she'd never been good at languages. All she knew was that his words warmed her heart and tingled her nerves.

A shadow dimmed the sun overhead. Both Chitto and the Spirit Goddess looked up and saw an eagle circling directly over them. It called out the song of its species, but both Chitto and Sophia-Emma also heard other familiar words. "This is my beloved daughter, of whom I take pleasure."

With those words, Sophia-Emma postrated herself on the grass around the small sink-hole and communed with the Father and the Son. For a few moments she was lost in ecstasy. But Chitto knew hardly anything about her mission, other than the *animus* and *animae* jargon. Nevertheless, her Father had told her less than an hour ago that Chitto would be her first disciple. She assumed that meant Chitto would be that person.

"Chitto?" she asked him, "Does all this seem odd to you?"

He shrugged his shoulders, like this was something he witnessed everyday.

"My spiritual Father told me a few minutes ago that you would be my most beloved disciple. I naturally thought you would be happy with that. But I won't force you. Do you remember the stories of Jesus?"

He shook his head in the affirmative. "And you remember that Jesus had twelve disciples?"

Another similar nod.

"Will you be that with me? As you know, I have no money. Maybe we'll have to be homeless, eat from dumpsters. I have a feeling that lots of people won't like us, may call us names or eventually kill us. But take it on faith, Chitto—and I know I've been around for an eternity—earth isn't even in the same league as to where we go after we die. It's like you're in a cocoon now. And butterflies emerge from cocoons. Humans can experience their own metamorphosis."

Already Sophia-Emma saw a disappointment coming on. Chitto didn't look impressed.

"Chitto, how old are you?" she asked, not willing to give up on him so soon.

"Nineteen," he said. "I am glad with you about your mission, but I'm not so sure I'm ready to piss everyone off just yet. And look at me, I'm not a God like you. I'm officially still a teenager. Someday I want to have a lover, have sex, see my cousins in Oklahoma. I bet if I work for you, I won't even get personal days off, will I? I think I need a less complicated job for now."

"If that's the way you want it, fine with me." Sophia-Emma quipped, knowing that others would say yes later. "Let's say I give you a few days to think about it. Besides, you need to teach me about the plants around here that heal, the dumpster-diving, how to get back in touch with the indigenous people whose blood still flows in my veins. I have so much to learn from you and your people."

"Okay, I stay with you while you're in this area, but I can't make any promises beyond that."

"Fine with me. Let's get on with why we're here, huh? But first things first. I need to pee. Can we also do something to mark this place? This is my baptismal ground where I went to the holy underworld and spoke with the Father and Son who revealed my mission. Now if he would only show me a plant to wipe my butt," Looking at Chitto, she saw that her joke-making ability hadn't improved post-baptism.

Chitto handed her a couple leaves from a lamb's ear plant growing wild along the road. Another proof, Sophia-Emma realized, that the Father's wondrous works of creation were amazing.

As she wiped, she noticed some blood on the leaf. Again she was reminded, both physically and emotionally, of the early morning's awful and humiliating gang rape. She wanted to lash out, kick each cracker's balls. Instead, she knew she'd be called to turn the other cheek.

"Even these you must invite to be your disciples," the Son whispered in her ear.

"With buddies like you, Jesus, I can see why you have so few other friends," Sophia-Emma balked. "And hey, no way do I want to even see those faces again, even if I were allowed to slap them."

"I'll deal with them," he told her in their own spirit language. "I've got it."

By the time she got closer to where Chitto was piling rocks on rocks, designating her baptismal ground as sacred, she ran over to him and knelt before him. "You're my substance, dear Chitto." She kissed each of his dusty fingers. "I'll always honor your generosity and protection you gave me today."

He looked at her like she was crazy, and maybe she was nuts about this mission, especially if her rapists would work with her on her mission one day. For now, she didn't want to think about it.

"So where to now?" Chitto asked.

"I hope you can accompany me to Promised Land, an old plantation belonging to my grandma Louise Foster. My mother grew up in the Big House on Promised Land. But before I visit my grandma, I need to go to the old slave cemetery over by the Alabama River. I've visited there before with Tillie and my mother, unbeknownst to Grandma. Tillie is the lady who had taken care of her. It's at the horseshoe bend area where the Cahaba meets the Alabama River. This will be treacherous in a way because Grandma has never claimed me. She won't be violent, but she may be obnoxious as only she knows how. But first, let's visit little Sofie. We've communicated since we were babies."

As they walked closer to the old cemetery, Sophia-Emma's stomach did flips.

"Do you hear the wailing?" she asked Chitto.

They stopped walking and made a point to blot out birds singing and rivers rolling by. In the old cemetery, they heard what sounded like the wind rushing through a cracked window pane. They picked up their pace. What both saw wasn't good. Mixed in with the wailing sounds coming from the graves of oppressed black and red bodies were noises from construction equipment. Bones separated from skeletal bodies laid in a pile over by the fenceline. Even Chitto plugged his ears. Sophia-Emma reckoned her grandma was hearing chaos, as well.

She found Sofie's grave, just as she remembered it a couple years ago. Both spoke in whispers. She was fearful of the stranger with Sophia-Emma, and asked her old friend who this man was. Sophia-Emma assured her that Chitto was a new friend who believed in the Great Spirit like they did. She assured her that she would protect her grave here for as long as she walked the earth. Maybe even one day in death, she would find space beside her. They kissed through the earth.

In tears, she ran to Chitto, who also had tears of his own flowing down his face. In reverence and silence, the two walked hand-in-hand to the plantation house. Tillie was out in her garden. She hobbled over to, dropped her cane, and after realizing who was visiting, kissed Sophia-Emma while laughing from her gut.

"You know, I had to look at you three times," said the old woman after her laughing finally subsided. "It's been so long, and how beautiful you've become! Is this young man here your new beau?"

"No Tillie, just a good looker I picked up in Selma. Chitto, this is Tillie. And Tillie, meet my new friend Chitto. We decided to walk along the river to get here. Nice walk. Sure could get down on my knees for a tall iced tea," Sophia-Emma begged as they walked up the wrap-around porch steps.

"I think I can manage that, sweetheart," Tillie said. "I also got some great chocolate chip cookies, too, if you two not afraid of expanding your waistline too much." She laughed at her joke. "Sit a spell. You must be tired after that long walk on this hot day." Tillie practically pushed both visitors onto two tall dove-white rocking chairs.

Chitto did a three-sixty degree scan of the house, garden, and out-buildings. "Do people still live like this in Alabama?" he asked.

Sophia-Emma nodded. "Can't give you a rundown on how many plantations have continued to operate all these hundreds of years, but Promised Land is probably nearly the oldest. My mama is the only blood descendant. But she and Grandma had a fight after my mama found me out in the pasture when I was a newborn. They never made up. Mama and Tillie tell me Grandma's going to will this historic place to a church in town to use as a conference center when she dies. I think that'll be soon. Gosh, the old woman must be near eighty now. Would love to bring her some healing today."

When Tillie came out to the porch, tea and cookies on a tray, she saw the two young people quietly praying. Being a good spiritual person herself, she sat down and joined them.

"What we praying for, my chile?"

"Grandma," Sophia-Emma answered. "Don't you think she's been miserable for long enough? I know Mama would love an opportunity to walk in on her, share a bottle of wine, and tease her again like she did before I come along. I feel it my fault for their riff. If I know I would split up a mama and her daughter by being put in the back pasture that fall day, I mighta told the Father to give me to the Lunds down the road."

Tillie looked at her like she must've run into a tree branch on the way there. "What you talkin' 'bout, little girl? Your Father? Did you find your daddy? We still ain't found your real mama either. I think you got none."

“Tillie, I’m kind of new talkin’ ’bout what I goin’ tell you, But Chitto here, he know what happened today on our journey. You see, things at home in Africatown have gone crazy. And I always had some special talents, you know, like talking with my eyes, you and me. So I thinks if I get up here in these parts near the river, the old slave graves, and commune with my birthin’ critters that brought me here, maybe I might get a handle on what God expects of me. I needed some directions, you know.”

Tillie was back to talking with her eyes again.”

“Just wait,” Sophia-Emma told her. ”You understand in a minute. So where was I? Yeah, that’s it. Down the road, a little before we got to the Cahaba, I slipped into a deep hole of mystical waters. I think I drownin’, but I ain’t. I didn’t need to breathe like a human—sorta like a mermaid—I spoke with God the Father and Jesus. They reminded me that I be the Holy Spirit. I be incarnated as a woman to show humans the importance of feminine energy on Earth. Anyway, before our reunion today I had forgotten that I was pushing for this not too long after Jesus’d come back to join us in the heavenly realm, like two thousand-more years ago.”

Tillie was now convinced Sophia-Emma was out of her mind.

“Have you found some moonshine in these here woods, or that ol’ marijuana? Take a long sip of that tea and rest awhile. I no dummy and you no Holy Spirit. Not even a dove or a pigeon, for that matter.”

“Yes, ’fraid I am,” Sophia-Emma insisted. “I ’member it all so well now, being as one with my partners, the Father, and Jesus. But after creation—that long ago—I saw that women, though they were created to improve on the Creator’s first try—Adam—they became the disempowered energy when it came to equality of the sexes. And things not gotten any better. So now I know my mission here to help men and women discover their long abandoned powers by using their feminine energy.”

“You crazy, chile, I still say so.” Tillie slapped her hand on her knee, now laughing her head off.

Chitto spoke up in his new friend's defense. "But, Miss Tillie, I was there when she came back from the deep water. Before then she had a high fever and I'd gone to find help for her. I found nothing, and was going to use some Creek medicine and chants, but the fever and other injuries, they gone when she emerged from the water. I then baptized here as her God had instructed."

Sophia-Emma hoped Tillie hadn't picked up on the word *injuries* Chitto had just uttered. She didn't give her time to think.

"And get this, Tillie," Sophia-Emma interjected, "as the water ran down my body, that eagle, maybe the one who showed me to Mama on my first day of life, he hovered over us, and said . . . guess what?"

"I s'pose something like 'This is my son . . .'"

She interrupted, "No. 'This is my daughter, of whom I find pleasure.' Ain't I right, Chitto?"

"That is how I remember what we saw—and heard."

"So, Tillie, even with a witness sitting here with us, you still think I crazy?"

Tillie didn't answer. She wouldn't look at her visitors either. Sophia-Emma wondered if she was afraid of them.

"Can I visit with Grandma today?" she asked.

"Oh, chile, I don't think she be ready for that story you just tell me."

"She as ready as she ever be," Sophia-Emma countered. "Why, she ain't seen me since I just a few days old. I think it 'bout time she come face-to-face with the God she loves. I promise, I be gentle. I not come to berate her, but to redeem her from all her bitterness, to help her see a new light of wisdom in this world, to help her find her True Self. You see, she been living a life that a sick society forced on her, a philosophy that only white-skinned people be worthy of God and privilege. It's time she see under this beautiful dark skin, and love all humankind like a mighty ocean wave, embracing the shore over and over, taking away impurities and hatred while it leaves love and peace."

"You know, she not been well lately, Miss Sophia-Emma. Maybe it's good for her to have one last chance to see her granddaughter. But I need to be in the room with you, and if I see her become agitated even a little, I'll kick you out faster than a steam engine heading downhill. I don't care if you're a god or a goose."

"Gotcha, Tillie," she assured her.

"Say friends," Chitto interrupted. "I don't think I'm up to this reunion among family folk. Miss Tillie, you mind if I wander around the place a little, maybe see if there are any remnants from my people over in the fields and by the river?"

Tillie invited him to wonder at his heart's delight, but she warned him that anything he found she wanted to see, since this wasn't really her land.

Sophia-Emma walked over to him and gave him a hug. Then she whispered, "This was your people's land first. Take whatever speaks to you."

As she followed Tillie up the winding stairway, trimmed with aged dark wood perfectly sculpted and collecting dust from decades of neglect, Sophia-Emma felt the stares from portraits of generations of privileged elites along her right side, she was in awe, wondering what other sights the people in the pictures had seen as they hung there through the years. She could also imagine her mama as a teen blurting out angry, cruel words to her mama, just like she'd done with her a few nights ago. No way for a Spirit Goddess to act, she told herself.

Tillie turned around before they approached her grandma's threshold and whispered, "Stay here a minute while I prepare her for you. And please talk like you a white woman. Just a suggestion, by the way."

"Okay," She begrudgingly whispered back.

"Miss Foster, Miss Foster, I have a special guest who's traveled a long way to see you."

She peered inside to see her grandma's reaction. She was so small and bony. Her head was nearly bald, but her blue eyes shone like Christmas tree lights. Tillie motioned for her to come in.

"Miss Foster, let me introduce you to Sophia-Emma Foster-Jones, your granddaughter."

Smiling, Sophia-Emma walked over to her bed, She reached down and gave the old lady a warm hug. She felt like an old rag doll whose stuffing had dried up. Louise Foster tried to pull away from the hug, but her granddaughter wouldn't let go. Finally she relaxed into the warm embrace and began to cry.

A sudden awareness of who she was hugging seemed to overpower the grandmother. She stiffened up again, saying in a gruff, but weak voice, "Tillie, get this little whore out of my private bedroom and my house. I don't know her and I don't want to see her again. Of all the nerve—all grown up, thinking you can fool me. Out!" She pointed to the door.

Sophia-Emma stayed and responded, "Grandma, yes, I've changed a lot since you first saw me. Just recently, God had changed my hair overnight to red. My mama, your daughter Amanda, said my red hair color was exactly the shade of red my great-grandmother had when she was a young woman. I saw her portrait on your wall. Mama was right."

Her grandma turned her head away from her and responded, "I'm not listening to you anymore. No mood to discuss hair. Tillie, bring me my medication."

But Sophia-Emma was in no mood to let her off the hook. "I'm sorry, Grandma. You haven't heard the best part of my story yet. I'd just healed my mentor in the ICU in Mobile. I was scared to death and ran away to Promised Land to see you and discover who I am. If you have faith along with my faith, and Miss Tillie's, I think you too can be healed."

Mrs. Foster looked over at Tillie, still standing in the doorway. "She's a charlatan. I knew Amanda was doomed when she picked up that Heinz 57 baby out in that dirty field. We should've let that old eagle take you home as ground meat for its babies that day. Now out, and never set foot in this house or on this land again. Tillie: Cigarette, please."

The old lady went about swallowing her pills and lighting up as though Sophia-Emma wasn't there, but Sophia-Emma knew she was wondering about her.

"Grandma, I'm staying here in your beautiful room as your handmaiden. I can heal you at this moment, if you want, or I can wait until you can't take this pain any longer. I know you're a woman who knows her scripture impeccably. As you know, many biblical women had their handmaidens, usually from other tribes and nations. If you don't want to accept me from your tribe, let me serve you as a handmaid from a foreign tribe. I promise I'll be here to wait on your every command. I'll comb your hair, polish your nails, massage your tired body. I've missed you so much. I've come to make amends for all the times my mother disrespected you. I'm not here for revenge, but for reconciliation. I've missed my grandma so much."

Out of nowhere, Louise started to laugh. Sophia-Emma could take that. She could see that her grandma was softening, even though the old woman herself hadn't realized it yet. She even continued to tell her visitor to leave, but her granddaughter ignored her commands. Instead she asked Tillie to bring up her favorite wine. After a few sips, she let Sophia-Emma style her hair. But she continued to order the visitor out of the room. Surprisingly, Sophia-Emma did leave for a few minutes. But during that time, she made a bowl of vegetable soup for her and sprayed some WD-40 on her wheelchair hub and spokes. She told Chitto, who had returned from his stroll around the plantation, that she was softening her grandmother up. If he wanted, he could head back to Selma. He declined, saying he had more exploring to do. She said she would be staying until this gruff injured woman found joy in her life again. On her way back upstairs with the food, Sophia-Emma decided she liked being a goddess. She didn't have to protect her ego anymore.

Not surprisingly, her grandma pushed the food away. But her granddaughter noticed that she'd finished off her wine.

"Haven't I told you to be gone?" she growled. "I heard you and your young man talking downstairs. I know what you're up to. You want to steal my precious items tonight. I can call in an armed guard to shoot you right now. You won't get one dime from me, you little whore."

A few days ago Sophia-Emma would've probably socked her in her toothless mouth if she'd said anything like that in Africatown. Today she didn't let it soak in. That woman in bed was a bereaved mother with no one caring about her any more. She had to pay Tillie to care for her, although there existed a loving connection between the two.

Sophia-Emma slowly inched her way closer until she was close enough to hold her hand. She brought the wheelchair over and said, "You must show me around the old place. Tell me stories about why you love every square inch of your home place."

Her grandma frowned and muttered a "hum-rump," as the teen helped her into her wheelchair and draped a blanket over her legs. First place they visited was the garden.

"Get me a couple of those snap beans," Her grandma ordered. "And over there at the well, I want a cool cup of water, what the farm hands would drink."

She complied.

"A wonderful garden," Sophia-Emma said. "Do you grow what we grow over in Africatown?"

"How would I know? I don't know what those people in that Africa town grow. Your mama always ate watermelon into October. Do you think that's why she was drawn to you, a little darkie?"

"No, I think she loves all skin tones,hair textures and nose sizes. She looks under all that and sees folk as folk, red blood rushing from heart to lungs to veins and . . ."

"Take me to the barn," Her grandma stopped her mid-sentence.

Sophia-Emma pulled open the big door with pulleys on it. They walked into the huge ancient building, smelling of straw, hay, and manure. The neighbor-help were milking a few cows and feeding their calves with bottles. Guernseys, her grandma told her, "make the best whipping cream and butter."

This was Sophia-Emma's first look at the Lunds, the so-called Melungeon neighbors "freeloading" off of Promised Land. For some reason, the visitor wanted to talk to one of the dark complexioned youth, possibly brother and sister. Perhaps later. Her heart went out especially to the girl. When her eyes met the girl's, they connected.

A couple horses blew their nostrils at them. Sophia-Emma wheeled her grandma as close as she could so her withered hand was able to pet the solid black mare.

"I want to show you the spring house, where we used to keep perishables before ice boxes and refrigerators were invented. And we also have a veggie cellar where we stored food for the winter, like apples, cabbage, squashes, and potatoes. We never grew hungry out here on this estate," she bragged.

Nearby were the pecan orchard, the round horse ring and jumping field, and the work house where Sophia-Emma learned even more about what made plantation life profitable. This was where before the Civil War slaves made pecan furniture and other crafted items that brought high prices in cities up north where they had no access to pecan.

No visit to Promised Land was complete without a visit to the family cemetery up on the highest point of the estate. As she huffed and puffed to push the old woman up the hill to the old oak tree and the burial sites of generations past, she saw a few decaying old shacks off in the distance and asked if they were chicken coops or pig pens.

"Oh no, that's where we housed our servants," Louise said.

"You mean the slaves?" Sophia-Emma asked.

"There you self-righteous folks go again," her grandma sounded perturbed. "They were like members of the family, present at childbirth, working in the Big House and the fields. They never went hungry. Some of the women even nursed our babies. Their young-uns played together with our little white children. Don't let anyone ever tell you this system didn't work. We worked together in harmony for hundreds of years, Sophia-Emma."

The Sophia-Emma of yesterday wanted to set her right about her last statement, but the fact that she'd called her by her real name, made her granddaughter happier than she was angry.

Once up at the cemetery, her grandma directed her to her husband's grave and then to her two boys' graves.

"Now there you have two of the bravest and most handsome boys you ever laid eyes on. The youngest died, after that Black president of yours poured more troops into Afghanistan. (Sophia-Emma knew that her uncle had been killed in war before Obama was president, but she didn't correct her.) You know, your mother was always a pretty girl, too, and just as smart. But she got in the wrong crowd. Ruined herself. Got you. I can't stand to think about it."

Even as a Spirit-Goddess, this was too much. "Grandma, I believe your daughter, your Amanda, who we call Loving, was especially chosen by our Creator to be the mother of one who can change the world by bringing women's voices into the market square and the family home. Your daughter saved my life and taught me skills she learned as your daughter. If you could see her today, you would be so proud. And listen to this."

She moved a few steps to be in front of her grandma, grasped both of her hands and met her eyes. "She now also has a son, your biological grandchild, blood of your blood. He's six-year-old Christopher. And he's also a handsome respectful boy who'd love to have you show him around this great expanse of land someday."

She could see tears welling up in her eyes. "A son, you say? A white son?"

"No, he's of African descent, son of Alan Jones. He's a brave man. I wish you could meet them both."

Her grandma remained quiet. Sophia-Emma kept pushing her to look at the other graves. The sun was about to set. Fireflies were blinking and sparkling. Tillie was ringing the bell out on the porch.

"Time to get back," the granddaughter said. "Or we can stay and hear your ancestors—family and *servants*—speak to us. You know, the spirits of Promised Land are speaking to us. I heard them today. They're worried that their grave sites are being destroyed over by the river from new construction."

"Oh no. I completely forgot about those old gravesites. Let's see what we can do about that tomorrow. The church is doing some building over there." She didn't seem to comprehend the disrespect her comment was confirming. "I'll call them first thing tomorrow and tell them not to disturb those graves."

"I spoke with one of those spirits—Sofie is her name—in that cemetery this afternoon. I know, you wonder who talks with the dead? Mama and I do. Her mother Cecilia is buried in Africatown now, where many slaves who had worked here before the war moved after they were freed."

"Now, young lady, you're getting a little too wacky for me." She clicked her tongue and shook her head as though there was no hope for her weird granddaughter.

"She's still up there in her grave," Sophia-Emma said, "and I don't think the graves there are that deep." She knew this because her daddy had already dug up Cecilia over there, and that was what he had told her. But she kept her mouth shut, knowing that her grandmother had already been exposed to more than she could handle in one day.

As they entered the house, they smelled fried chicken and heard Chitto playing Shupert on the baby grand. Grandma Louise and Chitto exchanged glances, even smiles.

"Keep playing," her grandma insisted. "I love to hear *Serenade*."

Tillie screamed from the kitchen. "Let's all eat in celebration of our wonderful guests."

Chitto frowned, but joined all of the family at the table. Besides fall-off-the-bone chicken, Tillie served fresh wilted-leaf lettuce salad from the garden with crispy bacon, along with a huge bowl of fresh green beans and potatoes and gravy. For dessert, she gifted her diners with apple pie topped off with the scrumptious whipped cream from the Guernseys out in the barn.

"Are these apples from the trees Mama always talked about?" Sophia-Emma asked. "She'd tell me how she'd sneak out to them when you and Grandma were busy. I wish she were here with us now. I can imagine that happy sneaky smile on her face."

Mrs. Foster moved her napkin up from her mouth to wipe her eyes, blotting the tears in her gentile way. Sophia could see Tillie had cut her dinner into tiny pieces.

"Hey Grandma, I have a terrific idea. Listen before you speak so I can finish the idea. I suggest the four of us go visit Mama and Christopher. We can take your car, Grandma, and be there in no time. You and Mama can visit and you can meet your grandson. Oh, I'm so excited. Tillie, don't you think this family needs a reunion?"

Tillie gave Sophia-Emma a tentative smile and then moved her gaze over to her grandma.

"Grandma, I can show you all the nicest places in Mobile. We can go down to the Gulf, eat gumbo, crawdads, oysters, and shrimp."

Her grandma frowned, showing she wasn't excited about the idea. Some heavier persuasion was needed.

"Before you give reasons why you can't go, Grandma, listen some more, please. It's about time you leave this gorgeous house for a few days and make new memories. Think about it. You and your only living child will again smell, touch, see, hear, and even taste each other once again. Hell, you two haven't shared a word since I was no bigger than a possum. I know Mama's ready to make up. And I can see in your eyes that you're ready, too."

"I can't leave here. Look at me. I'm ready for the grave myself. I can't walk. I can hardly eat. I take dozens of prescriptions. Besides y'all live in a colored neighborhood, I hear. I can't go there. I may be mugged or raped."

Sophia-Emma wanted to tell her about how she had been gang-raped by white young men early that morning, but that would rattle her too much for now.

"You'll be perfectly safe with us, Grandma. Tillie will be with us—won't you, Tillie? And I'll be with you. School's still not in session for a few more weeks. Mama won't let you out of her sight, and little Christopher, he'll be so proud to have you there with us. Plus, just as I healed a lady in Providence ICU yesterday, I can heal you, too. So don't worry about that. It's all free, if you have faith. I want to heal you regardless of whether you go with us or not. I'm not here to show you all the diseases you've brought onto yourself up to now. No, I only want you to be happy with your family—what's left of it—again. We visited your brave boys and your husband this afternoon. Now let's visit the living. Let's all be healed and celebrate our women power."

Chitto, meanwhile, was playing some sad concerto on the piano. He seemed to be deep in thought.

"And you, Chitto," Sophia-Emma yelled over to the man at the piano, "surely you, too, can appreciate woman power and come with us to Africatown tomorrow. I'd love to have you meet my earthly family and to verify what happened to us today. Not the bad stuff, just the good, huh?"

"Remember," he responded, "I haven't said I'd be joining your mission once you go back to Mobile."

"Oh yes, I guess you did say that. Haven't you made up your mind yet?" Sophia-Emma was showing that even a teenaged Spirit-Goddesses could get a little tipsy after too much wine.

Chitto kept his hands on the piano keys and refused to look up, even though his new friend started pleading with him to help her with her new mission. He just played on.

Chitto, the nice guy, surprised her. He seemed to become mesmerized by the fireflies, partying outside in the courtyard. "I'm not going with you to Mobile. There, I said it. I have work to do here with my mother, my dog . . . stuff like that." He returned to his concerto.

The mission wasn't getting off to a great start with her man who was supposed to be second in command. "Okay, I know today's been rough. Take some time. We'll talk in a few days."

"We will talk when I want to talk. So just give me a ride back to Selma when you leave, and we'll call it even, okay?"

She wanted to say, no, it wasn't okay, but her feminine instincts told her not to threaten Chitto's sense of his power, as well. She couldn't command him to be her disciple. Someone would surely show up to take his place. She put this problem on the shelf for now.

Turning her attention back to her grandma, she asked, "Are you ready to be healed?"

Her grandma looked over at Tillie. "What do you think, Tillie?"

"Mrs. Foster, I think it's about time you experience some wellness and happiness in your life. Time to let go. I say no harm trying. But remember, we must all, each of us, have faith. And this young lady here, she's probably nervous, too."

She answered Tillie. "I used to be, but now I'm confident that my Creator, the Father, wants to heal my grandma so she can be happy with us. Y'all ready?"

Sophia-Emma didn't know if she should get olive oil or bless some water, or have her grandma dress in a certain way. She decided that she didn't have time for making things pretty and right. The energy was already leaving her heart and flowing toward her fingertips at that moment.

"God wants to be one with you, Grandma. You are God's lover. God admires your beauty that surpasses age. There is an aura around you at this moment."

With her signature hug, she squeezed out of her body all the hurt, anxiety and bad memories, and filled it instead with her fruits of love, gentleness, faithfulness, goodness, patience, self-control, kindness, and joy.

Sophia-Emma stood in front of her grandmother, took her hands and pulled her up to her feet. Then together they walked to the piano. She sat on the bench by Chitto and began to play, as though she'd been playing everyday of her life.

"I can't believe it," Tillie exclaimed. "She hasn't played the piano since before you were born, Miss Sophia-Emma. This is truly a miracle."

"But be careful, Grandma," Sophia-Emma warned. "If you ever doubt our love, tell us. Because once doubt enters your heart, it can push out all the other fruits that showed themselves in you a few minutes ago." The entire room, including Chitto, seemed to exhale in unison. Mrs. Foster and Chitto were now playing a duet.

"Now I say we all go to bed after we help Tillie with the dishes. Okay, folks?" Sophia Emma questioned.

Later that night she called her mama. "We're coming home, Mama," she announced. "All of us—Grandma, Tillie, even me. I now know my mission."

Chapter 29

The next morning, before the rooster was up to crow, or the meadowlark had spread its wings to sing with joy, Sophia-Emma was up finding her way around the old plantation's outdated kitchen. She'd found the old percolator, similar to one that Miss Mildred had shown her in a box of cast-aways out in her garage. Back then she'd become fascinated by the aluminum pot with one big straw-like tube that rested on the bottom of the pot, the basket with holes in it rested on the tube about two-thirds of the way toward the top of the pot, which was topped with another holed flat piece. Over all of these was the actual lid with a clear cupolo knob-like widget that fit into the very top of the lid.

She filled the small basket with ground Folgers coffee up to where the coffee stain from previous brews stopped. Same with the water, up to the water mark on the inside of the pot. She lit the gas stove and looked for some cups and some cream and sugar, which she assembled on a tray.

Looking out the kitchen window, she saw that the lights were on in the old barn where the Lunds milked the cows mornings and evenings. Before heading off to Selma later in the morning, she felt led to talk to the young people about her age—give or take a few years—who did the milking. Maybe they knew something about a mystery that had perplexed her for her entire life.

Sophia-Emma noticed a small hint of pink off to the east as she softly and carefully made her way out to the barn, trying to not wake up anyone in the Big House while also not startling the milkers. Nevertheless, the cups and spoons, the Mason jar of cream and the sugar bowl seemed to want to do a contra dance on the tray. She had forgotten to put on her shoes before leaving the house, and the gravel on the driveway to the barn let her know it every step she took.

The milkers heard her knock on the door. Assuming it came from Tillie, asking for more cream for a dessert, they took their time answering. Finally the boy opened a side door. He was surprised to see someone he'd never met before there with freshly brewed coffee ready for them.

"Hi," Sophia-Emma, a big smile on her face, said, "I noticed you two milking yesterday when I was wheelin' my grandma around the place. You mind if we take some time for some coffee and chat a spell?"

"I don't know. These cows here, they kinda rambunctious. When we get 'em in their stalls, we gotta move fast," the boy said. "And then, well, ma's got breakfast ready for us in a li'l bit. So, you're the ol' lady's granddaughter? You sure don't look like them Fosters."

"That's kinda what I want to talk to y'all about over coffee. We can do this fast or slow. Y'all call the shots."

By now, the girl had come to join her brother. At least that was what Sophia-Emma assumed was their relationship.

"Yeah, looks like we three here about the same shade, if you know what I mean. S'prised that ol' bitch you call your grandma let you set foot in her house. We never been anywhere closer than her porch. Bet it real purty in thar."

"That's all a long story," Sophia-Emma commented. "Here, let's sit down on these milk crates and get some hot stuff in us and I'll tell you a little secret."

"Well, just a couple minutes. We don't have time to be neighbor-like, you know," the boy said. "By the way, I'm Elijah. My sister here is Sarah. Yours?"

"I'm Sophia-Emma Foster-Jones," she said as she poured the steaming liquid into the mugs on the tray, which she had put on a crate by itself. She showed the Lunds the sugar and cream. They took a little of both.

"Why I come out to see y'all this mornin' was, well, to see if you might know more about me than I do. You see, a long time ago I was a baby found in that pasture 'tween the Big House and the river out back. My mama, the woman who later adopted me, she rescued me out there. She was Mrs. Foster's daughter, Amanda. Ever hear of her?"

The two looked at each other. Sarah spoke first. "Can't say I can help you much, Sophia—sorry, forgot your middle name—all I know is what I hear the older folks mention off and on. Somethun' like that wild girl we took in. She had no kin 'round these parts. Called herself Madie—short for Magdalene—she not right in the haid. Story is once she sleepin' out in the woods 'tween Mrs. Foster's place here and ours, and while she dreaming, she saw a big light all around her."

"Aw, c'mon, don't tell her all that bullshit," her brother scolded his sister. "She goin' think we believe in witches and fairies like most other folks in these here parts think. Sophia, what it come down to, is Madie got knocked up. No one stepped up to say they the daddy. Don't know what came of her. My ol' lady, she saw her a couple times. One time, she had a belly on her the size of a watermelon, and the other time, she was as skinny as a fence post. The only thing she could think was maybe she had that baby and it died. None of us ever saw one. Of course, we too young to have our own memories from way back. We just tellin' you the old story we hear off and on from family reunions and stuff like that."

"Well, maybe I'm that baby she had. I would sure like to meet up with her. See if we much alike, you know what I mean, don't cha?

Would you mind if I walk through those woods out back to see if maybe I can find any old stuff she might've had when she roamed around?"

"Oh, if I you, no way would I go out in those woods. We always come here by that dirt road out yonder. Those woods, they hainted twenty-four-seven," Elijah warned. "But if you're dumb enough to go wandering off out there, don't blame usens if you never find your way back. That what happened to Madie. But then, they say she never wanted to come back any hows, cuz, you know she kinda lazy and wanted to be with the critters out there."

The two of them laughed at the naive city girl as they got the flow started from the cow udders by squirting each other with the warm sweet liquid before hooking them up to the milking machines.

"Hey, one more thing," Sophia-Emma added as she stacked the cups back on the tray.

They looked back.

"Did Madie have a boyfriend?"

"Naw," said Sarah. "She hated menfolk. She was one of 'em folks who, you know . . ." She blushed.

"Gotcha," said Sophia-Emma. "Sure nice gettin' to know you two. Your milk is so good. My grandma, even though she sometimes seems kind of uppity, brags about y'all all the time."

By now, the Lunds were busy calming the cattle down and attaching the milk tubes of the milk pumps to their tits. Sophia-Emma knew they'd said as much as they were going to say. It was best to leave and get ready for her trip back to Mobile.

But both Sarah and Elijah had given her a lot to chew her cud on, just like the cows.

When Sophia-Emma walked back up the steps to the Big House, the first thing she did was rub her sore feet. Country life, she'd decided, wasn't all singing birds and crowing roosters. But yet, she felt a call to go walk in those woods where maybe at one time a mother she'd never known once called home . . . or maybe still did.

No one seemed to be up yet, not even Chitto. She'd leaned on him a lot yesterday. She could see why he was sleeping in . . . unless he'd already left and was walking back to Selma at this moment. She snuck into the bedroom that was once her brother Matthew's room. She let out a sigh of relief when she found Chitto's naked body face down on top of all his blankets, as though he'd looked at the bed last night and collapsed there fast asleep before touching it.

Finding paper and pen in Matthew's desk, she wrote him a note saying she was going out for a walk in the woods. After she returned, they would take him home and the rest of them would go on to Africatown. She signed it with *xxxx, Sophia-Emma.*

She then slipped into her mama's old bedroom and changed into a t-shirt and a pair of Dickies bib overalls she wore as a kid. After slipping out for a second time, she took off in a run for the woods, not far from the milking barn.

The dew was still heavy, so in no time from her waist down, she was nearly soaked. Her overalls clung to her legs. Her objective was to find some type of artifact—clothing, eating utensil, a campfire, even bone fragments—left from this Madie. Had she been named in honor of Mary Magdalene, she wondered , the one loved more than all of Jesus's disciples? What a perfect name for a woman who may have birthed her. But why would she have abandoned her baby?

Hour after hour, she looked and hoped for even the smallest of tokens that would be something that her supposed mother once had in her hands. Since it was only late summer, there was a carpet of green beneath her feet, probably covering many years of stories that lay on the ground. The weeds and young shrubs did a good job of hiding whatever relics nestled on the floor of the forest.

The sun was now in the middle of the sky, signifying about one o'clock by Daylight Savings Time. She had to get back, even if she walked out empty handed. But she was beginning to enjoy the ambiance of the woods—mushrooms in colorful sculpted designs, fragile but boisterous mosses so verdant that she wanted to sleep on them, lichen arranged in curly waves as it embraced limbs, stumps, and rocks. When she glanced up into the clouds above her at the tall oaks, loblolly pines, elms and cottonwoods she couldn't help but feel that they were all bending down to shade and comfort her on this humid stroll.

But she couldn't deny that sense of other worldliness she felt, just as the Lunds had warned her. Often she swore someone was following her, maybe Chitto. She'd turn around and no one was there. And the noises, not the wind blowing through the trees or squirrels chasing one another across crunching leaves. No, this was a noise of someone watching her. Better to get on back, she told herself.

Using her Goddess guts, she steered herself, still empty handed, to find her way back to the Big House. She could only imagine how worried everyone was about her. No telling if her grandma had by now slipped back into her negative perspectives. She might even by now feel her granddaughter had abandoned her.

Her time of prayerful aloneness, but oneness with her partner-Gods, coming to an end, she picked up her speed and was soon hearing the cows mooing in the nearby pasture. Sophia-Emma lost herself in the sounds of farm life, so much that she didn't see the remains of a primitive lean-to against an old-growth cottonwood. She tripped over a limb that stuck out near other limbs and branches weaved together by some human. At first Sophia-Emma was stunned by her fall, adding new scratches to her body since her rape the day before. Her ankle didn't feel right, but upon seeing the lean-to, all of her attention was directed instead to the decayed structure. She peeked under the lean-to, pushing away layers of fallen leaves arranged into a soft nest-like ambiance. Then she noticed some carvings on the old tree. One stick figure seemed to be a baby. Another was of a larger figure with a round middle.

Sophia-Emma saw that she was onto something here. Someone had lived in this lean-to. She dug around the base of the tree until her fingers sensed a fragment of something vertical covered with something that didn't feel like leaves, but more fibrous, like some type of husk. She used a stick to remove the object, gradually loosening it from the roots intertwined around it. Finally, with a big grunt and a tug, she fell backwards, but with the object in her hand. She had no idea what the object was or even if it was worth taking back with her. Her immediate impression was that it was an old corn cob with corn husks wrapped around it. Probably no big deal, she told herself. But maybe others at the Big House would have other impressions.

By now she was close to the fence separating the barnyard from the woods. She was about to climb over it when she thought she heard someone singing a lullaby behind her back in the woods. Then the tune faded away. She wanted to go back and search for the elusive voice, but she pushed that thought out of her mind. Sophia-Emma surmised that even Goddesses sometimes imagined hearing and seeing things that didn't exist. Maybe she was probably just hungry. She again looked at her found object in the full sun and held it tightly, hoping the energy that had been put into it would speak to her.

She was still clasping the cob and its husks when Chitto, Tillie and even her grandma met her on the wrap-around porch of the mansion.

"About time you come back," her grandma, without her wheelchair, announced on behalf of the others. "We'd thought you got chewed up by whatever haunts those woods out there. What is it you have in your hand, young lady?"

"I don't know, Sophia-Emma said. "Thought maybe some of you could tell me." She held it out for all to see.

"I'd say it's a terribly dilapidated corn husk doll," Tillie offered. "Even I could make a better one than that. But no telling how old that one is."

Sophia-Emma looked at it again. "Yea, it could be that. Maybe the woman who bore me made that doll for her little baby before she changed her mind and left me out there in the pasture."

Epilogue

Corn husk creation tucked away in her grandma's silver Cadillac's glove compartment, Sophia-Emma asked Tillie to be the driver for the day. She admitted that she indeed did have a driver's permit, but it was for identity purposes only.

First stop was Selma, where they'd drop off her protector and fellow traveler Chitto. Sophia-Emma's gut ached as they drove by the intersection of Water Avenue and Highway 80. She still hadn't told any family members about her rape yesterday. Maybe she never would. Even goddesses didn't want to relive painful experiences.

Chitto requested to be dropped off at the Rebel Café where she'd first seen him with the gang that later knocked him out and sexually assaulted her. How she wished she could lean on him the rest of her mission.

"Yo, don't know what would've become of me, or what will become of me, if you hadn't saved me yesterday," she told her new friend on the sidewalk outside the café. Please change your mind and come with us. I beggin' you. I'll promise you eternal happiness, if you please stay by my side, maybe just a little while. Don't think I can do anything without you."

The entire time Sophia-Emma pleaded, Chitto shook his head, basically saying, there wasn't a chance.

"You know I could've died out there in those briars if you hadn't rescued me and watched over me on the journey. At the moment when

I hated every man and their unbridled sexual violence, you came and saved me like the Good Samaritan."

Even though he wouldn't budge on his choice to stay behind, Sophia-Emma knew she'd never give up on him. Bigger miracles were known to have happened.

"You don't know me, girl. I've crossed lots of bridges and buried myself in many holes this year. Too many obligations. My mother needs me here to support her and my sister. They're probably worried sick about me at this moment. Just get on your way. I have faith in you."

"Someday, someday, we'll find each other again," she promised as both left to go separate ways.

She wiped away the tears and returned to her grandma's idling sedan. She was ready to get this town and this café out of her mind. Yet this was also a part of God's heaven. Maybe she'd have to work on changing her mind and in time develop a real love for it.

"Someday, someday," she whispered to herself.

Finally on the road south, her tears made way for laughs and anticipation, with some anxiety added for balance. Her grandma, relaxing in the back seat, took in the sights along the way, except when she criticized Tillie's slow driving. She also talked about tapering off a few of the myriad of medications she was taking. Both Tillie and Sophia-Emma suggested she check with a reputable doctor first. Nevertheless, they all spoke of that little miracle that had happened at Promised Land yesterday.

Before they knew it, they were seeing signs on I-65 for Mobile and then on the 165 Bypass for Plateau. The only Google Maps mention of Africatown was the historic cemetery in her hometown.

Upon reaching the front door of Sophia-Emma's little house, her mama simply stood there behind the repaired screen door. She frowned and turned her head away from her mother for what seemed like an eternity. In turn, Louise Foster motioned Tillie to start the car again so they could go back home. Just as they heard the purr of the engine, Loving opened her arms to her mama.

"Mama, can you love me after all this time?" She reached down and gave her mother a kiss. It was a wet one. Both their faces flooded with tears. A stronger embrace followed—a scene Sophia-Emma swore she'd take with her back to heaven and cherish forever—the two mamas together.

"Greetings from Promised Land," her grandma managed to say while her snot flowed into her mouth along her deep wrinkles. Then came the apologies, remembrances of old times, swearing, touching, and arguing. Basically women being women.

Once her grandma was convinced that Sophia-Emma's mama wasn't going to kick her out of the house, she turned her attention to Christopher, the only male around. He looked on from his Legos, overflowing onto the kitchen floor from the dining room.

"Here's my handsome boy," Loving remarked and urged her son to sit on his grandma's lap.

Christopher at first looked at his mama and refused to move. But after some gentle coaxing and promises of two dips of ice cream, he came around, cautiously edging his way over to his grandma. When he was within a spot where he could plant a kiss on her furled cheek, She in turn, smacked another wet kiss on his lips.

With everyone settled into place at the Jones's home, Sophia-Emma decided to take care of some unfinished work elsewhere in the hood. First, she and Little Guy rushed over to Miss Mildred's, whom she found in her bed, Crazy Dog was at her side, not looking so crazy anymore.

"Let me see you, chile," Miss Mildred said. "In case you still concerned, my boy here, he's turned himself in. He's going to serve his time, but if he leads police to the drug king-pins, they tell us he'll get a reduced sentence. And when they release him, they'll put him in a witness protection program, moving him some place where he can start a new life." She reached for his hand with both of hers. "We had ourselves a good talk, my boy and me, and when he decided to go straight, I get well again, just like I did in the hospital when you visited."

Sophia-Emma stepped back and took a long look at Miss Mildred. "You didn't need heart surgery? Mama told me you had a setback after our meeting in the hospital, but you look right well now."

"They tested me when I was downhearted that you'd left so fast. I got over that. I just started thinkin' again about how y'all cured me with that powerful hug, young lady. Never forget that, I sure won't."

Sophia-Emma smiled, relieved she'd had something to do with Miss Mildred still being alive. Even though she was still in bed, her mentee knew in no time she'd regain her strength and go about cooking her scrumptious breakfasts in no time.

She shifted her focus and managed a faint smile for Crazy Dog, who gave her a handsome smile back. She could see now why so many women in the hood wanted him for their boo, even those not into drugs.

"Girl, when I sees how you love my ol' lady here, and how your hug bring her back to life, well . . . I know there be power in you that even Ma and me know nothin' about. I wanted it. So I'm straighenin' my life out, and I'm gonna do your daddy a favor, too. The guys over there at headquarters, they tell me if I talk, they get him out as part of the deal. Crazy Dog's done his first miracle, little girl."

She was reminded then that he was the same old egotistical Crazy Dog she hated that night he came by her house. But his good news caused her to cut him a little slack. "Crazy Dog, you done good."

Miss Mildred smiled and nodded with her agreement.

"Oh, I took a little trip to Selma," she confided," and I learned there that I had some behavior problems myself that needed some fixin'. So I guess we all turned some big corners in our lives, huh? And guess what, I brought my grandma back. She and Mama are real mommy and daughter again."

"I suggest you catch up with your friend Harriet now," Crazy Dog said. "We got that meeting at the church planned to a T. I gonna tell folk about why and how the GED program broke down. But in the meantime, we're starting our own program. And guess who'll run it?"

Sophia-Emma's godly mind went blank. She had no idea.

"The Afghan, who just moved into the hood. He a professor, and he tell me he's run such programs before coming here. His daughter, Amala, she been invited by Harriet to go with her to recruit new students. Check it out with Harriet and Bulldog. Bet they be at her place now."

Sophia didn't get a chance to share with Miss Mildred about her experiences in Selma, but with Crazy Dog there, she'd do that later when the two of them were alone, which she hoped would be soon.

But for now, she, with Little Guy at her heels, was headed over to Harriet's, to check the story out. She found her with Bulldog kissing on Harriet's front porch. Sophia-Emma yelled at them and interrupted their spell.

Harriet, after signaling her best friend to mind her own business, finally pulled herself away from her new boyfriend and got down to business. She reported that all the panelists had committed to showing up at the accountability session, except the mayor, which was no surprise. Regardless, the meeting was ready to go.

Sophia-Emma nodded as Harriet described the entire set up for the event, but somehow, all she could think about was what a perfect pair the two lovers seemed to be.

"And by the way, Bulldog and I have hooked up," Harriet added, as though her friend couldn't tell.

"We both love using four-letter words and doing other four-letter stuff, if you know what I mean."

Sophia-Emma was stunned and even realized her still human pride was a trifle jealous.

"So I guess you don't need me at the meeting," Sophia-Emma tried to sound grateful, but she somehow felt not needed anymore.

"Oh, y'all come," Harriet insisted. "We find something for you to do, like maybe setup or cleanup. But really, we got it, girl."

Sophia-Emma smiled, realizing that from now on, her life would be changing. The old Sophia-Emma had empowered others to work for change in the community. Meanwhile, she'd be discovering new paths now that she knew who she really was and what her true mission on this planet would be.

She was happy to help set up and clean-up in Africatown.

Little Guy, meanwhile, saw her for the same Sophia-Emma he'd known for the summer months. Wrapped in his glistening black fur, the little critter welcomed her back home with puppy licks all over her once bruised and wounded body. He loved her like he did the first time they became buddies.

For a moment she was convinced that this little ol' world might be a good place. It should be, she thought, because so many had worked before her to make it so. But she was determined to help make it better.

Nevertheless, today was a day to celebrate for so many reasons. No one, not even she, knew what trials she would face in the years ahead. But as a woman with the Spirit-Goddess within, she was determined to bring about a new birth of energy, and her goal would be another four-letter word:

Love.

Sophia-Emma reached into her overalls right pocket and fingered the old corn husk doll treasured there. A gift of faith, hope, and especially love, possibly from a mother to her daughter.

After all, wasn't that the feminine way?

Discussion Questions

1. Do you think as a teenager you would be more like Sophia-Emma or her friend Harriet?
2. Do you know about the origins of the people who settled in your hometown? Please tell.
3. At the beginning of the story who did you think Sophia-Emma was? An angel, prophet, goddess, or a confused teen?
4. What would you do if your parent seemed to be shifting too many responsibilities on you?
5. Discuss reasons Sophia-Emma's father doesn't look for ways to get out of prison.
6. Talk about important mentors in your life similar to Miss Mildred in Sophia-Emma's life.
7. If you had the power, what kinds of miracles would you like to perform?
8. Discuss the rape event. Could she have done anything differently to have avoided the assault? Should she have sought out the police? Why or why not?
9. What impressions do you get about Chitto? Do you think he should have followed Sophia-Emma like she asked?

10. Have you had super spiritual events in your life that you would like to share?
11. Do you think women could teach men better ways to improve the world?
12. Why do you think Sophia-Emma felt driven to go back to Promised Land?
13. What is the significance of the old corn husk doll that Sophia-Emma finds?
14. Compare female characters of this book, such as Loving Foster-Jones and her mother, Louise Foster, Sophia-Emma, Harriet, Chaos, and Miss Mildred. Who would you describe as an angel? A betrayer?

Acknowledgments

This second book in *The Goddess of Promised Land* series is the result of my annual attempt to write at least fifty thousand words every November as a participant in the NaNoWriMo (National Novel Writing Month) challenge. I've participated since 2015. I want to thank all my family, friends, and neighbors who have let me spend nearly thirty days in solitude as I struggled to write nearly two thousand words a day to reach my goal.

However, there are a number of people who I especially want to recognize and thank. To start, thanks to my detail-minded editor, Mindi Friedwald, an author herself, whom I trust with my every written word. In addition, I can't forget the talented members of Jan-Carol Publishing, Inc.—publisher Janie Jessee, communications director Savannah Bailey, and graphics designer Tara Sizemore for her creative work with the novel's cover design. Their patience in working with this aging novel writer has given me hope in our sometimes-crazy world.

More appreciation goes out to my long-time fellow author, friend, and critic Clare Hanrahan, whose gifted writing has resulted in such books as *Conscience and Consequence* (2005), *Jailed for Justice* (2007), and *The Half-Life of a Free Radical* (2016), all published by Celtic Wordcraft.

Much of my research on Africatown and other Alabama locations mentioned in my novel came from research on the internet. Some helpful sites included *Africatown, USA* by Alabama Representative (First District) Sonny Callahan (https;//memory.loc.gov/digging lib/legacies/

loc.afc.afc-legacies.200002671/), and State of Alabama Engineering Hall of Fame (engrhof.org/members/cochraneafricatown-usa-bridge).

Lastly, a never-ending thank you to my five children and eight grandchildren who have been just a phone call, or a few miles drive away, always accessible to encourage me on the long road that finally reaches publication. Blessings and blissings to all of you.

About the Author

Rachael Roberts Bliss grew up on a traditional farm and went to church every Sunday and Holy Day at St. Patrick's Catholic Church in Dunlap, Iowa. She knew she wanted to be a writer when she saw tears in her father's eyes as he read her last school newspaper editorial in the *Dunlap Reporter.*

During those middle years between book learning at Estherville Junior College (now a part of Iowa Lakes Community College) and The University of Iowa, and retirement nearly fifty years later, Bliss helped create and raise five children. She worked in television and print media but found more fulfillment working for social justice nonprofits that focused on hunger, the environment, poverty, and peace and justice. Her last job was as an Americorps VISTA volunteer in her sixties.

Now living in Asheville, NC, Bliss has in recent years taken courses in photography and writing at Asheville-Buncombe Tech Community College and the University of North Carolina-Asheville's Great Smokies Writing Program. When she's not pecking away on her laptop, she's playing grandma with her eight grandchildren or demonstrating for peace and justice at home and throughout the world.

You can keep up with her ups and downs on:

@PeoplePowerGran

rachaelrobertsbliss

TURN THE PAGE FOR AN EXCERPT FROM THE NEXT BOOK

The Goddess of Promised Land: Revelation

You have merely begun to read about the ever-changing life of Sophia-Emma Foster, or the Spirit-Goddess. Next up, meet preacher and mother Sophia-Emma in *The Goddess of Promised Land: Revelation*. The newness and enthusiasm of living the life of Spirit-Goddess has worn down our hero, the woman who was to lead the world into a new way of living, one guided by the Divine Feminine. In this book, she's missing. Is she dead? Or has she intentionally disappeared? No matter what, a shake-up is coming. Could her search for the love of one she once hated be on the horizon? Is this any way for a Spirit-Goddess to act?

THE GODDESS
OF PROMISED LAND

REVELATION

Write down, therefore the things which you have seen, and the things which are, and the things which will happen hereafter. (Revelation 1:19)

Press-Register:
SPIRIT-GODDESS SOPHIA-EMMA FOSTER-JONES BURIED

The Holy Ghost

Night had fallen in Africatown, Alabama's historic cemetery, where all the graves pointed east. The old-timers—former slaves—were the last Africans kidnapped and taken to America to become slaves. Their captors had been ship owner, Timothy Meaher, and his ship Clotilda's Captain William Foster in 1860. They had been brought to Alabama to bow down to white people for the rest of their lives supposedly, but the Union victory in the Civil War had freed them five years later. They stayed put in the Mobile Bay area, formed their own town and named it Africatown. Other former slaves who had come over on the Clotilda with them but who had been sold elsewhere, rejoined them after the war, as well.

They never forgot the old folks back home in Africa. So, when they died, they wanted to face home, to be resurrected one day back in Africa.

Tonight, however, a body many called Sophia-Emma Foster-Jones, also faced east, buried with the people she loved. But only her body was there. Her soul was floating above the grave, mourning as a Ghost, intent on reviving this body one more time and breathing her life into the limp body, wrapped in a swaddling cloth for adults. But the Ghost couldn't reach that body, the body she loved more than the heaven above. She abhorred the idea of letting it decay.

This was nearly midway through the twenty-first century. Science itself was on the verge of playing God. It had brought animals—cats and dogs of mourning owners—back to life. That was all she wanted. One little request. She longed for her body back. And Sophia-Emma, too, was being missed. Disciples by the dozens had mourned for days. They'd lain on this grave throughout the days, hoping for a miracle. Finally, they'd given up, moved on to find other gods, ones who professed to live forever. Tonight, the only griever was Sophia-Emma's spirit, the Holy Spirit herself. She had only emerged from a solitary mourning bush to give honor to the body resting in the grave.

The Ghost was glad the crowd had disbanded. She needed some one-on-one time with the body that had served her well for so many years. She'd never had a chance to thank the human. They had been separated too quickly. A good death wasn't possible when there was no warning of separation—body from soul—for all eternity. If the Creator wouldn't help her, she would help herself. Wasn't that what women had been doing for millennia? First, by asking those identified as men for their approval and assistance? Not getting such, then going out and doing what had to be done themselves? Women like Esther and the Virgin Mary, Mary Magdalene from biblical times to Elizabeth Barrett Browning, Agatha Christie, Joan of Arc, Mother Teresa, Queen Victoria, Dorothy Day, Jane Goodall, even Emma Goldman. Different times, different acts of independence. Now it was her turn.

As the Holy Ghost, she blew and blew the dry dirt piled over the shallow grave. In recent decades, the people had learned that bodies buried in shallow graves were far more able to nourish life above than bodies buried in deep graves. Also, so near the Gulf as this cemetery was, gravediggers would hit water before they reached six feet down. So, the feat of digging up her body wasn't impossible, even for a Ghost. She yearned to enter Sophia-Emma's body one more time, to feel and hear the familiar heartbeat, the steady uplifting of the chest with each breath, to experience the burp, the fart, the warmth of blood rushing through her veins, the love of another individual.

As a lonely spirit without any of these bodily functions, existence was just that. Nothing like life itself. And Sophia-Emma's body needed her. They'd been together, functioning as one for far too long—yet for such a short time—looking at it as a Goddess not used to counting time.

A whiff and then another. A cloud of rain moved some dirt. The rounding up of little nocturnal animals dug in the wet Earth. They knew not why they were digging. The rain knew not the spot, nor the gushes of air blowing dust. But in unison, they worked together. Hours later, the soul viewed the body, caked with mud. The soul saw the shape of a mature human with narrow hips, prominent nose, cheekbones, feet and arms, all waiting in expectation for a soul that had separated way too soon.

Sophia-Emma's Godly Spirit caught the odor of decay mixed with the scent of sweat that still lingered from a once-alive body. The soul knew that each individual, just like every snowflake, had its own taste, look and smell. Even death couldn't completely remove it. It was an awkward combination—sweat and death—but one a Holy Ghost could endure and even love.

As the Spirit was about to become again whole with the body, she could see a live human coming to stand from the grave. Suddenly the Ghost sensed this wasn't a good time for a reunion.

The Spirit was unsure—yes, even God herself sometimes didn't know appropriate actions at particular times—of what to do next. This person indeed was a living human being. But it looked to be a male. If she were to speak to him, he would just think that his imagination was playing tricks on him. Men, after all, still weren't inclined to trust their intuition. For now, he had picked up a shovel that'd been left nearby by another more recent grave. He started shoveling the muddy Earth back over the grave.

This too wasn't in the plan. Yes, Sophia-Emma had died way too soon. Yes, she could be raised from the dead. But even a Holy Ghost, a Spirit-Goddess who spoke in tongues and caused others to do the same; who gave out gifts and fruits to common humans when they were perceptive enough to receive them, sometimes even she was helpless in changing some people's minds, especially those of males.

Upon seeing a male emerge from the grave instead of Sophia-Emma, all the Ghost could do was grieve once more. The male paused for a moment, as though he heard something strange. Not long enough, however. The Holy Ghost could tell that his rationality was getting the best of him. He probably didn't believe in Ghosts, tongues or miracles. He just knew that he was filling an empty hole. A good man's responsibility was to leave a cemetery in good condition for those who would follow.

After stomping on the filled grave, now ready for its next occupant, the man left the grave site, looking confused and well-rested. He seemed to be heading for the closest bar or convenience store.

But the Ghost—Sophia-Emma's soul—was devastated. Meanwhile, dawn was about to be born again. Unlike the coming day, her body, wherever it was, would further deteriorate as the Earth's natural elements aided by the baking sun and bugs and worms worked together to turn a beautiful body into dust and bones. Yes, all of this would enable another reincarnation of sorts on the Father's favorite planet in this solar system. The Holy Spirit knew that in the end, what was naturally happening would be what Sophia-Emma's would probably want from a useless body.

So, Holy Ghost turned around and decided to put together the story of Sophia-Emma's life. She would infiltrate the lives of those still living and some who had died and left their body behind. She would then weave the words to come from those friends into Earthlings' hearts for eternity.

"The sons and daughters will prophesy, your old will dream dreams and your young will see visions." (Joel 2:28)

The Ghost knew this project would be difficult, considering how Sophia-Emma for so long had tried to soften the hardness of human minds. She did experience some success, but also she mourned too many failures. Even some women whom she'd been sure she could empower to birth a new Earth, turned their backs on her. Thought she was an opportunist or just delusional.

It seemed that it was all up to Sophia-Emma's soul, the Holy Spirit herself, to renew the Earth, leaving an endearing true story of what feminine energy, determination, and love could achieve.

Now the story of Sophia-Emma had to be told as only those who crossed her path could.

www.ingramcontent.com/pod-product-compliance
Lightning Source LLC
Chambersburg PA
CBHW030115260626
47156CB00008B/2661
9781954978959